I0672705

To Probe A Beating Heart

By

John Breen Wren

To Probe a Beating Heart

This is a work of fiction. All of the characters, names, incidents, organizations, and dialogue in this novel are either the products of the author's imagination or are used fictitiously.

Library of Congress Control Number: 2011909307

Printed in the United States of America

Cover Design By Katie G. Jones

ISBN 13 978-0-9889371-0-9

ISBN 10 0988937107

For Lois

Acknowledgements

I would like to thank all those who helped me progress through this, my first novel. My wife, Lois who read the first several attempts, Melanie Rigney and Sarah Collins Honenberger for their early editorial comments and Tanya Besmehn for her help in preparing the book for this revised issue.

The characters in the novel are fictional and any resemblance to anyone living or dead is purely coincidental.

INTRODUCTION

The Clann quietly opened their eyes and ears . . .

In 1876 in a small town in central California, Liam Rynne, a young boy, went missing on a warm June afternoon. It was assumed after a few days he had been taken by some wild animal and would never be found. Three years later while clearing land for a new road, Liam's remains were found buried not far from his home. The area was, at the time of his disappearance, unsuitable for anything and remained untouched during those intervening three years.

Based on the condition of the bones, the spattering of blood on his clothes and the damage to his skull, it was determined he had been severely beaten and murdered. Liam's killer had buried him in a shallow grave and covered it with rocks to keep animals from resurrecting his bones. His shirt, belt and shoes were still identifiable, and the matter immediately became a murder investigation. After some questioning of the family and friends, several conversations with the local population and a bit of actual police work, a suspect was identified. Upon hearing the site had been found, one Carl Mason decided to pursue his fortune "back east" rather than California and left town in a hurry in the middle of the night.

Liam was dead, Carl had run off and the local authorities had neither the will nor the resources needed to initiate a long-distance pursuit. As Liam's family had no money and no prominence in town, the authorities were disinclined to continue the pursuit of Carl and the case was shelved. It did not end for Liam's family, however. The Celtic Clanns of nineteenth century America were not as tight knit as the sixteenth century European Clans, but a "Clann" kinship was still respected in many families. The family has always been of prime importance within the Irish communities. The relationships cross many divides and it is still common to know of a "cousin" several times removed, but a cousin, nonetheless. The kinship and resulting support of the family, or the Clann, is a factor in many an introduction, or a helping hand to someone a bit down on his luck, or to a group traveling across the country to new beginnings.

So, it was with Liam's family. The word passed from father to son, brother to brother and cousin to cousin that Liam's killer was getting away with murder. When word spread across the country like a cold wind, this cry of injustice spread throughout the Clann and crossed to other families, other Clanns. The thought of such an injustice against one of their own, unpunished, incensed the Clanns and inspired a number of them to keep an eye open and an ear alert, because, sooner or later, someone might see or hear of Carl Mason, and justice might be rendered.

Actually, most people figured Carl had gone somewhere else and they would not see or hear of him again and poor Liam's family would not find that small modicum of justice to which they were entitled. Whatever the circumstances, however long it may take, the Clanns remained sufficiently vigilant and Carl was eventually found.

As the story goes, a distant cousin of Liam's had seen a picture of Carl and spotted him while traveling through a small town in Kansas in 1880. The local authorities were notified. Slow reaction by the police and few resources in the family allowed Carl to run again, this time to Oklahoma. It made the newspapers in a few states and he was located again by another family member later that same year. This time, three rather large and rough "cousins" took it upon themselves to seize Carl, secure him with rope and chain and secret him back to California. They immediately took him to James Rynne, Liam's father, for disposition. James was not sure what to do. After some consideration and discussion with his brothers, James determined since the local authorities had not done their jobs initially, the family would now handle Carl's punishment. The family tenet was very basic, lacking in sophistication and fairly literal. They did not want to simply murder Carl. He had to be "punished" appropriately for his actions. They rejected hanging, shooting and poisoning as too quick. They considered stoning him, which would allow everybody to participate, but no. No, it had to be more meaningful. "Liam was missing for three years," said his father, "perhaps Mr. Mason should go missing for that long."

James' brother, Samuel suggested a reasonable and equitable punishment. So it was, three years later, a young attorney with a Boston law firm, a relative of Liam's family, several times removed, was anonymously contacted by one of the Clann and advised that his distant cousin's killer was ready to be returned to the system that had failed to find or punish him. Carl Mason's remains were found in a deep and open pit several miles from the location of Liam's shallow grave site. The Clann had done what the authorities had not.

The Clann MacLoaghaire is a very loose grouping of families and individuals. They continue to the present day and as in the case of Liam, they remain ready, willing and able to respond to injustices that the authorities can't or won't address. These incidents are very few and far between, but nonetheless very real. In the fall of 1991, a little girl of the Clann disappeared from her neighborhood of Cleveland Heights, Ohio without a trace. The predator, seen in a rainstorm from a distance, could not be identified and the Clann quietly opened their eyes and ears, patiently observed, gathered information and waited for an unknown individual to make a mistake.

*　　*　　*

One

Starting life with a negative balance . . .

All stories have a beginning and no matter how far back you go, a starting point seems forever flexible. We will begin this story with the development of the predator himself. He began his life within unfortunate circumstances, beginning with his very conception, continuing to and beyond his birth and childhood.

*   *   *

It was late in the summer of 1967, and Nadia Lupasco, a slight, almost attractive girl with large dark eyes and pitch-black hair, had just finished her last year of schooling in Darza, Romania. She was looking forward to becoming a member of the working population and living in Bucharest. Like many unfortunate young girls, she trusted the wrong young man and a night of pleasure led to an unwanted pregnancy. Stelian, a tall, athletic young man with dark hair, and eyes to match, was a promising young football player. His dream was to go to America where he would become a rich and famous pro-athlete. He flirted with Nadia and charmed her into his hotel room and his bed. She fell easily for his come-on lines and boasts of making it to America, and even imagined herself at his side.

Stelian perceived Nadia as nothing more than a one-night stand, and he was gone in the morning before she woke, never to be seen again. That one night, the first ever away from her home and the subsequent fight with her mother together with the threat of a beating at the hand of her father, further darkened her horizons. Nadia was not brave, nor was she very strong, but she decided that she was now eighteen and did not have to put up with this treatment from her parents. Quietly, she packed a bag with her few better outfits, took all the money she could find in the house, secreted herself to the kitchen where she took a loaf of bread, a block of cheese, a knife and a few apples, and walked quietly out the door. She would never return. She would never see her mother or listen to her screaming again. She would not face her father, nor would she have to hear his rants or suffer his beatings. Nadia took the train to Bucharest where she would start a new life, a better life.

A week of flop houses and diminishing money led Nadia to visit several restaurants in search of a job as a serving girl. She found a job and earned enough to pay rent in a cheap boarding house where some of her new-found co-workers lived. As time passed and the daily routine became more mundane, she started having a drink or two at the bar every night before going home. After ten weeks on the job, she noticed that her belly was beginning to swell. She drank more, cared less and started to bum cigarettes from her friends. When offered a line of white powder for the first time, Nadia knew she should have declined, but was seduced with the thought of sweet oblivion. One line led to another, and she was soon addicted. The drug was free at first, but once she was hooked, there was a price to be paid. She had very little money and the bill was settled in cash when she had it, but more often on her back, and in time it no longer mattered to her.

At an early stage in her pregnancy, she attempted an abortion with the aid of one of her co-workers. That failed abortion attempt, her addiction to the white powder and securing her place of employment by sleeping with her employer made her existence so shameful that she often thought about allowing herself to fall into the river and float away. Her pregnancy continued to full term, complete with the evident effects that the alcohol and drugs had on her undernourished body and her developing baby.

When the baby was finally born in April 1968, she gave him up immediately to an orphanage, not wanting to be reminded of that night, nor the glib young man. In filling out a form at the clinic asking for names and such, she wrote Stelian as the child's first name, a name she did not like, and Lupasco was entered by the clinic as the surname. The name meant nothing to her and she just wanted to be away from the clinic, the baby and the memory of that night and the previous nine months. Nadia drifted back to her serving duties and resumed her destructive path of drinking, smoking, doing more frequent lines of cocaine and very slowly dying.

Young Stelian's first year was spent in an orphanage in a small village outside Bucharest. It was a wretched place with substandard care and the occasional vermin scurrying through the nursery. Food was never adequate, and the children's sickly pallor, combined with slight statures and vacant eyes, evoked sympathy from the few who ventured in. It was heart wrenching to witness, and even more so to live it.

Nadia continued on her self-destructive path, Stelian the elder, unaware of his offspring, had left town and young Stelian was alone in this cold and unforgiving place. His parents never gave thought to their child starting his life with a negative balance.

*   *   *

Two

Then he heard a voice . . .

Young Stelian was nearly a year old when an American couple came to the orphanage looking for a baby to take home to complete their family. Ellie and Allen Swall had been married for six years and as much as they tried, they were not successful in having children. Allen wanted a son to brag about, Ellie wanted a daughter with whom she could have afternoon tea. Most of all they both wanted a bright, healthy child that would make them proud and complete their family.

Adoption was not a consideration until the doctors confirmed there was no chance for pregnancy. Adoptions in the United States were difficult if one's history was less than perfect, and next to impossible if there were multiple flaws in your record. However, foreign adoptions were relatively easy and less expensive in the long run. Both European and Oriental sources were considered, and the European market won. It would please the Swalls to have a child that resembled them. Allen was of Mid-European descent, Ellie was mostly Hungarian with a touch of Romanian, she had dark brown eyes and long black hair. Her skin was naturally dark, she always looked as if she'd just spent a week at the beach. At 5'8", she was long and lean and would easily draw the attention of men and women alike. Allen was tall and athletic with dark hair and eyes, his olive skin tanned easily in the summer sun. Together, their appearance made them perfect candidates for the role of parents to young Stelian. Since money was often tight, multiple trips to Romania were out of the question, a decision had to be swift and so, young Stelian would be their vehicle for realizing their dream of parenthood.

Stelian Lupasco was adopted by the Swalls and went to America. America, the place his father had desperately wanted to see his dreams to fruition, and the place his mother often imagined escaping her tedious life. Now the dream would be young Stelian's. He was far too young to understand the concept of a new country, of a new family, but he was bright enough to comprehend that life had become more pleasant. Welcoming arms that hungered to hold him, a full belly and a warm bed had become everyday occurrences and he felt somehow safe and wanted. However foreign those feelings were, he came to like them very quickly. His greatest challenge now was in communicating, Stelian could not understand anything they were saying.

Names were important to Ellie, and Stelian was not an acceptable name for their new son. She had thought of a number of names during the years she and Allen tried to have children and she had a favorite. Allen had his wish, a son, and he was not about to deny her the choice of a name. Ellie had fond memories of her grandfather, a kind man who never arrived for a visit emptyhanded. His efforts to make birthdays memorable with fancy presents and trips to Disneyland, capped off with the keys to a new car at her high school graduation, made his passing all the more difficult the following year. His final gift was a modest inheritance that would provide a small but regular income for the rest of her life. She wanted to name her son Averell in his memory. How could Allen argue?

Averell's first year was one of learning new words, new faces and a sense of comfort and security. He now had someone to hold on to and feel the warmth of another being. He now slept through the night with no fear and no hunger. He now awoke in a sunlit room to Ellie's smile and gentle greeting. He was learning what love was.

His new home was a single-family residence in a middle-class neighborhood of suburban Syracuse, New York. The houses were built in the twenties and thirties and featured block foundations, clapboard siding, large windows, high ceilings, crown moldings, coal-fired furnaces and poor insulation. Home improvement projects were often undertaken to correct a number of these energy sucking features, and brightly painted walls along with new appliances made these homes more desirable to the up-and-coming young professionals. The Swalls had purchased their house in 1964 after the installation of a new gas fired, forced air furnace with space for an air conditioning coil to be added later. Summers in Syracuse were not known for excessively hot days and window fans were less expensive than having an air-cooling coil and condensing unit installed. The Swall's home was square with a covered front porch that ran the width of the house and an average front yard. Allen had planted flowers to complement the boxwoods that reached the floor of the porch, some three feet high.

The first floor housed a living room with a woodburning fireplace, a dining room, kitchen and a small den. The second floor held four bedrooms and a large bathroom with a walk-in shower next to an ancient cast iron clawed foot bathtub. There was an unfinished attic that was used to store off-season clothing, family keepsakes and holiday decorations. The basement was dark and damp, nothing more than the furnace, washer and dryer and a small freezer would provide reason to venture down there. Ellie had been petitioning for the washer and dryer to be relocated to the den to save time and energy on laundry day. Allen had begun moving his books and financial records out of the den and up to a spare bedroom on the second floor.

By Averell's second birthday he had learned new words and the "terrible twos" gained new meaning for the Swalls. His curiosity quickly outgrew his small frame as he would get into everything, no matter how Ellie and Allen tried to keep things from his eager reach and strong grasp. He found a demented joy in tormenting the family cat, the harmless act of pouring milk across its back soon graduated to Ellie's mug of hot coffee one Sunday morning and caused the frightened feline to dash from the house and into the street where it met a terrible fate.

Nothing was spared, Ellie's cosmetics were fodder for amusement on a rainy afternoon, Allen's socks proved fun to dip and fish from the toilet, spilled powder and the emptying of Ellie's favorite perfume atomizer would earn Averell a stern scolding and an hour of confinement in his room. As his transgressions increased, so did the punishments, rising to a spanking or slapped cheek.

By the age of four, Averell had worn his parents down, no longer the apple of Ellie's eye or the pride of Allen, he was now the little monster that made messes and tore up newspapers. He spent many hours in his room, alone, repeating the new words he had heard stream from his parents' lips, "Damn it. Damn it. Damn it," very quietly to himself.

For all the negative, there was Averell's ability to read. He knew the alphabet when he was three and could match words and pictures and recognize a number of words before his fourth birthday. Children's books were a way to keep him quiet and out of the way and both Allen and Ellie picked up different books for Averell for just that reason. Mostly books about animals and dinosaurs, but he could struggle through a newspaper article or a piece in a magazine, if it looked interesting enough. With all the time he spent alone, Averell did a lot of reading and he enjoyed it. Each time he was sent to his room, he was told to clean it. "There is a place for everything, and everything should be in its place," was the order given at the beginning of each punishment. Averell became a very neat individual, almost to the point of obsession. His room was spotless, his books were not only placed on a shelf, but they were also in alphabetic order.

* * *

Travel had not been one of Allen's main job responsibilities until a promotion and a bump in pay called for an increase in his leadership role for several teams in various locations. The largest group was in California, and he needed to be in direct contact with them on a regular basis. Ellie never liked Allen's traveling while she sat home alone, and now she had the additional burden of an unruly child. Whenever Allen determined his presence was needed out west for a project meeting, Ellie complained loudly and cried even louder. Allen was powerless. His job demanded face time with his team and the trips were unavoidable regardless of his wife's disapproval.

The common routine was a fight the night before his departure, followed by days of Ellie being unhappy, short-tempered with Averell and often punishing him with tongue-lashings and confinement to his room. Allen's perceived desertion was unpleasant for everyone, including Allen, often setting the tone of his trip on a sour note.

When Averell was banished to his room, he'd often withdraw into himself and curl up in a corner, where the walls would hug him on either side, giving him a feeling of safety. "I'm safe here, damn it," he'd mutter to the vastness of the room before him.

Then he heard a voice say, *"Damn it."* Nobody was there, and he did not understand.

One trip would have Allen returning late, having not spoken to Ellie, he wasn't sure what to expect on his return. Often a chilly reception would lead to days of silence and hard feelings. On other occasions, she seemed happy to see him and they'd quickly patch up the last argument and hustled Averell off to bed, so they could do the same. This time, to his relief, she welcomed him with open arms. Allen had picked up three new books for Averell in the airport in California and left them in his room thinking he was already asleep. It was late for a five-year old boy, but Averell was not tired and when the door closed, he turned on a light, picked up the books and laid on the bed, on top of the covers. As he browsed through the books one at a time, previewing the pictures, he could hear them bouncing on their bed, laughing and talking. When there was silence, he got up and made his way to his safe corner and started to read.

Allen mistakenly thought Ellie's attitude toward his traveling had shifted, but the following trip would prove him wrong. Tears were replaced by expletives that were a constant stream from Ellie's lips. "That son of a bitch," and "bastard" were common references and new to Averell's ears. Practice words for his alone time when banished to his room. He didn't know what the words meant, only that they were forbidden to say. When he used the word "bitch" in front of Ellie, he was sent to his room for the remainder of the week. Spilled milk and the slip of another word resulted in more punishment. No matter what he did to incur the wrath of his mother, the punishment always involved his being relegated to his room for the remainder of that week.

With each trip, Ellie became more withdrawn and the new punishment for Averell was to simply be ignored. That was almost worse than a beating and he found himself going to his room and the comfort of his corner. He squatted down and mumbled, "Damn it."

And a voice repeated, *"Damn it."*

Again, nobody else was in the room and Averell was confused. He didn't understand who was repeating his words and that disturbed him. He didn't know where the voice was coming from. Perhaps the voice was his mechanism for dealing with his confinement, or the unreasonable punishments he had to deal with by himself.

* * *

On day five of a six-day absence for Allen, Ellie found a babysitter, Charlotte, and went out to meet friends at a local restaurant and bar. Dinner and conversation had a very relaxing effect on her and when her friends started heading home, she ordered another drink. Alone at last, Ellie addressed the bartender, "One more time, and be generous."

Charlotte was fourteen and acted more like eighteen. She was tall and slim with large seductive eyes and a body that would soon attract the attention of boys her own age and much older. She fell asleep around 2:00 AM and Ellie woke her at 8:00 AM when she came in.

"Sorry for the late return," said Ellie, "I got into a conversation with the bartender that lasted until about 3:00 AM and they tell me that I fell asleep in mid-sentence."

"No problem," said Charlotte "I had a completely open book last night, and now you owe me for another five hours." They both laughed, and Ellie paid her giving her an extra ten. "You must have had a VERY good night," said Charlotte.

"Yeah, I should do that more often," she giggled.

***The occurrence of an auditory hallucination is experienced by something in the neighborhood of fifteen percent of the population at some time during their lives and experiencing an occasional voice repeating single words or simple phrases is not that alarming. Continuation of these episodes beyond the occasional simple utterance* *becomes concerning and the development of a psychotic condition that could negatively affect an individual's ability to cope in the modern world increases in probability.*

"As far as I know, you were home before midnight, and I fell asleep on your couch." Ellie pulled out another ten and Charlotte smiled knowingly and said, "Thank you."

Charlotte left, and Ellie went to her room, undressed and stood in the shower for a few minutes, then laid down on the bed and caught a quick nap. Averell was in his room leafing through a book. His door was open, as was Ellie's and he could hear her in the shower cursing as she washed herself off. He could only make out a few words, the ones that got him in trouble when he used them. He gently closed the door to his room and squatted in his corner.

Allen arrived home that evening to Ellie's stern and disapproving face. There would be no make-up session. Allen was tired and announced he was going to take a nap. Ellie was furious, "Your flight touched down at 4:12 this afternoon and you want to take a nap? I've been cooped up here for the last week and I need a break from the brat, you watch him for once. I'm going out … to a movie."

Allen was tired and had no patience for Averell. Allen pushed him away and called him a "little bastard." Averell was confused, he knew it was a bad word, but he didn't understand what he had done wrong. He went to his room and squatted in his corner, mumbling all the obscenities he could muster. Ellie was gone for about five hours and didn't want to talk about the movie or anything else when she returned home. She went straight to the bedroom, showered again and went to bed. Averell was awake, laying on his bed, looking at his ceiling and wondered why she used the shower again. He fell asleep.

It seemed the more often Allen went on business trips, the more often Averell was punished for offenses against some rule or other. It also often meant another book. So, Averell spent most of his time in his room where he crouched in his corner looking through his books. Allen's trips became more frequent, and money more abundant, which meant Ellie could utilize Charlotte for her many outings. The reunions between Allen and Ellie were more predictable, often ending in reconciliation—until the next time. The routine seemed to work its way into their lives and become accepted.

The first phase of Allen's project was soon complete, and all the documents were in a six-week review period with the client. No travel was required during that time, but the next phase of travel loomed large in Allen's mind, although he avoided discussion of it at all costs. They were getting back on track, the arguing stopped, and they actually enjoyed a few movies and dinners out. Then, magic happened. Ellie was feeling a bit ill in the mornings, and she felt somehow different. She went to the doctor and discovered she was pregnant. A complete surprise to all, including the doctor. Perhaps their reconciliations after each trip created a more perfect field for the sowing of the seed. Allen was confused, but happy and Ellie was happy, yet not quite as confused.

It was an uneventful pregnancy and as the time approached, Averell was pushed more and more into the background. The time he once spent with his mother in the middle of the day was cut shorter and shorter until it disappeared. The more time he spent alone, the more he withdrew and the more he acted out. Averell was alone in his room more often than not and he continued to talk to himself, muttering the forbidden words and losing himself in his books again and again.

Allen was not practiced in problem-solving and resorted to a swift swat on the most available cheek in response to any bad behavior displayed by Averell. Ellie found it easy to send him to his room, Averell learned to be alone, to play alone and to find comfort in being alone.

When he would quietly speak the forbidden words, the mysterious voice would continue to echo, "Damn it."

"Damn it."

"Bastard."

"Bastard."

Allen's trips resumed, minus the tears from Ellie. Averell became numb to her indifference as Charlotte made a few extra dollars.

*   *   *

THREE

How many crimes could a five-year old commit . . .

When the due day came in May of 1973, Ellie asked to be taken to the hospital, *quickly!* Allen called Charlotte, helped Ellie into the car, told Averell to let Charlotte in when she arrived and probably broke a few speed limits getting across town to the hospital. They made it to the emergency entrance in time and Ellie was rushed into a labor and delivery room where everything happened quite fast. It was a girl. A very little, very pink little girl. Allen looked at her through the glass partition with amazement. He was a real father. Ellie called her Sarah. Life was about to begin for Sarah and change for Averell. Life would also change for Allen and Ellie.

Sarah had blue eyes and strawberry hair. She was petite with a defined twinkle in her eyes. Allen wondered where the blue eyes and light hair came from, as his coloring was more, swarthy, and Ellie's was the same. He also did some math and determined Ellie became pregnant during the period when he was flying in and out of town on a weekly basis. Ellie was aware of his musings, she knew he suspected something, but she said nothing.

Sarah became the center of Ellie's entire world. Nothing else seemed to matter. Sarah was perfect. She was doted on and boasted about to all of Ellie's friends. Meanwhile, Averell seemed to fade into the backdrop more and more every day. One evening after dinner, Averell crept toward the kitchen and overheard his parents in conversation.

"We never should have gone to Romania."

"It was your idea, your mistake."

Averell was confused, the word "mistake" lingered in his memory, and he vowed to look up its meaning in the dictionary on the living room shelf that Allen had introduced him to. The next time he was alone, he would look in that book. "Mistake," Averell muttered to himself.

And the voice echoed, *"Mistake"*.

Averell avoided contact with Ellie, Allen and especially Sarah as often as possible. He didn't understand his feelings toward Sarah, but he knew that when she came home from the hospital, he was pushed aside. He didn't like her, but he could do little about it. If he hurt her, he would be severely punished. If he complained about her, he would suffer Ellie's wrath. It made no difference, he concluded it was best to just stay away from her.

It did not take long for the tension in the house to rise. The air was thick with mistrust. Allen started working late, Ellie didn't complain, and she seemed to look forward to his travel.

Averell took advantage of an opportunity to pull the dictionary off the shelf and look for the words he had heard. He looked through the book and found the word "bastard", he struggled with the meaning as he had both Ellie and Allen. He continued to look up words he knew were directed at or uttered in reference to himself and each definition made him angrier. *Why would they say those things about him?*

As Averell wondered about the words he was learning, Allen wondered about Sarah. He had a little private time one Saturday morning and took Averell to the library. "I have to look up a few things, you go and play in the toy room." Averell did as he was told. In time he became bored and looked around for his father. He found Allen sitting at a table with his head in his hands. Averell feared he was crying and thought it best to return to the toy room and wait for Allen to come get him. Allen had checked a medical book that covered blood types. He knew that he was type A, he knew that Ellie was type O and that Sarah was type B. He now also knew that Sarah was not his daughter. He found Averell sitting on a bench, waiting. "Come on," he said, "let's go home." His voice was sad, and the ride home was silent.

When they arrived, Ellie asked Averell where they had been, and Averell replied, "The library, I played with the toys and daddy read a book that made him sad." Allen heard the comment and decided this was as good a time as any to voice his discovery.

"I was looking through a medical book of blood types. It seems as though your blood type and mine cannot make a baby with Sarah's blood type. What do you think about that?" Confronted with this information, Ellie calmly suggested that Allen move out and allow her to raise Sarah alone. Averell was not mentioned.

Allen was furious and took the opportunity to do what he had been thinking about for months. He often kept a bag packed and ready for his next trip. He went to the bedroom and gathered a few more his belongings, including a cash reserve he kept in the dresser and returned to the living room. Ellie was sitting on a chair, holding Sarah. "If that's what you want, then that's what you will have. I'll send someone for the rest of my things," he said as he headed for the door. He walked out without another word and never returned. He arranged for a friend to retrieve several boxes the following week,

In October of that year, Ellie filed for divorce. It was finalized the following April without dispute. Ellie now was alone with Averell and Sarah. She seemed happy with this arrangement and soon had a new group of friends who called on her with some regularity. Allen was doing quite well with his new position, didn't contest the divorce settlement and sent the required checks every month through the courts. That payment, plus the monthly stipend from her grandfather's estate, kept Ellie from having to work. She was quite pleased, the only thorn in her side was Averell and he had learned to stay out of her way. He would play alone or sit and read for hours on end. He would even come to dinner late, after Ellie and Sarah had finished, and he accepted the cold food and warm milk as fair trade for avoiding contact with them. As he grew older, it became clearer and clearer that he was not wanted.

His increase in age brought an increase in chores. He cleared the table after meals, swept the floors and did the lighter work outside. Ellie always seemed able to find someone bigger to cut the grass and clear snow until he could handle the lawn mower and heft a loaded shovel in mid-winter.

Other than the increase in chores, Averell's existence changed very little. He was usually ignored, just pushed aside in favor of anyone or anything else, especially Sarah. He was not important, but now he was not punished as much.

*   *   *

Four

Keep the key . . .

Steve Danker was a tall, slender man with sandy wind-blown hair, blue eyes, large gnarly hands and a very rugged weather-beaten outdoor complexion. He showed interest in Ellie almost as soon as Allen walked out the door. Steve owned a general contracting company and was very generous. He would frequently buy Ellie little trinkets with diamonds or pearls, gifts that often opened the door to her bedroom. Steve started spending a lot of time at the house, he'd show up with a bottle of wine and the intent to stay for dinner—if not the entire night.

Steve treated Ellie like a princess, seemed to genuinely love Sarah and initially was nice to Averell. After a few weeks his kindness toward Averell began to wane. When he referred to Averell as a "brat" one evening, the boy retreated to his room with the dictionary in hand.

"Brat," muttered Averell as his finger traced the meaning.

"Brat," said the voice.

Steve knew Averell spent a great deal of time in his room to avoid contact with the rest of his family and came after him one morning. He raised his voice and accused Averell of making his mother cry.

"You're a little bastard, you make her cry. I don't like you, kid, and if it was up to me, I'd send you back to Romania." Steve delivered a firm kick to Averell's bottom. It was not a hard kick, it hurt his feelings more than it hurt his bottom, and he did not cry. As Steve was about to continue the verbal assault on Averell, Ellie called him, and he turned and left the room. The words and kick combined were the final straw. Averell thought to himself, "I hate you."

"I hate you," repeated the voice.

Steve moved in with Ellie, Sarah and Averell in May 1974. His blue eyes and sandy hair made it easy to assume he was the cause of Ellie's pregnancy two years prior. Steve and Ellie joked back and forth about him being Sarah's true father and Steve was sure he was, but Ellie's escapades during that turbulent period of her marriage to Allen left the question very much unanswered in her mind. Of course, he could be the father; she didn't know, and she didn't care. She now had a man in the house to provide for her and Sarah again, and Steve thought he was Sarah's true father.

Allen knew about the new living arrangements and decided he would move closer to his main project in California for the time being. He might even stay in California, if all went well. None of his family would miss him, they never talked, and he felt no real connection to any of them. So, in February of 1975, he put a deposit on an apartment in Sacramento. He was ready for new beginnings, determined to forget the past, he planned to buy a fancy car and reap all that California had to offer.

Steve became a permanent fixture in Ellie's house. He had moved some of his belongings in, clothes, tools and furnishings. Ellie often mentioned the prospect of marriage and all the advantages, and in time Steve concurred. They married in September of that year and Steve gladly adopted the two kids, Sarah and Averell. After all, Sarah was his, and Averell was part of the deal. Thus, in March of 1975, both Sarah and Averell took Steve's last name, Danker. Ellie wanted him legally tied to Averell, giving her a few more options and Sarah was the bait he could not refuse. This was good news to Allen, his alimony payments ceased and since Steve adopted both of the children, his financial obligations to them were over as well.

Averell began first grade at the local public school that Fall. During the registration process, a pile of paperwork was required to prove Averell's validity as an American citizen and he noted where the papers were kept. Ellie was not concerned about security, fire, or theft, and the papers were kept in a shoebox on a shelf in her bedroom. He planned to go through them and learn more about himself when the opportunity presented itself.

Life went on, the Dankers were a family, at least for a while. Little disagreements and Steve's wandering eye ate into the day-to-day activities and soon he was staying at work later and later. As Steve became more remote, Ellie called Charlotte more often to babysit while she also went out, alone.

So, it went on, Steve drank too much and was loud and abusive toward the rest of the family, Ellie was paying an extra ten to Charlotte more often than not and both Sarah and Averell got the worst of it. Even Sarah at this point experienced some negative treatment from Ellie. Sarah used to find it easy to join Ellie in bed in the morning for a short snuggle and sometimes for a brief nap. But if Steve was still in bed, Sarah was not allowed in. If Ellie was somewhat hung-over, Sarah was not welcome. The more Steve spent time out with friends, the more Ellie went out and the more she was either hung over or exhausted. Averell had never spent time in bed with his mom, and he found it deeply satisfying to see Sarah denied the same.

Their depraved behaviors when apart led to dismissiveness when together. When sober, they argued, and hurled accusations at each other. Steve continued to physically and emotionally abuse Averell, and Ellie tolerated it. Steve crossed the line one day when he swatted Sarah for some minor infraction and Ellie exploded, "What the hell are you doing? How dare you hit my daughter!"

"That's right, your daughter, she ain't mine, is she?"

"I really don't know!"

"I do! She's not my daughter, and that little Romanian bastard is not my son."

Averell heard the argument, and stayed hidden in the next room, under the dining room table, listening. Later when he was back in his room, he tried to write down all the words he had heard once more.

Bastard, damn it, Romanian, adoption; he couldn't spell them all, but he sounded them out and printed them on a piece of paper. As he looked at the paper, the voice said, *"Bastard, damn it."*

The wars continued. Ellie and Steve were frequently coming home at the same time, early in the morning. One night Ellie asked another man to spend the night in her bed, the thought of getting caught made the experience all the more thrilling. Her suitor left the house as dawn was breaking and Steve came home around two hours later. Ellie tried it again with another man and again Steve was oblivious. Soon she played the game at least twice a week. The neighbors knew, but Steve didn't have a clue.

This went on for a few months and finally Steve came home early one evening only to find a stranger in his house, holding a pizza box as Averell was getting the newspaper and mail off the dining room table. It was late May and the weather was warm. A breeze freshened everything, and Ellie was upstairs opening as many windows as she could to rid the house of stale odors.

"Who the hell are you?" demanded Steve.

Ellie's friend Dan replied with the same question.

"I am Steve Danker, and this is my house!"

"Oh, okay pal, I'm outta' here." Dan bolted out the door and was hurrying to his car as Ellie flew down the stairs.

"What did you do?" she demanded.

"Who was that, and what is he doing in my house?"

"Your House?!" Ellie protested. "This is MY HOUSE! And you are welcome to leave it anytime you want. The sooner, the better."

Sarah was frightened by the yelling and she ran to Averell. He led her up the stairs to her room and told her to sit in the corner where she would be safe. "If you are still scared, you can get into bed and get under the covers, that's safe too."

He then went to his room, sat in the corner and listened to the argument raging on the first floor. He didn't like listening to it, but he wasn't going to go downstairs and try to get past them to get outside. Averell looked across the room to his window, where it opened onto a flat roof over the garage. He often wondered what it would be like to escape onto the roof, he moved to the window and opened it. The screen came off easily so, he crawled out and sat on the roof, losing himself in the Spring breeze.

He stood and walked carefully across the flat surface, fearing he might at any second crash through and find himself in the garage. He carefully approached the edge and looked to the ground. It was a long way down and he was tense. He noticed a tree growing close to the opposite edge and made his way there, the tree's branches served as stepping-stones to a height he could safely descend to the ground. An empty garbage can would serve to elevate him to the lowest branch to climb back up and make his way back into his room—completely unnoticed.

Averell sat on the roof for a long time until he no longer heard the arguing on the first floor. He crawled back in through the window, replaced the screen and made sure there was no sign of his venturing out on to the roof. He went downstairs and found Ellie sitting in the living room reading a newspaper. The pizza was still on the table.

"Go set the table for dinner" she barked.

"Okay, is everybody going to be here?"

"Just the three of us, Sarah, me and you."

"Okay."

Dinner was quiet, the pizza had cooled down and the soda was warm. Sarah was still a little scared and behaved accordingly. Averell was curious about Steve but didn't ask. After dinner he cleaned off the table, loaded the dishwasher, swept the kitchen floor and straightened up the living room. He found several of Steve's tools near his chair and under the couch. He took them to his room and thought about how Steve used them and handled each one. A pair of pliers, a boxcutter, and a pair of wire cutters. Averell went back downstairs and joined Ellie in front of the television.

Suddenly Ellie stood up, tossed the newspaper to the floor and addressed the children, "I'm going out for a while, Charlotte will be here soon."

"Okay," said Averell.

"Okay, Mommy," said Sarah.

Ellie headed up to her room. A short while later, Charlotte arrived, and Ellie left without a word.

"Should we watch television?" This was Charlotte's standard question. Averell said he had something to do in his room and Sarah just nodded.

Averell pulled the shoebox from Ellie's closet shelf and opened it. The papers inside were confusing and full of odd names; Swall, Lupasco, Nadia and Stelian. None of the names meant anything to him,

It was around nine o'clock when he heard Charlotte bringing Sarah up to bed and he asked her, "Is mom home yet?"

"No, probably not for a while."

"Okay, I'm a little tired and gonna' go to bed."

"Okay by me, makes my life easier."

Charlotte finished putting Sarah in bed and hurried downstairs. She was on the phone immediately to a boyfriend and, shortly afterward, there was a knock at the front door. Averell was very much awake and heard the knock and then footsteps climbing the stairs and the sound of Ellie's bedroom door closing. He peeked into the hallway and heard some giggling. He went back to his room and crawled out on to the garage roof and made his way to the bedroom window, he looked in and saw Charlotte and a boy about her age, naked on the bed. He moved suddenly and made a noise.

"Shhh, careful," cautioned the voice, *"careful."*

"What was that?" said the boy.

"I don't know," said Charlotte, "maybe a squirrel."

Averell crept back to his window and into his room. He closed the screen, straightened the curtains and climbed back into bed, under the covers. He mumbled, "Safe, I'm safe." He lay there awake for a while saying "Safe, I'm safe." After about half an hour he fell asleep, still hearing the noises in the other room. He woke when he heard the shower running and thought that Ellie had come home. Then he heard Charlotte say to the boy, "Donnie, go downstairs and turn on the TV, I'll be there in a minute."

"Okay." He lumbered down the stairs, with his shoes in hand and his hair sticking out in all directions. He was still thinking of the last hour and he smiled as he turned on the television, sat on the couch and tried to straighten his hair. It was a losing effort and Donnie settled for his baseball cap to hold his mop in place. He tucked in his shirt and started to tie his shoes when Charlotte joined him. They were in front of the television when Ellie returned around midnight. She paid Charlotte the usual rate and was about to give the extra ten when Charlotte said, "No, we're even tonight." They looked at each other and smiled at the thought. Charlotte ran out to her boyfriend's car. Ellie thought back to when she and Allen first started dating, Ellie was younger than Charlotte.

She went upstairs and turned on the shower, noting the damp towel and spray in the shower stall. She laughed as she undressed and stepped into the shower. Averell was listening and opened his door to look.

Hearing the shower, he went into the hallway and noticed the door to the bathroom was open enough to see in. Through the frosted glass of the shower stall, he could see Ellie standing in the stream of water. Her back toward the door. She could not see Averell and he watched as she stood motionless, allowing the water to run over her for what seemed like a very long time. Then as Ellie reached to turn off the shower, Averell crept back to his room, closed the door and crawled into bed. About five minutes later he heard Ellie go into her room and close the door. He got out of his bed and crouched in the corner. "Why did she stand in the shower so long?"

"Why?"

Steve returned in the morning, went into the bathroom and stood in the shower like Ellie did, letting the water run over him for a good five minutes. He dressed and headed out to work. He said nothing to Ellie and gave Averell a look that said, "You're stuck here, I'm not."

Over the next two weeks, Steve began to gather his things in boxes and load them in his truck. Each trip to work took him to an apartment on the other side of town where the boxes were deposited. Ellie was aware of the slow secretive moves but said nothing. The time he spent in the house was uncomfortable for everybody. There was little to no conversation. Stares and short slighting comments were the rule of the day. Ellie slept in the bedroom and Steve spent nights on the living room couch. Sarah was constantly with Ellie and Averell hung around Steve. When Ellie was not around, Averell asked Steve questions about the words he had heard.

Steve had nothing to gain or lose and answered the inquiries with the best information he had. "Romania is a country in Europe, where you were born. I don't know the name of the town. Your name used to be Stelian Lupasco before Allen and your mom adopted you and brought you here to America."

"Why do you stand in the shower for a long time?"

"To wash away my sins, kid."

"Stelian?" said the voice.

"That's all I'm going to tell you, now go find something to do."

This was not what Averell expected. He took the information and sat in his corner trying to figure it out.

Why would his real mom let someone else take him?

Was he a bad baby and nobody wanted him?

"Bad baby," repeated the voice.

Was his real mom still in Romania?

Who was his real father?

Did he have any brothers or sisters?

What's a sin?

"Sin?" said the voice.

The questions kept coming to his young mind. Questions but no answers. He had mixed feelings about wanting to learn more.

Steve had moved everything he wanted to take, or thought he could take, and approached Ellie, "This ain't workin' out and I don't want to be here no more."

"So, leave, nobody's stopping you. There's the door, use it." Ellie was holding on to Sarah in a way that seemed to say, "She's mine and you can't have her."

Their voices grew louder and Averell went to his room and closed the door. He could still hear the argument and went out on the garage roof. After a while he heard the side door open and Steve came out, still grumbling. He took his keys out of his pocket and got into his truck. He sat there for a minute and took a key off the ring and threw it on the ground, started his truck, backed out the drive and drove away. Averell went over to the tree and climbed to the ground, walked over to the driveway and looked to see what Steve had thrown away. The light from a kitchen window reflected off something and Averell picked up the key and put it in his pocket. He climbed on the garbage can, to the tree, the roof and back into his room. He sat in his corner again and questioned no one in particular.

"What should I do?"

"Keep the key," answered the voice.

"Who said that?" The voice was strangely familiar, but no one was there in his room but him.

"You don't know?" said the voice.

"No!"

"You can call me, Stelian."

"Where are you, I can't see you."

"You don't have to see me, no one can see me and only you can hear me. I am wherever you are, I'm inside you," said Stelian, the voice.

Averell was scared, this did not make any sense. He got up and went downstairs and into the living room where Ellie was watching television with Sarah.

"Can I watch?"

"If you're quiet," said Ellie.

Averell sat there until he was sleepy and had difficulty keeping his eyes open. Ellie was engrossed in her program and hardly noticed Averell getting up and going to bed.

The next few days were unusually quiet around the house, Averell went to school each day, came home and stayed relatively close to Ellie or Sarah. No more voices, no more fear. He started to relax. He went to his room and read or played by himself again.

* * *

Five

We got new neighbors . . .

The summer passed, and a new school year began. Averell was now in the third grade, he was eight and feeling more independent. He wanted to try new things, he especially wanted to play baseball. He did not develop physically as many others had, he was shorter than most and not yet very strong. He wanted to be like other boys. The sport that was least demanding in size seemed to be baseball, but he wasn't very good at it, finding it difficult to connect bat to ball. He planned to practice, but his enthusiasm for the sport quickly waned.

Several weeks passed and Averell was feeling comfortable, feeling safe again. Then Steve called to argue with Ellie about a lawsuit she had filed against him, she planned to sue for support. The conversation was loud and the pair traded insults like machinegun fire. The battle raged for a good fifteen minutes when Averell escaped to his room. He could feel his world once again collapsing around him and he wanted to get out of the house. He went out the window to the roof, then to the ground and down the street to a large, wooded area two blocks away. He could no longer hear the fighting, now all he heard were the birds singing. It was so much nicer, he wanted to stay and never return home.

Averell had never been in the woods and was a little tentative. The trees were tall and close together. He could see small openings where the sun broke through and areas that were mostly bushes. He moved deeper into the woods looking back periodically to note his path. He hadn't realized the vastness of the fourteen-acre plot that had been a farm years before and had been left untouched since the farmer went off to war in the forties.

The farmer never returned and his family abandoned the property. Averell was looking for a place to rest when he heard voices. He was in heavy undergrowth and could see an opening ahead. The voices were getting louder and easier to understand. It sounded like several boys, about his age. His curiosity got the better of him and he crept a little lower, hiding his presence. He laid on the ground, looked through the leaves and could see four boys. He recognized them from school, they were older than him, and each had a reputation of a troublemaker. Averell was eight, these boys were at least ten and one of them was twelve, he was in the eighth grade. He stayed quiet and listened. He caught most of the words, several of which he was not allowed to say, even though Steve uttered them often, as did Ellie. The boys finally got up and took their leave.

Averell watched them leave, and then walked home and entered through the kitchen. Ellie was in the living room watching television when she spotted Averell, "I called you five minutes ago, where the hell were you?"

"I was outside," Averell answered, being vague to protect his secret way of escape.

"Get the table ready for dinner. You and Sarah will eat together, I'm going out," said Ellie.

"Okay." Averell was eager to end the conversation before any more questions were asked.

When the weather turned cold and rainy, Averell avoided the dark, damp woods. He had several new books and was content to stay at home and read or play by himself. Ellie frequently took Sarah out to the store or to visit a friend, but Averell was rarely brought along and was frequently left alone.

One afternoon that Fall, a large moving truck was parked in front of the neighbor's house all day as movers carried boxes and furniture out to the truck. Averell was curious and began to wonder who might move in. The answer came a week later on one of the few pleasant October days that year. Another truck parked in the same place as the other had and the movers carried furniture and boxes back into the house. Averell sat on the front porch and watched the activity. As he watched, a car pulled into the driveway. The new neighbors had arrived. Two younger girls and a boy that looked to be a year or two older than himself climbed out of the car, the girls breezed into the house, while the boy took his time and upon seeing Averell, gave a wave. Averell waved back, and the boy turned from the house and approached Averell.

"Hi, I'm Jimmy, we're movin' in today." Jimmy was a few inches taller than Averell, had short dark hair, quick blue eyes and a smile that put one at ease. He seemed to have no qualms about approaching a stranger and Averell wondered if he'd made friends this way often.

"I'm Averell, I live here."

"What kinda' name is Averell—never heard it before?"

"It's just a name," Averell shrugged.

Jimmy instantly regretted the awkward exchange and quickly changed the subject.

"Wanna' see my new house?"

"Sure," said Averell.

Averell had never been in that house. He had watched the people who lived there sometimes and often wondered what it was like inside. They walked in the front door, dodging the movers as they crossed the threshold. The floors were wooden and polished to a high shine and the walls were freshly painted with a coat of off-white. The overhead molding and baseboards were all a natural varnished dark wood, and the house was similar to Averell's in size and room configuration. Jimmy led him to an empty room on the second floor that he said was going to be his.

"I get my own room. My sisters have to share a room. What about you, you got your own room?"

"Yeah, I have a little sister and she has her own room too."

"Cool."

They sat in Jimmy's empty room and talked about moving and trucks. Jimmy was a nice guy, kind of big for his age, which happened to be the same as Averell's. Jimmy liked baseball and his dad had encouraged him to try all sports. So, he planned to check out the basketball team when he started school. Time passed quickly, and Averell lost track. He heard his mother calling him and he assumed it must be about dinner time, and she wanted him to set the table.

"That's my mom, I gotta' go."

"Okay, see ya in the morning for school. You can show me around," Jimmy said with a grin.

"Yeah, okay, sure. See ya," Averell headed out of the room.

"See ya," Jimmy called after him.

Averell ran home and breezed in through the kitchen, "I'm home."

"Where have you been?" asked Ellie as she opened an envelope. It was the first of her new alimony checks from Steve. The amount looked right, she had gone after more than Allen had been paying, and she got it.

"We got new neighbors, and there's this kid, he's my age, and he's a nice guy, and I'm gonna' show him around school tomorrow."

"That's nice, now set the table," she snapped.

After dinner, Averell looked out the window wondering about his new friend. Maybe he could show Averell how to play baseball. He was excited, he figured that this is what "happy" felt like.

In the morning, Averell met Jimmy out front and they walked up the street toward the school. When they arrived, Jimmy had to go to the office and get all signed up. "I'll see you later, maybe in a classroom if I get through the office stuff."

At lunchtime, Jimmy came into the cafeteria and spotted Averell.

"Hey, I go to the next class, you can show me the way."

"Sure," Averell was feeling good—proud that he was needed.

Jimmy was too late to sign up for the basketball team and he did not want to start football for another few years. So, the fall and winter passed with the two boys getting along, doing homework together and earning a few dollars shoveling snow. Averell was on top of the world.

Spring came, and with it, the baseball tryouts. Jimmy started practicing with a tennis ball, bouncing it off his garage door and catching it in his glove. Averell tried, using Jimmy's glove, but he was not very good at catching, and his throwing was even worse. When the tryouts started, Jimmy was a natural at either shortstop or third-base and he was able to pitch, but he preferred third. His slot on a team was a no brainer, the kid was good, able to fill several slots and better than any of the others. Averell, on the other hand, was terrible and was laughed at by the other boys.

"Hey, cool it, he's tryin'," barked Jimmy, "more than some of you."

The coaches liked Jimmy's attitude and his standing up for a friend. "The kid is good, young, but good. I like his efforts in leadership," said the pitching coach.

"Agreed, let's give him an 'A' on his shirt and see if it turns into a 'C' on next year's team," said the head coach.

The whole staff concurred. Jimmy was a leader. They also agreed that baseball was not in Averell's future.

One of the assistants offered, "Maybe Averell could be a manager, take care of the equipment."

"You think he would go for that? I mean, most kids think they should be starters, and anything less, well they get pissy and some even cry 'cause they aren't going to be the next Mickey Mantle," said the coach.

"Let's set the team and then ask Averell if he wants the manager's job. If he takes it, we minimize the damage, if he says no, then at least we tried, what else can we do?" The other coaches agreed it was the best way to handle the awkward situation.

When the roster was announced, the head coach called Averell into his office and explained the situation. "You aren't that good with throwing and catching, but you try hard and we like that. We would like you to be involved with the team and we have a need for someone to help with the equipment and watch the score during a game. We would call you a manager. Whatta' think 'bout that."

Averell was smart enough to know the coach was right, he was a terrible player. He also knew the coaches wanted Jimmy to play and be happy and since Averell was his friend, that was why Averell was offered the job. He knew from the beginning he was not going to be on the team, but he wanted to be part of the group. His hope was that he might be put on as the last man, more as ballast than player. So, when the coaches offered him the manager's spot, he was thrilled. He could be part of a team, he would be one of the guys, he would fit in, it was all good. All Averell had to do now was convince Ellie he should be allowed to be involved with the team.

When he got home and asked Ellie, she did not ask what he would be doing, she didn't care if he was a player, a manager or even a cheerleader, all she thought about was that it was another way to keep Averell out of her hair and she approved. Averell sensed her approval was more to benefit her than himself, but he didn't care. He ran out of the house and over to Jimmy's to tell him he was going to be with the team as the equipment manager.

Jimmy was surprised that anybody would be so excited at being equipment manager, but he gave Averell his first high five, and they laughed as they practiced a few variations that could be used when somebody scored a run or got a hit. The smile lasted on Averell's face until he fell asleep that night.

As the practice sessions passed, Averell proved to be good at his task. He kept things in order, fully accounted for all the equipment and was treated like one of the guys. The coach showed him how the score book was kept and allowed Averell to try it out during the three scrimmages that preceded the scheduled games. During those games he kept track of the scoring, at bats, hits, runs and errors. He also learned how to track the action on the field and enter it in the book.

"Averell, nice job. The book looks pretty good, we have our first league game on Tuesday, why don't you stay next to me during the game and keep the book. Before the game we have to set the line-up and figure who will come in for the pitcher in the fifth inning. So, you will call the names of the guys, who's up, who's on deck and who is in the hole. You'll keep track of the hits, runs and the errors. Are you okay with that?"

Averell was in his glory, he liked calling the batting order at the beginning of each inning and keeping the guys on deck and in the hole during the innings. Even better was giving high fives as the guys came off the field. He was given a task and he did it well, the coaches were happy with his work and Jimmy was proud to see his friend shine. The baseball season ended when the school year ended. Jimmy and most of the other boys played in a community league over the summer. Those teams were overloaded with kids who wanted to play. Most were not good enough to make the school teams, but they were all better than Averell and he did not stand a chance of playing on one of the teams in that league either. He would have been happy to be an equipment manager on Jimmy's team, but the coach had a daughter who enjoyed being around the boys and had done the job the year before. So, Averell was relegated to the role of spectator. After the community league had run its course, Jimmy went away to a sports camp for two weeks in Olean, New York and Averell stayed home.

* * *

Six

It tasted terrible, stringy and tough . . .

It was July, his friends were all involved in baseball and Averell was looking for a distraction. He was now nine years old and thought of himself as much older, more mature. When he noticed a group of older boys going into the woods, he decided he would see what was going on. He was quite adept at hiding and moving through the brush quietly. He followed them at a safe distance and watched as they set up a circle of logs to sit on and a smaller circle of stones in the middle, which they piled with small twigs and the larger sticks. Each of the four found a larger log and set them nearby, ready when needed. Then they sat around and started to talk. Averell crept closer and when he achieved a good vantage point, he listened to the conversation.

"I got it, we just have to set it up and stay clear, when it trips, we will hear the rattling around and we can check it out," said George, the tall one of the bunch. "It has a thing like a wall that moves with a lever and it lets you squeeze the critter and hold him still and you can do things to him."

"That sounds fancy, but, okay, let's set it up then," replied Tom, the heavy one.

"Where should we do it?" asked George.

"How 'bout over in that open area, there." said Frank, as he pointed. He was the smart one, thought Averell.

"Yeah, that looks good," agreed Tom.

Don didn't say anything. Averell thought of him as the quiet one. The boys went into the clearing and set their trap.

"Now we wait," said George, and they all went back to their seats around the unlit campfire. It didn't take long and the trap was sprung. George and Tom ran over to the trap and came back with a rabbit in the small cage.

"Hey guys, dinner," said Frank. "Somebody, start the fire. Then we kill it, skin it, put it on the spit, cook it, and then eat it." The rabbit was not about to go peacefully, and when the tall one reached inside the cage to grab it, the rabbit bit his hand. A little blood flowed from the cut and George then angrily grabbed the rabbit and broke its neck.

"Yeah, I'll start the flames, you skin the little bastard," said Frank.

There was that word, *bastard*, again. Averell didn't like these boys, and they didn't know how to kill the rabbit. George had to use his hands to twist its head around. These guys are stupid, except for Frank. He started the fire and Averell watched as he rearranged the small twigs and built a progressively larger pile of sticks, then he lit a small wad of dried grass and pushed it beneath the wood. The fire gave off very little smoke and probably was not visible from outside the woods.

The other three boys were skinning the rabbit and making a mess of it. There was blood everywhere and it was difficult to see any variation in the body parts. Frank took a green stick and sharpened one end on a rock and pierced a small piece of the rabbit, placed it over the fire and laughed at the other boys.

"You monkeys couldn't cook a hot dog without screwing it up."

"Yeah, well if you're all that smart," said George.

"George, I am that smart, and you're dumber than a bag of rocks. Here let me help you."

With that Frank showed the rest how to select a green stick, sharpen it and skewer a piece of meat, and cook it. The boys cooked and ate as much of the rabbit as Frank said they could.

"The rest is not good for eating, and if you had been more careful skinning it, we would have a rabbit skin that could be used for something else, like a coat."

"Damn small coat," said Tom.

Frank looked at him and said, "You need more than one, dummy. You catch enough of them and sew the skins together. Then you can make a coat."

The quiet one smiled, but still said nothing.

Averell was fascinated by the whole process. He wanted to try it. As he was thinking that through, the boys got up and prepared to leave.

"We should gather up all the bits that we didn't use and throw it away so nobody will know what we did."

"Okay Frank," said George. He cleaned up all the pieces he could find and wrapped them up in the remains of the hide.

As the boys were leaving, Averell noticed that the trap was left behind, forgotten. He waited until the boys were out of the woods, then went back and picked up the trap. He wiggled the movable partition, looked at the spring mechanism and thought about bait. Perhaps a piece of an apple or some candy. As he was thinking about bait, he found a place to hide the trap and left it there. He did not want to explain it to Ellie, and even more importantly he did not want the boys to see him with it.

The boys were back in the woods the next day and Averell once again crept up on them to listen.

"I'm sure it was right here" said George, "I know it was."

"You're a bonehead, you sure you didn't toss it when the little bastard bit you?" said Frank.

"No, I dropped it, right here."

They spent a few minutes looking in the brush near where George was standing. No luck, no trap.

"Could someone have found it and taken it?" asked Tom.

"I guess," said Frank, "let's get out of here. C'mon Don, let's go." The quiet one was still looking in the woods for the trap. He turned, waved and caught up with the others.

They left, and Averell followed shortly, staying well behind and out of sight. He went back that night after dark and waited to see if anyone else was there. Nobody. He remembered the fire sequence and did it just as Frank had done. He built a small fire just enough to give him light. He sat on a log and thought about the words he had heard, about Ellie, Sarah, Jimmy, Steve, Allen, then as he was about to put out the fire, he heard Stelian's voice.

"Why don't we just live out here, in the woods?"

"Who is that?" He already knew the answer.

"Stelian."

"I don't want to talk to you, go away!"

Averell quickly put out the fire and headed home. When he got there, the door was locked. As he was about to push the doorbell, Stelian's voice said, *"Use the key, you don't want to wake Ellie."*

He pulled the key from his pocket and very quietly opened the door. The clock in the kitchen read 12:06. If Ellie heard him, she would explode in his face and punish him. He closed and locked the door, crept up to his room, took off his clothes and noted the smell of the campfire. He dressed for bed and crawled under the covers. In the morning when he went downstairs, Ellie was drinking coffee and he said, "Can I wash some clothes?"

"Yeah, go ahead," she said, waving him away.

Ellie gave no indication she knew Averell had been out late and he was fine with that. He took the opportunity to get all his laundry done and when he thought he was finished, Ellie told him to do four more loads that she had piled in the hallway. They were Sarah's things.

"Wash Sarah's clothes, damn it," said Stelian.

Several days later, Averell found an opportunity to go back to the woods. Ellie had gone out, Sarah went to bed at 9:00pm and Averell announced to Charlotte that he was tired and was going to bed. She seemed pleased and picked up the phone to make a call. She waited until Averell went up the stairs and she dialed a number.

Averell had a Swiss army knife that he put in his pocket, he had also taken an apple from the kitchen, found a small flashlight and some matches he had hidden in his room. He turned out the lights and waited until he heard Charlotte and her friend come up the stairs and go into Ellie's bedroom. When he was sure that Charlotte was getting busy with her boyfriend, Averell unhooked his screen and started across the roof. He couldn't resist and walked over to the bedroom window and peered in. Charlotte and her boy-friend were in the bed, naked.

"They shouldn't be doing that," said Stelian.

Averell shrugged his shoulders, turned and left. He got to the campsite and set a small fire. Then he retrieved the animal trap and set it up in the clearing.

Stelian asked, *"How long do we wait?"*

"Until it snaps, we'll hear it," said Averell.

It took an hour for the trap to spring. It was a squirrel, a grey squirrel. He knew squirrels could bite and he had to be very careful. So, first, he had to kill the squirrel. He wiggled the lever on the side of the cage and the middle wall moved. He squeezed the squirrel against one exterior wall and with the animal immobilized, he locked the partition in place. He then used a flat rock to sharpen a stick to a fine point. The squirrel was very agitated and would not settle down. Averell maneuvered the sharpened stick to the squirrel's neck and pushed. The squirrel thrashed with its mouth open making a choking sound for a minute then no movement at all. Just to be sure Averell pulled the stick out and repositioned it where he thought the squirrel's heart would be and pushed hard and fast. The squirrel twitched briefly but ceased all movement after that. Averell felt a warm sense of pride wash over him as he looked at his work. He pulled the sharpened stick out of the squirrel.

"That was pretty cool," said Stelian.

Averell opened the cage and shook the squirrel out onto a log. He opened his knife and made a clean cut from the squirrel's throat to the crotch exposing the creature's insides to full view. He did not know which bits were edible and which were not. Not sure what to do, he sliced out a piece of what appeared to be meat and skewered it on a sharpened green stick and held it over the fire.

"That looks good, get another piece ready," said Stelian.

"One at a time," said Averell.

When it appeared that it was fully cooked, he took it away from the fire and blew on it before taking a bite. It tasted terrible, stringy and tough. This was not what he expected, and he spit out the rest. It was getting late and Averell thought it best to be home when Ellie came in. First, he had to get rid of the evidence. He collected all that remained of the squirrel and put it in the fire and sat back to watch it burn.

"It smells funny, maybe you cooked the wrong piece," said Stelian.

The smell of burning fur and flesh did not repel him, he sat calmly, watched and listened as the little animal crackled and sputtered as it burned. Averell had to add fuel several times to keep the fire going, trying to turn the body to ash. After a while, he gave up and with a stick he pulled the half-burned body parts out of the fire and loosened the soft earth under a bush making a hole where he placed the remains. He found several stones that he placed over the remains, then pushed the dirt back in the hole and stomped it down with his foot.

He returned the trap to its hiding place and made sure he had all his tools before heading for home. It was nearly midnight when he approached the edge of the woods and he saw an older boy with a girl walking toward him. He hid himself and watched as they looked around before going into the woods. Curious, he followed at a safe distance and they went directly to the campsite. They stopped, and the boy looked around with a concerned expression on his face. He put his hand in the fire pit and quickly withdrew it.

"Somebody else has been here, recently, this pit is still hot."

"Come on Jeff, let's get out of here," said the girl.

"Okay, let's go," he replied with an angry and disappointed look. Averell waited for them to leave and started for the street again. He stopped short and peered through the leaves and saw Jeff with two other boys and Sandy talking. They were looking around as if searching for someone. Averell sat down to wait them out. As he waited a car passed the woods, it was Ellie coming home. He wanted to get home just in case she opened his door to check on him. Not that she ever had before, but why take a chance? He picked up a few stones and threw them one at a time back into the woods. The boys heard it and charged into the woods with Sandy close behind. Averell then crept out of his hiding place and walked quietly across the street and down the block to home. When he was as far from the woods as he could be and still see the place where the boys were talking, he turned, paused and looked. They were still in the woods. He was halfway there.

He climbed up on the garbage can to the tree and on to the roof. He was getting pretty good at this maneuver. He walked quietly across the roof and opened his window and crawled in. He undressed and put on his pajamas and turned down his covers. His hands were filthy with both mud and blood. He needed to clean up. He heard no sounds from downstairs so he opened his door and went into the bathroom. He washed up and since he was making noise, he flushed the toilet and opened the bathroom door to go back to his room. Ellie appeared at the stairs coming up and apparently going to bed.

"What are you doing?"

"I had to use the bathroom."

"Get in bed, it's late."

"Okay," answered Averell.

He crawled into bed, pulled the covers up on himself and thought, "I made it, I'm safe."

"Yeah, safe," agreed Stelian.

He lay there in bed, thinking about the squirrel and seeing its eyes as he pushed the stick through its body. The animal's reaction was fascinating - the need to get free, the urge to bite or scratch back at him, how it would fight to stay alive, the fear of attack. Averell was breathing heavier, excited by the memory of that moment when the squirrel's eyes went full wide, then blank, when it stopped breathing. It made him tense up, breathe heavily and perspire. The excitement, the thrill, the final moment of life and he was in control. He wanted to do it again, he wanted to do it now. He wanted to feel that control over another being's destiny. His body was tensing, and he was sweating. He got out of bed and paced back and forth in his room, calming and cooling down. Then, as he relaxed, he sat in a corner with his back to two walls. He quietly said, "Again, I want to do it again."

"Again," said Stelian. Averell lowered his head and fell asleep in the corner.

Sunday morning came with a beam of light from his window crossing his face. It was early, around 6:30 and Ellie was surely still asleep. Averell stood and looked around his room and remembered his episode with the squirrel. He wanted urgently to do it again and started to dress. Sarah was awake and playing in her room. She would certainly wake Ellie and he would be tasked with, God knows what.

Averell finished dressing and started down the stairs when Sarah came out of her room and dropped a plastic cup with little pink Lego pieces all over the floor. Averell went back to Sarah "Shhhh, mommy's still asleep, let's be quiet." He picked up the Legos, led her quietly down the stairs and asked her if she wanted breakfast, "Then we can watch some cartoons, okay?"

"Okay," responded Sarah, happy to have someone looking after her in the early morning hours.

Averell poured cereal in two bowls and they sat at the kitchen table and ate their breakfast, quietly. When finished, Averell cleaned up the kitchen and turned on the television. As they sat there, watching cartoons, a man came down the stairs with his shoes in one hand and a set of keys in the other. Averell was surprised, and Sarah was afraid. "Who's that?" she whispered.

Averell was frozen in place as the man went quickly out the door and Ellie came down the stairs with her robe flying open behind her.

"What are you doing?"

"We're watching TV," said Averell.

"Why aren't you still in bed?"

"I woke up and Sarah was hungry, so we had breakfast," said Averell.

Sarah looked at Ellie and said, "Mommy, who was that man?"

"You should still be in bed."

Ellie was angry that her visitor had been seen and she did not feel like explaining. She diverted attention from her friend by criticizing Averell for getting up early. Averell thought that he had done a good thing, looking after his sister, but it appeared he only served to annoy Ellie.

"Go to your room and stay there until I call you."

Averell went back up the stairs. About an hour later he heard some movement in the hall outside his room. Then it stopped. He put aside the book he was reading, quietly opened the door enough to see Ellie and Sarah walking toward the stairs. They wore closely matching outfits of denim shorts and blouses, a pair of white tennis shoes completed their ensembles. He went back to his room and picked up his book. When he heard the door open and close with a click, he moved to his window where he could see them climb into the car and pull out of the driveway. He wondered where they went, but felt it was just as well that he be alone.

By noon, Averell was hungry and went downstairs to make a sandwich. He sat at the kitchen table and ate, then cleaned up and went up to the top of the stairs and sat down and waited. At one point he needed to use the bathroom and as he came out, he met Sarah in the hall.

"You couldn't come 'cause Mommy says you're bad," Sarah chided.

"Averell, I told you to stay in your room until I called you," Ellie's voice was stern.

"I had to use the bathroom," countered Averell.

"Averell get in your room, and stay there, understand? I will call you when I want to see your face!"

"Mommy said you're a bad boy. She hates you," said Sarah.

"She hates you," repeated Stelian.

Three hours later Averell was called downstairs and Ellie said, "Set the table for dinner."

"Set the table," repeated Stelian again.

*　　*　　*

Seven

Do you hate me now?

The week passed, Averell was allowed out of his room. The time spent in solitary was utilized in planning and preparing for his next visit to the woods. He wanted to have better tools for his sessions with the small animals that he captured. Sticks were crude, he didn't see them as dependable and they would be easily broken. He was playing with the wire cutters that Steve had left lying about and a hanger from his closet. He used the wire cutters to cut the hanger into two pieces about ten inches in length and bent one end into a loop with a short arm sticking out to one side. He thought about wrapping tape around the loop end to be used as a handle and cut the other end at an angle leaving a sharp point. He could use this as a probe to pierce an animal's skin. One was not enough, so he cut three hangers and bent the pieces into six probes of different lengths. These were his new probes, they wouldn't break, they would be easy to clean up and he could hide them in his room, or in the woods. As he sat in his room, he spread them out on the floor and pretended to select specific probes as a doctor would select a scalpel. Averell thought about Ellie punishing him for everything he did, he thought about Ellie scolding him for things he did not do. He sat in his corner and muttered words he knew he was not allowed to say and sharpened his wire probes with a stone he kept in his room.

He felt alone, and in pain. He thought about Ellie, he thought about Sarah, he thought about the squirrel. He thought about pushing a sharp probe through Ellie's neck. He could see the blood dripping on her white shoes, he could see her eyes, he could see her go limp. He smiled.

"She hates you," Stelian said again.

"I hate her." He sat in his corner thinking about going back to the woods. The next opportunity came when Ellie went out with a man and Charlotte was in charge. Averell waited until Charlotte was busy with her current boyfriend, then went out through his bedroom window, across the garage roof, to the tree, down to the ground and straight to the woods. He took a few minutes to check the area and be sure he was alone, then he built a small fire, retrieved the trap and set it up with bait, sat down with his probes and continued to sharpen them. It didn't take long for the trap to snap closed. Averell lined up his probes on a log and walked over to the trap. He had caught a gray rabbit, this one was going to pay for Averell's latest punishment. He used his new probes, first pinning the rabbit with the movable partition, then aligning the first of his probes, he slowly pushed it into the rabbit's abdomen. The second, third and fourth probes were similarly inserted into the rabbit's body and sometimes through its body and out the other side. He stared at the rabbit's eyes, the rabbit stared back. Averell inserted the remaining probes one at a time and watched his victim's eyes. Each probe caused pain, and that pain registered in the rabbit's eyes. Finally, the rabbit stopped resisting and Averell felt satisfied that his mission to kill had been accomplished.

"Do you hate me now?"

Later that night while sitting alone in his room, Averell cleaned each of the probes and carefully placed them back in his bag. These were his special probes, he had made them, he had sharpened them, he had used them, and he was going to use them again.

*　　*　　*

The next day he walked out of the house and started toward the woods with his bag of probes.

"Where are you going?" demanded Ellie.

"Outside," and he continued to walk without pausing.

"Where are you going? I don't like her," said Stelian.

"Neither do I," said Averell.

Ellie stood in the doorway and glared at him, then turned her attention back to the kitchen, muttering obscenities about the son she had once wanted so desperately.

* * *

When Averell arrived at the little campsite and saw the four boys sitting around the firepit talking, he could hear them in conversation about the injustices of adolescence.

"I hate my dad, he hits me and always bugs me to do chores. He don't give me no breaks," said George.

"Same here," agreed Tom, "we're supposed to be on summer vacation." He then turned to Don, "What about you, is your dad a jerk?"

"Nope." That was the first time Averell had heard Don talk.

"Nope," repeated Stelian.

"Look," said Frank, "the trick is to get up early, do a chore they're expecting you to do; cut the grass, clean your room—you know, just something to make them happy. They'll be glad something got done and they'll leave you alone."

Averell thought about that. It could work. Perhaps do a little something and Ellie would get off his back. It was worth a try.

The next morning Averell got up and went down to the kitchen. He set the table for breakfast and swept the floor. It was still early, and he went into the living room and straightened up, he dusted and was thinking about running the vacuum cleaner, but that would make too much noise. He noticed the windows were dirty and as he was headed to get the window cleaner, Sarah came down the stairs, "Do you want some cereal?" he asked.

"Yes, but mommy is still asleep."

"That's okay, she won't mind if we eat now," said Averell.

"Are you going to make her coffee?" asked Sarah.

"I don't know how," replied Averell.

"We should watch her and learn how," suggested Stelian.

"Good idea."

"What idea?" asked Sarah.

"Oh, I was just thinking about something."

"I don't like her either," said Stelian.

Sarah was looking at the cereal boxes, trying to decide which one she would have when Ellie came down the stairs. She walked into the kitchen and stopped, pausing to look around and saw all the work Averell had done. She said nothing. She walked over to the coffee pot and poured out the last of yesterday's brew, Averell watched as she rinsed the glass pot and refilled it with water. After pouring the water in the top of the machine, she threw away the old filter and grounds and placed three scoops of coffee into a fresh filter. She then sprinkled a dash of salt and put a pat of butter on top of the fresh grounds. She plugged it in and pushed the start button. She sat down next to Sarah and said, "Good morning Sarah, how are you today?"

Averell knew that Ellie liked a certain cereal that he did not, and it was on the table, obviously for her. Sarah had her favorite sweet cereal and Averell had the generic cereal that only he ate. Ellie still had not acknowledged Averell. The coffee finished brewing and Ellie noted a mug on the table, picked it up and filled it with her first caffeine fix of the morning. Averell finished his cereal, rinsed out his bowl and put it in the dishwasher. As he was walking out of the kitchen he looked back at the table. Ellie was engrossed in the newspaper and Sarah was looking Averell with an evil, twisted grin.

* * *

Averell went to his room and picked up his bag of probes, went back downstairs and started toward the door. Sarah was coming out of the kitchen, she looked at him and very quietly said, "You're a bastard and she hates you," then giggled and ran up the stairs.

Averell turned and walked out the front door as Ellie came into the living room. She was about to challenge him when she noticed that the room had been cleaned. As she stared at the room, he walked down the front steps and turned toward the woods. It had worked, Ellie didn't say a word and Averell was free—for the moment, anyway.

"It worked, we're free," said Stelian.

"Maybe, maybe it will work again, we will see."

He got to the woods and no one else was in sight. Perfect. He set the trap and sat down to wait, holding his probes, thinking about which one was best, and which one needed more sharpening. As he sat there casually scanning the surrounding area for a flat rock, he heard someone coming. It was three of the boys he had overheard before. No chance to hide, so he put his probes in the bag and put the bag under some leaves under a bush.

"Hey, look who's here, it's Skinny Danker," said Tom.

"Skinny?" repeated Stelian, incredulously.

"Yeah, what are you doin' here?" asked George.

"Same as us," said Frank, "lookin' for a place to hide from his dad."

"He don't got no dad—the guy ran away," said Tom, "and his mom is a ho."

"Not nice, Chubby," said Frank, "you get pissed when I call you fat, don't you think Danker has feelings too?"

"Hey, Danker, why does Lardo there think your mom's a ho?" asked George.

"Cause my dad says she has all kind a guys sleepin' there overnight. And that's bein' a ho," said Tom.

Averell didn't like anybody talking that way about Ellie. Even though he agreed to himself that she had a lot of boyfriends, still, that was none of their business. He glared at Tom.

"Hey Tom, you hit a nerve, Danker looks like he wants to hit you," said George.

"Cool it, you buttheads, he's just like the rest of us and your old man would jump in the sack with anything he could, so shut it!" said Frank.

"Hey, Danker we're goin' over to George's place and rip off some cigarettes from his old man, wanna' come?"

"I gotta' clean the windows today, but thanks."

The three stayed for another few minutes and were about to leave when the trap snapped shut. "Hey, that sounded like my trap," said Tom.

"Trap?" said Averell, "Trap?"

"Yeah, I lost it a coupla' weeks ago, did you find it?"

"What's it a trap for, I mean what do you catch with it?" asked Averell.

"You know squirrels and little things like that."

"What for?" quizzed Averell, trying desperately to take their attention away from the trap.

"Where is it? I heard it."

"Which way did you hear it from?" asked George.

"I don't know."

They all looked for a few minutes each went in a different direction, Averell went toward where he knew it was and pushed some bushes aside, "Nothing here."

A few minutes later Frank said, "You're hearing things, let's get some cigs, Hey Danker, last chance."

"No, maybe some other time."

The boys left, and Averell went to the trap. A squirrel was inside, appearing frantic and skittish. He picked up the cage and took it back to the campfire circle. He emptied his probes on a tree stump and carefully selected the one he wanted. He placed it where he thought it could go through without causing the squirrel to die. He pushed, and the squirrel barked at him, he pushed harder and the probe broke the skin and entered the squirrel's chest cavity. He slowed the probe and picked up another one. He set it at the connection of the front arm to the chest and pushed. The squirrel felt this one more than the first. Averell was enjoying the squirrel's eyes when his probe hit something and blood spurted out of the wound. The squirrel thrashed and stopped moving. It had stopped breathing and was dead.

"Very disappointing," said Averell, "I wanted this to last longer."

"Yes, much longer," agreed Stelian.

He decided he had to learn more about how things were built. How a squirrel was put together so that he could probe the animal without causing it to die, at least not until he was ready. He wanted to be able to avoid hitting a vein or a vital organ and end his fun. He wondered where he could find a book that would tell him that. Then he remembered going to a library with Allen. The library was his answer.

Over the next three weeks Averell got up in the morning and did a few chores, the house was constantly in order, the windows were clean, the floor was swept and the grass was cut without Ellie nagging him. She began to leave him alone to do as he wished. When he went out, she didn't question where he was going, she let him go. If he came home late, she said nothing. Averell was in charge of his own life and he enjoyed it. Nighttime was his chance to think about the woods, his probes, the library, anything he wanted without interruption. Almost.

"I know what you're thinking," said Stelian.

He imagined many things, as any young boy might. Driving a car, graduating from high school, getting a job, moving away from Ellie and Sarah, spending more time in the woods. He thought about girls his own age only once in a while and he didn't dwell on them. They were interesting, but at the same time more annoying than fun. He thought about using his probes on different animals. He thought about using them on Ellie. He thought about using them on Sarah.

On a very hot July night, Averell lay on his bed imagining using his probes on Sarah. He couldn't sleep, his room was very warm and he was soaked with sweat. He got out of bed and noted the time was 2:35am, he went into the bathroom, and soaked a small towel with cold water. He wiped himself down from head to toe, before heading back into the hallway. As he passed Ellie's bedroom, he saw a fan was blowing cool air around the room. He went to Sarah's room, and a fan was blowing air around her room as well. Both Ellie and Sarah were enjoying a deep sleep in their cool surroundings. Averell went back to his room and sat on the edge of his bed, "I wish I had a fan."

"Take the one from Sarah's room," suggested Stelian.

He opened his bag of probes and selected one, a longer one with a good handle. He held it in his hand and went back to Ellie's room. "I would like to push this probe through your eye," he thought.

"We could kill them both, tonight," said Stelian.

Averell stood there staring at Ellie for a long time, debating, longing to use his probe, but deciding not to. He turned and went back to his room.

"We could kill them both and say somebody broke into the house and did it. We could go out the window and hide on the roof," said Stelian.

"No, they would know. Too risky." He laid down on his bed and thought about killing them both and finally he fell asleep.

Every time Sarah heard Ellie say it, she repeated it to Averell, "Mommy hates you," and Ellie said it often. Sarah enjoyed repeating it and each time he heard those words, Averell thought about using his probes on Ellie and Sarah, but the opportunity did not present itself again as it had that July night.

Averell continued his pattern of doing chores to buy free time. While their hate for one another was mutual, each tried to stay out of the other's way.

Ellie frequently left money on the kitchen table and Averell wasn't sure how carefully she tracked the amount. He decided to test her and took two-dollar bills and put them under the table, when Ellie returned she picked up the cash and put it in her purse, not realizing it was two dollars short, then left the room.

As was the usual case, Ellie had plans for the evening and Averell waited for Charlotte to arrive. When Ellie left, went back into the kitchen and retrieved the two dollar bills he had placed under the table. He sat down in the living room and watched television until it was time for Sarah to go to bed. Then after Charlotte's boyfriend arrived and they disappeared into Ellie's room, Averell walked out of the house and down to the woods. He sat on a log and thought.

"We could catch a rabbit or a squirrel," suggested Stelian.

"No, not tonight, I have to think. I need a plan," said Averell. As he sat there, three of the boys showed up with some cigarettes. Averell had started a fire and was absorbed in thought when he was startled by their arrival.

"Hey, Danker, ain't it past your bedtime?" asked Tom.

"I told you guys to cool it with Danker, he's okay," said Frank.

"I do pretty much as I please," said Averell.

"Well, ain't you hot stuff?" said George.

"Yeah, kinda," said Averell.

At that all four laughed. "You're alright, Danker," said Frank as he dug out a handful of cigarettes. "Want one?"

"Why not?" said Averell as Frank handed him a cigarette.

"Where's Don?"

"He's in trouble with his folks," said Tom, "grounded for talking back."

"Yeah, and his dad probably slapped him around too," said George.

"He talks?" asked Averell.

"Oh yeah, he don't say much, but when he opens up, look out," said Frank.

All three laughed and Frank put the cigarettes on a log.

"Ever had one before?" said Frank, "Straight up, kid, if you have, that's okay. If not, that's okay too."

"Well, not really, but I have wanted to try one."

"Okay, here's what you do, DO NOT inhale at first. Suck a little smoke into your mouth and blow it out. Do that a few times and then inhale a little bit, a very little bit. You'll catch on."

Averell lit his cigarette and did as Frank told him, after a little while he took a very small drag and breathed it in, and immediately blew it out. A little cough, and he was ready to try it again.

"That's it, Danker, little drags. You're doin' good," said Tom.

"Yeah, real good," said Stelian sarcastically.

"One's your limit today, Danker. Maybe next time we see you here you can do two cigs," said Frank.

"Yeah, we don't want you should get addicted," said George.

Averell looked at Frank and said, "You know where the library is?"

"Yeah," said Frank, "You wanna' go there, in the summertime, when we ain't in school?"

"Yeah, I want to check out some stuff about bleeding," said Averell.

"Like what?" asked Frank.

"Like where can I cut someone and not make them bleed a lot," said Averell.

Tom frowned, "Cut someone? Who you gonna' kill? One of us?"

"No, no, I watched a movie, and somebody said in the movie, 'cut him where he won't bleed.'"

"I saw that flick, lotsa blood and guts," said Tom, "let's go to the library and check it out."

"It's too late, we could go tomorrow," said Frank.

"You can show me the way?" asked Averell.

"Sure, no problem."

The next day Averell met Frank in the woods, "Where are the others?" asked Averell.

"Not big readers," said Frank. He pointed to his temple, "Kinda empty upstairs." He grinned and placed an arm around Averell's shoulder. "We gotta take a bus to get there, you got any money?"

Averell pulled the two-dollar bills from his pocket, "Two bucks." Frank waved him away, "Naw, keep it, they usually want exact change, I'll cover you and we can even up later."

The two walked to the main street about two blocks away and caught the east bound bus. For the first time since his days with Jimmy, Averell was having fun.

*　　*　　*

EIGHT

Have you ever heard voices?

The library was much as Averell remembered it, large, full of books and very quiet. They went to the Information Desk and Frank asked the librarian where he could find books on the human body, she took them to the reference section and they started poring through the pictures and drawings of the body.

"There's a lot of stuff here," said Averell, "I can't remember it all."

"You can borrow books from a library, take 'em home for a week or two and bring 'em back," said Frank. "All you need is a library card, do you have one?"

"No, how do I get one?"

"You get your mom to come down here with you and she has to fill out a paper—and bingo, they give you a card."

Averell looked disappointed, "Okay."

"What, I told you, get your mom."

"That's the problem, her. She doesn't like me and won't do anything for me."

"Oh, okay, then we can do this a different way. Just let me do the talking, okay?"

"Yeah, okay," said Averell with renewed hope.

They returned to the main desk and Frank spoke to the librarian. "Excuse me miss," he said in a much more refined voice, "my cousin would like to apply for a library card. His mom is down in the car with a sprained ankle so, I brought him up here. What do we need to do?"

The librarian helped them fill out the application and said they should have Mom drop it off after she signs it. Frank said, "She's down in the car, I can run it down to her and come right back with it signed?"

"Well, yes why not, sure." The librarian was pleased to see two young boys so interested in the library.

Frank told Averell to stay put, he'd be right back. He borrowed a pen from the librarian and ran down the stairs and out to the parking lot. A few minutes later he was back, the name Ellie Danker was scrawled on the form. It had not occurred to Averell to sign his mother's name, but it was clear Frank was no stranger to forgery.

The librarian gave Averell a paper card and told him to look for the permanent card in the mail in a week or two. The boys walked out of the library with two books that Averell borrowed. Hel was impressed with the system, and he found Frank to be a nice guy and so he decided to trust him with a question.

"Frank, can I ask you something and you won't think I'm crazy?" as he asked the question, he knew it already sounded a little crazy.

"Sure," said Frank, "Hey, I hang out with three of the dumbest meatballs this side of the city, believe me, I hear crazy."

Averell relaxed a bit and said, "Have you ever heard voices when nobody is there?"

"Me? No, no never." Frank hesitated, then continued, "Well, almost never. Look, you ask me a tough question because if some people heard you or me sayin' that we hear voices, they may call put us in a rubber room, you know what I mean?"

"Yeah, sorta," agreed Averell.

"You're a nice kid. Sometimes your head is tryin' to tell you somethin' from deep down inside, and it comes out like you're hearin' stuff. But it is just you kinda' talkin' to yourself. That's not a bad thing, just don't get into no arguments, and don't tell nobody that it's happenin', okay?"

"Yeah, okay," Averell felt a little better about Stelian.

"So, you hearin' stuff all the time?" asked Frank.

"No, usually when I'm alone and trying to think."

"Okay, remember don't say nothin' to the guys about this, they don't understand," said Frank.

When he got home, Ellie was sitting in the living room reading the newspaper. She saw the books and asked where they came from.

"I borrowed them," he replied, and went up to his room.

Over the next two weeks Averell read through the books and made a number of trips to the woods, catching squirrels and rabbits and toying with them, torturing them with his probes, pushing the probes into and through their writhing bodies, watching their eyes as he played. He compared the pictures in the books to what he saw when he dissected the little animals. They did not always match to his liking and Averell realized he was looking at squirrels, and the books were based on people. He drew comparisons, but knew he needed better information.

Averell got to the mailbox each day before Ellie could and when a letter from the Public Library arrived, he pocketed it and put the rest of the mail on the dining room table. He took the envelope from the library to his room and opened it. There was his permanent library card. Armed with his card and a few quarters, Averell alternated between the woods and the library. His process of probing the animals became more directed, trying to insert his instruments and move them around for a longer period, always watching the animal's eyes, and piercing specific organs only when he had finished his investigation. He was getting better at his sessions because now he knew something about what he was probing. After an animal stopped moving, Averell would use the box cutter to make as precise a surgical incision on the animals, from throat to groin, as he could, to remove and review their parts. He continued to compare the animal's insides with what he saw in various books and read about the parts he recognized. He thought about the Library often and it became one of his favorite places. He was in control of what he did, what he read, what he learned. The only problems were when questions that arose, and he had no one to confer with. It occurred to him a science teacher at school may be a resource. He was now anxious to get back to school where he could ask his questions.

Ellie returned from the grocery store and put the bags, along with the change, on the table. Averell saw the opportunity and pocketed two quarters and two more dollar-bills. Ellie couldn't be certain, but she thought he might have a few coins—but decided to let it go, determining he wasn't worth her time and energy.

Averell got up in the morning, did a few chores and ran to catch the bus. One quarter was all he needed for the ride to the library. When he got there and turned in the books he had borrowed, he looked around for others. He found one on squirrels and pored over it for an hour. Then, realizing the time, he went to the check-out counter and handed the librarian his new card and the book. He then hurried out to catch the bus, using another quarter for the ride home.

* * *

Nine

That made the cat screech . . .

July gave way to August and Jimmy returned from baseball camp. The boys were nine years old and got along famously through the end of the summer break. September brought the new school year and the new football season. Jimmy still wanted to wait a few more years before starting to play football. He would try out for the basketball team this year, and since he had never played organized basketball before, he wanted to see how he would stack up against the other kids his age. Once again, he was a natural. Jimmy took to the game as if he had been playing for several years. The other positive with Jimmy was the ability to coach him. The same staff that coached the baseball team also did the basketball team. They remembered Jimmy and that he actually listened to the coaches and did as he was told. After a number of repetitions at almost any exercise, he had it.

Averell went to the first practice and the coaches knew what he could do with a score book for the baseball team. He could probably do the same with a basketball score book and he was warmly welcomed as a member of the team. As it turned out, Averell's value was more as a bookkeeper than an equipment caretaker, but he did both jobs and enjoyed it. Jimmy and Averell were locked in for the season. Sports at this age was still taken rather lightly, with the objective simply to learn and have fun, and that's what they did.

The team was not that good, but all of the boys enjoyed the season. They played their games on Tuesday and Friday afternoons. Half of the games were at their school and the others were at one of the other local schools. There were no extended trips and the boys were home by seven when they had an away game. The season was broken by the winter break when a great number of people traveled to visit relatives. Jimmy and his family drove to Philadelphia to visit his mother's family and Averell stayed home. Ellie was not big on holidays and especially did not like buying presents for Averell, whether it was his birthday or Christmas. She usually picked up a handful of books and Averell appreciated the gesture. This year was no different. Averell was given five books that dealt with animals and baseball while Sarah had a pile of clothes and toys. Once again Sarah delighted in telling Averell that she was the favorite and "Mommy hates you."

January and the resumption of school couldn't have come soon enough. Averell was again involved with the basketball team and spent as much time away from the house as he could. As the winter snows melted and spring brought out the baseballs and bats, Averell and Jimmy were ready. The transition from one sport to the other was no problem for either of them. Both having reached the age of ten, they felt like they had grown up—they were young men. This season, Jimmy was given a uniform with a "C" on his shirt and Averell was again the team manager and all was well. This season, the game was taking on a more serious tone. The team was now playing harder, playing to win. The lads expected to be pulled out of a game if they made mistakes. The coaches stressed teamwork and winning this year. The games were more intense and more fun when they won. At the season's end, their record was a little better than .500. They won more than they lost, but not enough to win their league. They actually finished third, which was not bad for a team that had never won that many games in a season.

When summer arrived, and Jimmy was again going to play on a community league team and go to camp, Averell steeled himself for the duration. He once again visited the woods, found his hidden trap and tools and again took to catching small wild animals.

One day about mid-summer, when he heard his trap slam shut, he went to check and found that he had captured a cat. The animal had a collar and a tag, it was somebody's pet. He did not read the tag, but he was curious about how a cat might be different from a squirrel or a rabbit. He was going to find out, he was excited about the prospect of probing a different animal, an animal that should not be afraid of people like a squirrel was. He'd never felt like this before. As he began his probing with the knife, the cat screamed, and he dropped the cage. It had startled him, but he was not deterred. He regained his composure and the cage, secured the cat with the movable partition and proceeded with his probing. He ignored the cat's screams and carried on, very deliberately, very carefully. It was precise, satisfying work, discovering things he could do that did not make the animals stop moving. Some other things were more dangerous for the animal. He was in the process of removing the cat's left front leg when it seemed to stop moving, stop resisting, stop being interesting. He took a probe and positioned it for a thrust into the heart.

"No, no, an easy push, just make sure it's not pretending to be dead," said Stelian, as if this were an operation.

"Yeah, you're right" replied Averell. And he gently pushed the probe into the cat's chest but not all the way to its heart. That made the cat screech and the game was back on. He continued with the leg removal.

"See," said Stelian, *"I can help."*

"Yeah, sometimes," replied Averell.

"Remember the key, I helped then too," said Stelian.

"I guess."

Averell had the leg almost all the way off when he heard someone moving in the woods. He had to silence the cat, now. He made a fast-final cut at the leg, pulled it off and quickly placed the knife at the cat's throat. Another fast cut and the cat went completely limp. There was not enough time to put out the fire and put his things away. He had to act fast. He quickly dumped the cat out of the cage and gathered up his tools and put them in the tree. Then he grabbed the cat by its tail and the loose leg and darted into the bushes. He crept quietly in the direction away from the campsite until he heard voices.

"Yeah, someone was here alright, Will. The fire is still going," said the first man.

"Yeah, Chuck, sounded like they were strangling a cat," said the second man.

"Probably those punk kids that hang out here and smoke and drink beer," said the first man.

"We probably scared the little bastards off," said the other, "we ought to put this fire out and keep an eye on these woods for a while, see who's been comin' in here."

"Probably, yeah, we'll do that, I got a good line of sight from my front porch. We can sit there with your binoculars and watch."

"Maybe have a beer or two of our own."

They kicked dirt on the fire, smothering it, and walked toward the clearing.

Averell was well ahead of them and moved quietly out in front of them. He headed down the street in the direction he knew the older boys had come from the other day and dumped the cat in a garbage container that had been put out for collection in the morning. He continued in the same direction and walked all the way around the block to his house to avoid the two men. He walked in the side door, not hiding from Ellie. It was still early for a Saturday night, well before ten. He quietly went to the bathroom, washed his hands and then to his bedroom. He went to the window and looked out at the cloudless sky. He was looking at the moon and stars and he said quietly, "Safe, I'm home and safe."

"Yeah, safe," agreed Stelian.

He laid on the bed for a few minutes, then got up and walked over to the corner. He squatted in the corner with his back touching the two walls, picked up his book on squirrels and started to read.

The next night, well before dark, he rode his bicycle past the woods and in the direction of the house where he had dumped the cat. Directly across the street he saw two men sitting on a porch drinking beer and looking around the neighborhood with binoculars.

"Hey, kid, come here," said Chuck, the first man from the night before. He was the taller of the two, and older looking.

Averell approached but kept his distance, "Did you call me?"

"Yeah," said Will, the second man, "you know who hangs out in the woods?" He was short, bald and heavy.

"No, the woods are kinda' scary, I don't like to go in there."

"Liar," whispered Stelian.

"But you have been in there, right?" asked the first man.

"Yeah, a coupla' times, not much though."

"You see other kids in there?" asked the second man.

"No, I kinda ran in and ran out, didn't go too far. Why?"

"Ah, never mind," said the second man, waving Averell away.

Averell got back on his bike and kept going, again taking the long way home. As he was pulling away, the first man called out, but Averell ignored him, pretending he did not hear him. He peddled a little faster. No mention of the cat, and all the trash containers were all back in place. He arrived home to find Jimmy had gotten back from his summer camp. Averell saw him talking to his father on the front porch and he waved. Jimmy waved back, but with a straight face. Something was wrong. Averell parked his bike in the garage and walked back around front. Jimmy was on his lawn heading in Averell's direction.

"Hey, Av, how you been?"

"Okay, what's up? You don't look happy."

"Yeah, well my dad has been transferred again, to Buffalo. About a hundred miles from here."

"Oh, so that means you're going to move," Averell couldn't hide his disappointment.

"Yeah, this happens every coupla years, I never know where to next."

"Doesn't seem fair, I mean to you and your sisters."

"We could bounce back in a few years, you never know."

"Yeah, well, if you do come back, I'll probably still be here, we have never moved, my dads have, but we stay here."

The boys had a week before the move and they did everything together. Then the day came, the truck arrived, and the movers did their job, hauling furniture and boxes. That evening, Jimmy got in his dad's car and they drove away.

The house had a "For Sale" sign for a few weeks and finally another truck arrived, more movers carried furniture and boxes into the house. When the family arrived, Averell was disappointed to see three girls get out of the car, no boys.

School began, and Averell was not asked to help with the equipment for the basketball team. The coach's son was now old enough to be involved and the job went to him. He went to a game after school and was ignored. His greetings to a few friends from the previous year were met with little enthusiasm.

* * *

TEN

Averell was about to be beaten up . . .

The next three years were much the same, spring and fall Averell was in school and needed time to study, he had no time for the woods or the small animals. He put his probes in a special place in the garage where Ellie and Sarah would never look. When school was out for the summer, Averell retrieved his probes and spent most of his time in the woods, alone with the animals. He became more efficient with the probes, keeping the animals alive longer and prolonging their suffering, watching their eyes longer and longer as they slowly died. Their pain was his doing and their eyes were his fun. Stelian visited more frequently and their conversations were more in depth, more interesting. Often discussions about cutting different parts from squirrels and rabbits would take place. Stelian would never stay longer than welcome. Whenever Averell told him to leave, he complied.

In the fall of 1982, Averell was in his first year of high school. He was now fourteen and a fairly good student. He was also somewhat interested in girls, although he did not understand why. He noticed them and they made him uneasy, he talked to them and they made him nervous. He found himself wanting to touch them like he remembered Charlotte being touched. It was a very confusing time. He decided to avoid them, that was the easiest way to get through the day. He sometimes looked at a girl and wondered what it would be like to have his probes, and a girl, in the woods.

Sarah was nine, and becoming even more of a pest, she knew everything. Averell could not tell her anything. She already knew everything worth knowing. She was bright enough, but not near as bright as Averell. She, however, boasted about every complement from her teachers, about everything she did right. At the same time, she found it only proper to be critical of Averell, after all, her mother was and she relished telling Averell that "Mommy hates you." She said it every time she heard Ellie say it, which was often. Each time, Averell would grit his teeth and think about Sarah and his probes.

In school, Averell had no desire to be a part of any definable group, he enjoyed being a loner that did not exist to others. Many of the non-jocks who wished to assert themselves would seek out someone like Averell, someone who was smaller and apparently weaker and somebody that nobody cared about—and proceed to beat him up. A classic process where acceptance was gained by dominating someone weaker. So, in the spring of 1983, when Brian Cooper wanted status as a tough, he needed a victim, someone he could easily defeat. A bloody nose was always a nice touch, especially if accompanied by tears and Brian's older brother Bobby had been encouraging him to accept the challenge. After school, while the crowd milled around outside the school, Averell noticed an attractive girl and was contemplating all the things he could do with his probes. Brian saw him and noticed that he was looking at Carol. He intentionally bumped into Averell and tried to goad him into a fight.

"Watch where you're going!" Everybody nearby knew what was happening. They all knew that Averell was about to be beaten up. A small crowd gathered to watch the spectacle. Averell did not respond, he apologized and tried to move on. Brian was bigger than Averell and had been in fights before. He knew he could take Averell and was not about to back down now, "And you're stupid." Still nothing. Then Brian grabbed Averell's shoulder to spin him around and said, "C'mon you stupid bastard, fight me." Averell was not easy to provoke but that was the one word that did it, he turned and swung his best punch right at Brian's nose. Contact. For Averell, it was lucky, for Brian, it was messy. Brian was bleeding, crying and running from the crowd, heading back into the school. Bobby, watching from a fair distance ran after his brother to check on him. He came back out and looked for Averell, but Averell had taken the opportunity to get a head start toward home.

"Danker. Where did he go?" demanded Bobby.

"That way," pointed several kids, not wanting to be on Bobby's bad side. He was much bigger than his brother and a lot meaner and was personally insulted that some scrawny little freak could beat up his brother. Family honor was at stake here and Bobby was about to put it right. He took off after Averell and the crowd, now larger, followed. He caught Averell about a block from his house.

"Okay Danker, now you're mine." With that, Bobby proceeded to beat Averell with his fists until Averell also had a bloody nose. But he could not make him cry. An adult came out of her house and yelled, "I called the police." That broke up the crowd and everybody went in different directions. Averell had been beaten, but he also gained the respect of the crowd for not crying or giving up Bobby's name.

"Are you alright?" asked the woman.

"Yeah, I'm okay." Averell picked up his books and headed home. Ellie was not home, so Averell was able to get cleaned up and toss his blood-soaked shirt and pants into the laundry. When Ellie returned from wherever she had been, Averell was finishing his laundry and had started his homework. Ellie noticed that his face was slightly bruised and asked, "Have you been fighting?"

"It's not a fight when the other guy is twice your size, and older," offered Averell.

Ellie had no pity, "Well, what do you expect when you offend everybody you meet?"

*　　*　　*

Summer came and now Averell was fifteen. He continued to visit the woods and mutilate animals. One night in late June he was heading into the woods when he saw Bobby with a girl coming from the opposite direction. They did not see him and to avoid another confrontation, he slipped into the woods and hid in the bushes. Bobby and the girl were going down the path toward the campsite. Averell followed and watched. They sat on the logs talking quietly for about half an hour when the girl stood up and said loud enough to be heard, "No, what if somebody comes?"

"Nobody comes here at night, Lisa," said Bobby.

"Well," said Lisa.

"C'mon, sit down."

They sat and talked more and started to hug. Averell figured they were about to do something and he wanted to leave before they started.

Then he heard Stelian's voice say, *"No, stick around, this could be very interesting, we may be able to use this."*

How? he thought.

"Let's wait and see," said Stelian.

When he looked again, they had taken off their clothes and were lying on a blanket. He dropped back down so as not to be seen, and he listened.

"I'll never tell anyone, I promise," said Bobby.

"Well, okay then, but just a little," said Lisa.

Averell slowly crept away and out of the woods.

The next day Averell wrote a note to George, one of Bobby's friends, as if he were Bobby, telling him about being with Lisa in the woods and doing more than he actually did. He embellished as much as he could, using every word he had heard. He also wrote to two of the other boys he knew were close to Bobby, bragging about getting Lisa alone and naked.

As in any teenage scenario, word spread like a bad cold. Everyone was talking about Bobby and Lisa being naked on a blanket in the woods. Word got to Lisa, she was furious, and embarrassed. Worse, Lisa's older brother, Mike, heard about it from his friends and, having no sense of humor whatsoever, proceeded to look for Bobby.

When Mark saw Averell and asked about Bobby, Averell told him he hadn't seen him since Bobby beat him up. "I'm gonna' kill that son of a bitch." Mark was a solid six foot two and heavily muscled. He had graduated from High School and had been accepted at Syracuse University where he was going to play football. He had been good enough in High School and was looking pretty good in the first round of summer workouts at the university. Then he hurt his knee and his options were surgery and rehab, then maybe football—or forget football and let the knee heal. He opted to pass on the surgery and got a job working construction. After two years of wielding a shovel and pushing a broom he was given a shot at operating a jack hammer breaking up concrete. Not exactly light work, but it was an increase in pay and he liked operating the machine.

"Works for me," said Averell. That made Mark smile for the first time since he heard the news.

"He's gonna' kill the son of a bitch. Ha, I love it," laughed Stelian.

Word reached Bobby about what supposedly had happened, and he was completely confused. He didn't write the notes. George showed him his note and Bobby said it wasn't even his handwriting. That would make no difference to Mark. He was intent on locating and beating Bobby to a pulp.

Bobby heard Mark was after him and tried to avoid him, "Maybe he will calm down in a day, or a week."

Luck was not on his side and Mark found Bobby. No amount of explaining did any good, no amount of pleading did any good either. Mark cornered Bobby and unleashed his rage. Bobby was soon in the emergency room, being treated for cuts and bruises, some of which required a few stitches, but none serious enough to require extended hospitalization.

Mark was arrested for assault and the whole matter was hauled into court before a judge. Both Mark and Bobby were over eighteen and Lisa was almost sixteen. It appeared someone was going to go to jail.

Probably both, and Lisa was grounded for the summer. Bobby had several stitches in his face, a few bruises and would have trouble walking for a day or two but all in all, he was alright. Even his father did not sympathize when he went to the hospital to pick up his son. Cindy, Bobby's sister, was with him, and she was also just sixteen.

Averell was picking up some things at the grocery store when he heard two girls talking about Mark and Bobby being in court and that the judge determined two weeks of community service would be sufficient for both of them. In spite of Bobby's pleas and both his and Lisa's denials about exactly what happened in the woods, nobody knew for sure what had happened and nobody even imagined that Averell was the source of the notes—the cause of all the trouble. He had evened a score in his mind and nobody knew. He was once again safe.

"That was choice," commented Stelian.

"Worked for me," said Averell and he laughed as he walked home.

He had stood up to Brian and won, he had taken a beating from Bobby and did not cry. He was not considered a tough guy, but neither was he to be pushed around. The rest of Averell's high school years passed without incident. He visited the woods a few times each summer and by the time graduation came around, he no longer felt the need to visit the woods. He put his probes in a bag and hid them in the garage behind a support between two wall studs.

After graduation Averell was unsure what he wanted to do. He was now eighteen and free to do what he wanted. Ellie told him that there was no money for him to go to college and he had to get a job. He was bright enough for college level work and his somewhat shady experiences with the critters in the woods, along with all the reading that he had done, gave him a leg up in anatomy or biology related studies. His grades would qualify him for most schools across the country, but scholarships that would cover everything were not a sure thing and Ellie was not going to help him. She was hoping he would either move out and be out of her hair or get a job and pay her room and board each month. Averell's choices were limited. He looked into military service and inquired about college programs during and after enlistment.

*　　*　　*

ELEVEN

An investigation was conducted . . .

Averell had seen recruiters at the high school during his senior year and visited with an army recruiter in a strip mall near his house. Giving it serious thought, he envisioned himself the perfect soldier. He liked the idea of living in the wild, off the land, hunting both food and enemies. He would learn about weapons, he would become a weapon, a killing machine. The thought of combat did not scare him; it rather intrigued him. The opportunity to kill another man before he killed you excited him. He decided to enlist and see what the army could offer him, both while on active duty and after his discharge. A three-year enlistment would allow him to save money and qualify for educational assistance. So, he took a bus to the strip mall, marched into the recruiter's office and filled out the required paperwork.

When he returned home and told Ellie, she didn't react, she just wanted to know how soon he would be leaving. He said he had to go to another recruiting center downtown where he would be tested and be given a physical. After that, he would be given orders defining where to report. Ellie wasn't moved in any way, she did not comment and returned to her newspaper. Averell looked at her for a moment and thought how good it would be to no longer have to put up with this treatment. He was angry with her but smiled and walked out of the room.

He visited the downtown recruiting office later that week and took the battery of tests. Upon finishing the physical, he was instructed to report to the bus terminal on Erie Boulevard in one week.

"You can bring a razor and a toothbrush, don't need much more than that. What you do need, we will give you," said the recruiting NCO.

Over that last week of civilian life, Averell dreamt of growing taller, building muscle and becoming a killing machine. He was five foot eight and weighed one hundred fifty-three pounds. He thought of the Green Berets, airborne, secret missions, danger and always, killing. The week passed, and Averell showed up at the bus station, on schedule, along with eleven of the other young men. One recruit was missing and the recruiter was not happy.

He barked a few final instructions about behavior on the bus and how to act when they arrived, then gave the group a final look and ordered them onto the bus to Fort Dix in New Jersey where their basic training would take place. Boot camp was more difficult than Averell had imagined. He had a hard time keeping up with the physical aspects and everything hurt. He had blisters, bruises, bumps, scratches and cuts everywhere. He stayed in the showers as long as they let him and began to lose his enthusiasm for the special forces training. His new goal was to survive basic training, then he would figure out the rest. He would not give up and quit, even if he could, he would finish what he started. He was actually rather good on the rifle range, shooting expert and able to strip down his weapon and reassemble it faster than most of the platoon.

Military basic training is dangerous, by virtue of its purpose. After all, this was the army. There is risk in every exercise and people do get hurt on occasion. Averell was learning to be a soldier, to engage in combat, so minor injuries were to be expected. On a day when his platoon was learning about hand-to-hand combat, he took a solid hit to his midsection from Al Davis, a fellow recruit, and he vomited. The drill sergeant told him to sit down and relax. Take it easy, let the pain pass and he could rejoin the others when he felt better. Even though Davis was a bully, always pushing people around, this was embarrassing, degrading, and he wanted to show he was equal to the others, but what could he do? The rest of the day passed with slight glances from the others and short laughs that made him feel smaller and inadequate. Over the following two days of hand-to-hand training, Davis threw cheap shots at three others. Each time the teasing was less and the looks of disdain were directed at Davis now, rather than his victims. This was his thing, this was how he grew up. He climbed over others to get what he wanted and punching Averell in the gut was just another step to his goal. Nobody appreciated Davis' approach and the entire platoon silently agreed that someday Davis would catch the short end.

While on a cleaning detail after the hand-to-hand training, Averell found a piece of wood about two feet long and hard as a rock. He kept it out of sight and secreted it back to the barracks. At night, he retrieved the stick and put it under his mattress where he could get to it quickly. It would serve him well if Davis, or anyone else, ever tried to rough him up again.

"Let's not wait for him to attack again. We could get him while he is asleep," suggested Stelian.

We could, thought Averell. "We might," he said quietly.

That night while everyone was asleep, and the fire watch had walked into the latrine, Averell crept over to Davis' bunk with the stick. He hit him three times around his right ear as hard as he could. He was thinking Davis might die from the beating, but that would be okay. Davis deserved to be hurt, even to die. Averell heard a noise and assumed the fire watch was returning. He left the stick next to Davis and quietly went back to his bunk, pulled the blanket up around his neck and shivered with excitement, even though it was nearly eighty-degrees. He laid there and listened for sounds, everything was quiet, no movement except the fire watch walking past. He waited for something else, but nothing happened. The fire watch never noticed Davis and the wounds around his bloodied ear. Eventually Averell relaxed, he had done it and now he could sleep. He mumbled, "Safe."

"Yeah, safe," Stelian mumbled right back.

At 06:00, the unit was rousted out of their sleep and were standing at attention in front of their bunks, everyone but Davis. Sergeant Connor yelled and screamed as he approached Davis' bunk. He stopped, stared and called for someone to get a medic and moved to Davis to check him. There was a drying pool of blood on his pillow and the stick was lying next to him. Davis did not move, he was breathing, but not moving. Connor yelled again "Hurry up, someone get a medic."

Davis was still alive, Averell was disappointed; he was safe because no one saw anything, safe but disappointed. The medics arrived, and

Davis was carried out. Sergeant Connor was not in a good mood. It was obvious Averell would be one of the suspects, perhaps a prime, but not the only suspect. Davis was a bully and had been asking for it for quite some time. Nobody cried for Davis and some were actually pleased that "someone else" had nailed the S.O.B.

An investigation was conducted, and Averell denied everything. He said he was asleep and knew nothing. He further stated he thought he heard something around 3:00am, but it could have been the wind. He really didn't know. Another of the recruits, Ed Crane, was also a prime suspect and the investigative team found him to be the least believable in his denials. He was arrested and charged with several offenses. He seemed pleased to be recognized as the one who nailed Davis. Even Averell gave Ed a thumbs up when he was arrested. The next week Davis was awake and able to talk. He didn't remember a thing. Another week and he was back in training with another platoon.

Ed was convicted of assault and was sent to a secure lock up pending his sentencing. Averell was pleased he had gotten away with it and someone else would spend time in prison for his action. Two lives negatively affected, he had retaliated, and nobody knew it was him. He was safe.

Time passed, and Averell made it through the several phases of basic training. The running, push-ups and other physically demanding activities were grueling, but he excelled at the rifle range. He was a skilled marksman when it came to hitting paper targets, and he imagined enemy soldiers running at him and his bullets searing into them. He was praised by his drill sergeant for the cleaning, care and use of his rifle, but when that phase was complete, the fun and the praise ceased.

After graduation from basic training and a brief stint in an advanced training program, he was assigned a job as a supply clerk's job at a base in Georgia. He handled orders for everything from pencils to equipment parts, and in time, was saddled with buying and distributing materials for the entire base. The job was not physical but did require a certain amount of organization. He became more detail oriented, fussing over sloppy requisitions and any disorder in the storage facility. His bookkeeping was near flawless, and he knew where everything was in the warehouse and how much to order at the end of each month. He was efficient but seemed to fade quietly into the background. Nobody really noticed him, but he didn't mind, he went about his business and got by. His life in the army was very routine, he did his job, lived in the enlisted men's quarters, saved most of his money and enjoyed a game of pool periodically but was not a very social person.

In the summer of 1987 Averell noticed an ad posted on the bulletin board in the enlisted men's club. It read, 'For Sale, 1983 Chevrolet Impala.' The owner was a sergeant who wanted to unload his car before being deployed. He made Averell a reasonable deal and Averell was determined to make the vehicle last, he became a stickler for scheduled maintenance, oil changes and kept it clean inside and out.

The time passed quickly, and after three years, his time served was complete. Averell had not once heard from Ellie or Sarah, not a card, nor letter, and he didn't write to either of them. He managed two brief vacations to a state park in Florida, where he had rented a one-bedroom cottage and took a tour of the swamp and visited an aquarium. His three years in the army had an upside, Averell was physically fit. He exercised daily, having learned to rise in the morning and run a mile before breakfast. He grew another inch in those three years and now stood at an even five-foot-nine-inches and now weighed in at an impressive one-hundred seventy-eight pounds, his heaviest to date.

So, three years of managing a warehouse resulted in fewer thoughts of heroism, and more of his discharge. He was never deployed and saw no adventure, he managed to stay out of trouble and was now ready to become a civilian again. He took his honorable discharge in July of 1989, loaded his car with his belongings, drove back to Syracuse and went to his mother's house.

New residents in the home advised that Ellie and Sarah had moved to a townhome a few miles west of the only home Averell had ever really known. Averell thanked them for the information and asked if he might check in the garage for something he had left there years ago. The new owner agreed he could take whatever belonged to him and allowed

Averell access to the garage. He went straight to the spot where he had hidden his probes. The bag was still there, coated in spider webs. He retrieved it and opened the bag. All six were there in their dirt and rust covered glory.

Averell wished the new owner luck in the house and drove away. He assumed that since neither Ellie nor Sarah had written and told him of their relocation, he was not welcome in their home and decided to leave town. First, he would drive by their new residence because he was curious. The Charter Woods development was newly completed by Danker Construction according to the sign at the entrance. Averell was looking at the numbers wondering which was their specific unit when a pick-up truck pulled into a driveway about five units down. It was Steve Danker. After all those years, Steve was back in touch with Ellie. Averell sat there for a few minutes watching as Steve went up the stairs, unlocked the door and went in.

"Cozy, he has a new key," chuckled Stelian.

"Yeah, they deserve each other," said Averell. As he was about to leave, the door opened an attractive blond teenage girl emerged. She seemed about the age Sarah would be. She wore a pink blouse, blue denim shorts and white shoes. The outfit familiar, as she had dressed that way often as a little girl. Soon after, a middle-aged woman with dark hair came out wearing a similar outfit as the young teen. Averell could only assume the pair was Sarah and Ellie.

"C'mon Mom, we're going to be late, hurry," said Sarah.

As Ellie walked across the parking lot to her car, she looked directly at Averell, but made no indication she recognized him as the son she had treated so poorly all those years.

Averell sat in his car and watched them pull out and drive away. He sat there for another few minutes and then started to drive away. "Well, they don't care, so I don't care."

"Yeah, we don't care," agreed Stelian.

"I hate them," said Averell.

"Yeah, we hate them," agreed Stelian.

Averell drove west on I-90. He arrived in Rochester and decided to spend the night in a motel. He would determine his next move in the morning after a good night's sleep and breakfast.

*　　　*　　　*

TWELVE

That is why we plan . . .

Morning had Averell up early and taking an abbreviated run before breakfast. As he returned to the motel, he noted the exercise room on the first floor. It had ellipticals and treadmills and he figured those might come in handy on hot or rainy days. He returned to his room and after showering and dressing he went to the front desk and asked where he could get a current Sunday paper with the want ads. The receptionist pointed to a drugstore across the lot, "They'll have everything you need, you can even get the New York Times if you get there early enough."

"Thanks," said Averell, as he headed across the lot and bought a local paper. He returned to the motel and went into the restaurant, ordered coffee and a bagel and began reading the newspaper, looking for work. He had plenty of time, but he wasn't one to sit idle for long. Averell liked to be productive. He scanned the various ads and landed on one for a traveling salesman, hawking office supplies. Travel was primarily northeast and as far west as Toledo. Customers included major distribution centers and an occasional strip mall vendor.

Office supplies were something he fully understood, having dealt with them for the last two plus years for the army. His military experience may have been more useful than he had expected. He answered the ad and was granted an interview for the following day. When he arrived, he was wearing his uniform, since he didn't have anything else that was suitable. "Pardon the uniform. I just got out and I'm still rebuilding my civilian wardrobe."

"No problem," said the personnel director. "I was in the army too. Where were you stationed?"

"Georgia, the state, not the country. All I did for three years was count, store, deliver, reorder, restock and estimate office supplies. I think

I was pretty good at what I did, but I decided to join the civilian world and do it out here. So here I am." He listed a few references at Fort Benning and gave the local motel as his address. The next afternoon he was called and after another short interview with Fred Dennis, the manager for whom he would work, they offered him the job. He had no reason to look further and accepted.

Averell's training period was a week in the main distribution center and two weeks on the road with Fred, meeting the significant contacts in each distribution center and several of the larger outlets. The job was easy, and Averell had time to do other things. He made his own hours and as long as he visited the supply centers and stores on a route that stretched from Albany to Toledo, all within a few miles of I-90, nobody bothered him. The locations were often convenient to shopping, restaurants and movie theaters, making downtime fairly enjoyable. He also discovered that several of the communities he visited had summer baseball leagues running from June through September. He found the local PONY leagues especially fun to watch. He attended games in Auburn, Batavia and Jamestown, New York, and felt a connection to them due to his Syracuse roots. He made a point of tracking the local schedules and even took his clients to a game on occasion.

By the summer of 1990, he had been on the job almost a year. During his frequent travels, an occasional forest off the interstate would remind him of his time with the animals in the woods. It was hard to believe that a full five years had passed since his last visit to the woods, he thought of the thrill of doing his probing, secreting all his tools and hiding the remains. The army, and now his job had monopolized his time, keeping him busy for the last five years. There was always something to do, and others to do it with, but now he had to find other distractions. Baseball and movies could only fill so much free time, and there was still gaps in his schedule for other things. His lack of fellow Army buddies to hang out with meant there was more opportunity for isolation and with that came thoughts of his former pastimes. As he went about his business, he would see squirrels and rabbits in parks and residential areas. The thoughts of playing with the little animals, poking and probing, cutting and dissecting were always there. Not as compelling as when he was in high school, but he had to admit that the urge to probe a beating heart was still present. But now he was older, and his activities should be more in tune with his abilities. He could use bigger and more complex tools. He could probe bigger and more complex subjects. He opened his bag of probes and remembered. *I always wanted to use these on Sarah and Ellie, now what is there to stop me? Nothing.*

"Could we do that, go to their new place and - ?"

"Yes, I remember standing in Ellie's bedroom with a probe in my hand, wanting to push it through her neck, but was afraid of what would happen to me. I would be punished. I dreamt about doing it to both of them, Ellie and Sarah."

"We could do it now, and who would know? Nobody."

"No, we would have to have a plan and be very careful. If we did it, we would be the prime suspects. No, we have to think, to plan and when everything is right, then we do them."

"Then we do them!"

"Yes, but first I need new probes, these are too small. They seemed bigger when I was younger. Now, for what we want, we should have bigger and stronger probes."

"I agree, we should go to the store and look at what they have," said Stelian.

"You mean, look in the medical aisle for probes? I don't think so."

"No, no, no, let's see what they have that we can use. You never know," said Stelian.

Averell went to a Walmart and walked around. He looked in the tools, in the pharmacy and finally in the housewares, where he spotted barbeque skewers.

"Perfect. Absolutely perfect."

"See, I told you," said Stelian.

"Yes, you did, and you were right. It's a set of eight."

"You shouldn't argue with me," said Stelian.

"I see that, it wouldn't look good either, would it?"

"Nope," said Stelian.

As he walked through the store in conversation with Stelian, he realized to others he was alone and he quickly quieted down.

The rabbits and squirrels of the woods in Syracuse were no longer appealing. Averell now had an objective, actually two objectives and he viewed other people as potential trial subjects with which he could practice. During every session in the woods when he was probing rabbits and squirrels he was secretly dreaming of Sarah and Ellie. He resisted the many temptations to push a probe through their necks while they slept and watch their agony. Now, he was thinking of them again, but he would take his time, he would plan, he would practice, he would become perfect and when he finally did it, no one would suspect it was him.

Visits to his client base would have him considering who might be his practice victim. He determined the circle was too small and with him the common thread with all his clients, it would only take a second victim to make him a prime suspect. This was completely unacceptable. His solution was to consider only random strangers. He could target them, then monitor their moves, assess the risk, plan the trap, implement the strategy and enjoy the process. He fantasized over a number of prospects, but he never carried the planning beyond that initial stage. When he was ready to begin, his strategy would want to be well thought out. A private location would have to be found and verified as safe. Averell knew that the planning should be thorough, every contingency considered and a "Plan B" for everything should be developed in the event of a mishap. So, as he went about his business, dealing with ordinary people in ordinary circumstances, he was constantly thinking of ways to get them into a potentially compromising position where he could control them, get them to a place where he could restrain them, then probe them, watch their eyes, open their bodies and see their beating hearts, then watch as the life blood flowed out of them as the fire left their eyes.

He thought about Sarah, bound and helpless. He envisioned Ellie being forced to watch as he probed Sarah. Each time he ran the scenario in his mind, he became more excited, his eyes widened, his muscles tensed, and he would begin to perspire heavily. Then, as problems with his plan surfaced, his mind would try to adjust quickly to address each flaw. His thinking progressed through various scenarios, finding the weakness, modifying his method and gaining confidence as he progressed.

"That is why we plan," he muttered to himself as he drove the interstate.

"So, we are constantly making a new plan, a better plan."

"Yes, each one is better than the last. We are getting close to our first subject."

On a July evening as he walked to his car after a movie, he spotted a man, apparently drunk, lying on the ground next to a dumpster.

"We could start with this guy, practice, remember, practice," said Stelian.

"No, it's too risky," said Averell.

"But that's part of the fun," said Stelian.

"No!" asserted Averell, "I want a woman, not a man. Besides, he's dirty and smells." Averell got into his car and drove to a nearby motel he had used before.

"Well, it's been, what two months? Welcome back," said the desk clerk

"How long are you with us this time?" asked the desk clerk.

"Just the night, gotta' get back on the road and be in Erie in the morning."

The clerk gave him a key and said good night.

Averell went to his room and was asleep almost immediately.

Morning came, and Averell was back on the road heading for Erie.

"We could have done that guy in the gutter. Who would know? Who would care?" said Stelian.

"I said no!"

The rest of the trip was relatively quiet, Averell turned on the radio but couldn't find a clear signal, "I should get a tape player installed. I should get a new car, with a tape player," he said, turning off the radio.

"Yes, that's a good idea." and again, silence.

He arrived in Erie and had time for breakfast before his eight-thirty appointment. He drove to the shopping center where the big box store was and parked near the front door. He walked down to a cafe a few doors away and went in. He was sitting at a table finishing his coffee when a man approached, "Averell, good morning."

"Hey Jack, how have you been?"

"Great, it's a little early, but if you're finished, we can get started, get a jump on the day," said Jack.

"Okay, all I have left is my coffee," said Averell.

"I'll grab a cup to go and we can get going."

"Sure, okay," said Averell.

As they were walking, Jack said, "So, how was your trip in this morning, heard there was an accident on 90 just north of here."

"Didn't see it, and I can't seem to hold a station on my radio for more than a few minutes."

"Yeah, I have a tape player in my car and I listen to whatever I want, no problems."

Averell was thinking he was about due for a new and better vehicle and replied, "I'm going to look at new cars this weekend, I'll make sure there's a tape player in whatever I get."

Their meeting centered around supplies and specials, but Averell found himself daydreaming about a new car. "What should I get?" he wondered.

That weekend back in his townhouse, Averell scanned the newspaper for used cars. Nothing appealed. That was disappointing and he was about to pour another cup of coffee when his ever-present companion chimed in, *"Well we could look at new cars."*

"I don't think so, too expensive," said Averell.

"We should look," said Stelian *"besides, we have enough money."*

After being totally frustrated by the listings in the newspaper, Averell got dressed and headed out to a dealer.

"I'm just curious, what do you have in a larger car? I'm in sales and travel a lot, and I want something big enough to carry my samples and get decent mileage."

"You're a family man, we have some minivans you can put the wife and kids in and have plenty of room for luggage," said the man with the amber teeth and limp handshake.

"I don't think you heard me, I'm in sales and travel, and I don't like vans. Not married, and no kids."

"Well, step into my office and we can check our inventory, my name's Earl, what's yours?"

Averell did not like this guy and was reluctant to give too much information.

"Davis, Al Davis," he said, thinking of someone he would like ol' Earl to meet.

"You liar," said Stelian.

They talked for another minute and Averell said, "Oh, look at the time, I gotta' run, pick up the kids, thanks for your time."

As he was walking away, Earl said "Hey! You said you don't have any kids…"

Averell got in his car and drove down the road looking for another dealer.

"A minivan, we should check them out," said Stelian.

He pulled into another lot and parked as a man approached, "Good morning, can I help you?"

"Well, I have a few questions," said Averell.

"Sure, my name is Tom Walters," he said with an extended hand, "anything special in mind?"

"No, not really," Tom's handshake was firm and Averell felt better about this encounter and continued, "I travel a lot, up and down I-90, I'm in sales, office supplies."

"So, do you carry samples and some demo spreads?"

"That and my luggage, and sometimes I stop in those rest areas and take a nap, so I was thinking about a larger car."

"Well, I hope I have something that will fit what you want. Have you thought about buying or leasing a vehicle? There are advantages both ways, depending on your needs and the programs they offer."

"I hadn't thought about it," said Averell. "I've had that thing about three years now," he gestured toward the seven-year-old Chevy in the parking lot, "I got it used in Georgia when I was stationed there. It has less than seventy-thousand miles on it and still rides as smooth as ever. Mileage isn't the greatest, but it has been good to me for the last few years."

"Well then, why don't we look at the several vehicles we have, and you can narrow it down to type. We have a pretty good selection of each so, type first, then color and extras. Whaddya think?"

"Okay, sounds good to me, by the way, my name's Averell, Averell Danker."

Tom took out a business card and handed it to Averell, "Just in case you want to come back and continue."

"Come back?"

"Sure, if I read you the right way, you are going to hit a few places, see what's out there and think it over. Hey, this is not a box of cereal. It's a serious financial commitment. You want to take your time and do it right."

"Yeah, yeah you're right."

Tom showed him economy cars, mid-size and full-size sedans and then suggested that they just look at the minivans, if for no other reason than to knock them out of the game.

"Okay, sure let's look."

The first was a loaded van with a sound system that was out of sight. The second had full tinted windows and a tape player, each had fold down seats in the rear that would allow hauling of rather large loads. He looked at a number of mini-vans and after an hour he said, "You were right, I have to sit down and think this through."

"Okay, no problem, let me give you some printed info, you don't want to carry all this in your head. I'll get something on everything we looked at."

"No, just the full-size sedan like that silver one and the minivans."

"Ah, see we have already narrowed the field. Just remember this is going to be your car, so get it for yourself, not for anybody else."

Averell took the info, thanked Tom and drove off the lot. He got about a mile down the road and pulled into a McDonalds, got a cup of coffee and started to look through the brochures. Within another hour Averell was back at the dealership looking for Tom. Another hour and he was driving off the lot in a new 1990 minivan with tinted windows and a tape deck/CD player.

"I like this."

"Yeah, me too," said Stelian.

* * *

THIRTEEN

Averell pulled the knife from his back pocket . . .

The minivan handled easily, more so than Averell had expected. His first few calls the following week were extended by his bragging about his new ride to his customers. "Yeah, it handles the road better than we thought, I mean better than I thought."

"Thanks, pal," said Stelian.

Always in planning mode, Averell offered several people a ride in his van to see how easily someone could hop in and be contained. Most declined the invitation but the few that did accept seemed to feel obliged to look at and touch almost everything. They were at one point or another, completely distracted and could easily be overpowered. "Very interesting," he mumbled to himself as he dropped off the last of his guests.

"Interesting."

Averell was again happy and engaged with his new toy, and Stelian's voice stayed quiet. Then, one day in Erie he had finished early and was debating whether to take in a movie or hit the road. He decided to check the local listings for theaters. Nothing interesting. Mentor, Ohio was just an hour and a half away and he didn't have to be there until noon the following day.

He checked his fuel gauge and noted he was still at about 3/4 tank. He decided to drive to Mentor and if nothing else, there might be something on television. The road was virtually empty, it was a beautiful July day, six days after the holiday and he cruised along with the speed control set right at 65, "No tickets for this boy."

He arrived in Mentor with no traffic delays, and the tape player had lived up to its billing, great sound and no static like his radio. Not sure what to do, Averell decided to drive around to a few movie theaters and see what was playing. He found one at a mall and pulled into the parking lot. He noted a bar near the theater and in the parking-lot was a man sleeping in his car, he assumed the guy passed out after an afternoon binge.

"We could do him," said Stelian.

"No, not safe."

"C'mon, we can catch this flick another time," Stelian argued.

"No!"

Averell got out of the van and crossed the parking lot to the theater.

"Theater two, please," and handed the kid a ten.

"Thank you, sir, it will begin in eleven minutes."

Averell took his change and headed to the snack bar for something to munch and a drink before heading inside. It was dark when Averell exited the theater, he was headed to his van when the sleeper staggered up to him and said, "Hey buddy, could you do me a favor, that som' bitch in the tavern won't sell me no more drinks. An' I need another drink." He looked to be in his late fifties; rumpled suit and smelling of cheap whiskey. His tousled, graying hair was matched with a two-day growth of whiskers.

Averell looked at him with disdain, "Well, maybe you shouldn't have one, you are loaded." He had seen this type before, in the Army. There were guys who drank just because they thought they were supposed to and others who drank intentionally to get smashed. Either way, it was disgusting. He helped the man maintain his balance back to his car and pushed him through the door. His keys were still in the ignition and the drunk slumped over in the front seat, closed his eyes and didn't move.

As Averell was positioning him in the front seat, he mumbled to himself, "Why don't you stay here, and I'll get you a bottle of wine from the drug store." Averell never intended to be taken seriously, he planned to get into his van and drive off.

"Okay, I'll wait here," came the surprising reply.

Averell got into his van, pulled out of the parking lot and started toward the highway where he had seen a string of motels earlier. He pulled up to a red light, stopped and was waiting for the signal to change. Then he heard it, somebody was pissed off and laying on the horn. Then there he was, the drunk. He had gotten out of his car and came up to Averell's door.

"Hey, where's that bottle? I gotta' have a drink."

Averell thought for a moment and said, "Sorry pal, the store was closed and I gotta' go." Averell pulled away, turned onto I-90 and sped up the road to a rest area. He pulled in and waited. If Sleepy flew by, he would wait a bit and go to the next exit. One way or the other he would be rid of the drunk loser.

As he sat there waiting a car pulled in behind him and parked. It was 'Sleepy'. He got out and came over to Averell's window, "Where's that damn bottle?"

Averell got out and led 'Sleepy' over to a bench near the restrooms. "Sit down and let me look in my van, I might just have a little something."

"Okay, I'll wait here."

Averell scrounged through a plastic container that he had kept in his car and had transferred to the van. He had a few tools, jumper cables, some duct tape, a roll of paper towels, and various fluids he'd used in his old car. Amongst the tools was a small knife which he put in his back pocket and then grabbed the duct tape and walked back to the bench.

The bum was slumped over, obviously still drunk. Averell said, "I don't have anything to drink. Nothing. And I have to go. Do you understand what I said?"

"Yeah, you said you were goin' to get a bottle an' you don't got it."

He stood and started at Averell. Averell said "Hey, back up! I don't want to do this."

"You promised," and he lunged toward Averell.

Averell pulled the knife from his back pocket and thrust it into the old man's mid-section. He pulled the knife up and out creating a large gaping wound that allowed blood to flow freely. Sleepy slumped, staggered and looked at Averell.

"Why'd you do that?" and he fell to his knees grasping his belly. Averell knew he had to finish this. He stepped behind the old drunk and grabbed his hair and with the other he drew the knife across his throat. A short, throaty gurgle and the drunk fell to the ground in a pool of blood.

Averell scanned the area, then grabbed his victim's ankles and dragged him into the bushes. It was late, dark and traffic was light. Averell went to the old man's car and used his handkerchief to take the keys and lock the vehicle. When he returned to the body, he pulled the old man's wallet from his pants, pocketed the two singles that were inside and scattered the credit cards to the ground where someone could find them, and hopefully use them, sending authorities on a wild goose chase. He then tossed the wallet into the bushes along with the keys, careful to wipe his prints from everything.

Back at his van, he saw his shirt, pants and shoes were partially covered in blood. This was bad. *First things first. Get out of these clothes and into something else*, he thought.

He grabbed a fresh shirt and a clean pair of pants from his suitcase and headed to the restroom. Once changed, he put everything with blood on it into a plastic bag and loaded it in the van. As he got back on the interstate, he took a deep breath and breathed a sigh of relief.

"Wow, that was cool," said Stelian.

"I don't think so."

"Sure, you do. We should go back to Erie and turn around. Maybe spend the night," said Stelian.

"Now, I agree."

He drove north on I-90 and pulled off at a motel near Erie. The receptionist greeted him, and Averell tried to appear calm.

"Just one night, and I will be on the road early. I want to be in Mentor by 8:30," said Averell.

"Yes sir, I got you in 108. The door to the lot is right across the hall," said the clerk.

Averell made it to his room, undressed and stood in the shower for about fifteen minutes with the knife, cleaning both himself and the fatal blade. Before going to bed Averell made some notes in his logbook. Anyone reading the log would think that he had spent the entire day and night in Erie. The tricky part would be in fudging some mileage over the next few weeks to absorb the additional trip from Erie to Mentor. He calculated it to be about 175 miles total.

In the morning he was on the road by 6:30. As he passed the rest stop, he saw Sleepy's car but nobody else. He kept driving. When he was a few miles outside of Mentor, he spotted a 24-hour coin-operated laundry. He pulled in and looked through the windows. Finding it empty, he took the bag of clothes and shoes and tossed them in a machine adding bleach and soap. The bleach ruined the clothes but had the desired effect. He ran them a second time again with an excess of bleach. An extra few minutes in the dryer and the clothes were ready to be disposed of in a Salvation Army donation box. Almost done. He then drove to his appointment in Mentor.

After the first appointment, Averell found a dumpster completely out of view and disposed of the bloody paper towels. He took the knife and dropped it in the dirt and rolled it around. He then placed it on a block and stepped on the blade breaking it at the hilt, perfect. He picked up the knife, went back to the van, and drove to his second appointment. There he saw another dumpster and tossed the knife away. After his final appointment that day he drove west to East Cleveland and up into Cleveland Heights. He liked this area and drove through whenever he had a chance looking at the homes and thinking that he might just move there one day.

He found another motel and signed in for the night.

"Nicely done," said Stelian.

"Yeah, very messy, but we were lucky." He turned on the television and sat on the bed to watch the news. There it was, the rest stop, the drunk's car, his wallet and keys and a stretcher with a full body bag. The police sergeant being interviewed said it was obviously a robbery gone bad. It happened on the north bound side and they were looking for suspects as far north as Erie.

Averell relaxed and thought about dinner.

"See, I knew we could do it. And you liked it, didn't you?" said Stelian.

"It was messy."

"Yeah, and -?"

"Alright, it was a little cool, but we can't do it that way again."

"What should we change?" asked Stelian.

"I don't want to think about it right now. I'm going to dinner, that was a lot of work and I'm hungry."

Averell went to the motel's restaurant and ordered a large steak with baked potato, some red wine and a little cheese. Dessert consisted of apple pie ala mode. A perfect end to a pretty good day.

The next day Averell was on the road again. After three more appointments in the Cleveland area, he was headed to Toledo. That is as far west as his route would take him and then he would turn around and try to arrange two or three appointments each day, all the way to Albany.

His new van was a pleasure to drive, he sat up high and listened to his tapes and CD's. Two weeks passed without incident, then Averell noted a drunk in a parking lot.

"That could be fun."

"No, I think it's dangerous, and our last escapade was not fun, there was no challenge and it was sloppy."

"So, what do you propose?"

"If, and I mean *if*, we do this again, we have to use the plan, make sure we have covered all of the possible glitches, as many as we can see. The whole process should be more like the squirrels, neat and clean. I don't like messy."

"Then, let's plan, it'll be fun."

"If we do it right. Yeah, it could be fun."

"It would be more fun if we did the ones we really want to do, you know what I mean?"

"Yeah, sooner or later I want to do both of them."

"Sarah and Ellie?"

"Yeah, as a matter of fact, I want to do Sarah first, with Ellie watching. Then, Ellie, while Sarah is fresh in her mind."

"Why don't we just do them now?"

"No, I told you, I want to be ready, I want to do someone else as a practice session, then, when we know what will work, then we do them. We will do them both, maybe a little to one, then a little to the other. Let them each watch as the other feels the pain, then switch."

Averell began building his toolbox; over a two-week period, he purchased knives, an ice pick, saws, and a few miscellaneous tools, always paying cash and collected in various cities, making him difficult to trace. He kept them in a toolbox in the van, along with his probes. Other items included plastic bags, rope, duct tape, rubber gloves, painter tarps and paper towels.

"We should only pick subjects that deserve to be probed, cut and killed."

"Who fits that bill?" inquired Stelian.

"We have to look closely at everyone we know. Some will be too close and doing them could be very bad for us," replied Averell.

"Well, I think we should consider someone very much like Sarah and Ellie," said Stelian.

"Yes, but maybe only one at first, so we know what it's like, then we can do two. We have to be very careful and not let any of the preliminary sessions tip our hand. When we do get to them, it has to be a surprise, they should not see it coming."

"What about Steve, he should be a target."

"He would be difficult, I don't want to deal with 'difficult'. He would be a physical challenge. Maybe if he was drunk, or if we could catch him when he was distracted."

"Maybe we should just pass on Steve and concentrate on the other two."

"Agreed, and if that goes the right way, we could re-evaluate"

"Yeah, but we will keep him on our list, right?"

"Oh yes, very definitely keep him on our list."

Averell enumerated a number of people he knew and loosely arranged them in order of best to worst candidate for the first session. The basis was similarity to either Sarah or Ellie and one Marlene Fielding came to the top of the list.

Averell had met Marlene at during a business stop in Toledo. She had no connection to him other than they were both in that one store at the same time. She was tall and of medium build, blond hair and blue eyes were similar to Sarah's, but her eyes were lifeless, empty, rather like a shark's eyes and her dismissive attitude toward Averell was applied to every man she met that day. Her name rose to his number one spot after Averell considered what several other people had relayed to him about her. She was divorced, and was constantly suing her former husband, apparently determined to break him financially, claiming that everything he owned was actually hers regardless of where it came from. The poor bastard had entered the marriage with a tidy sum of money, intending to save for the next twenty years, when he hoped to retire well before he reached his sixtieth birthday. Their marriage lasted less than two years and she filed for divorce, claiming abuse as the prime reason. The court ruling left the man broke and all but homeless.

Good enough, he thought, and if there was to be a prime suspect it would likely be the ex-husband or someone else she had insulted or injured, not Averell. He felt this subject would be safe, nowhere on anyone's radar.

Now to the planning. The appeal in targeting Marlene was partially to rid the world of an undesirable, but to make certain it was one who would evoke little sympathy from the general public. His plan was to monitor her and determine an opportune time to secure his prey, taking great care to not be seen with her in public and ensuring her guard was down. This was going to be a good test for Averell.

* * *

Fourteen

This is really going to hurt . . .

Marlene Fielding was a creature of some habit, going for an early morning run several times a week. A run that often ended as a brisk walk. Averell observed her over a period of several weeks, each time he visited Toledo. He had located a vacant building in an industrial park that was easy access from her route. He also noted that the local police visited that specific industrial park every day at roughly the same time, not to return until the next day. They had gotten very lax and removed the lock from a gate, allowing anyone who would venture the two hundred feet off the road along the fence line to gain easy entry. Several buildings within the park were not visible from the main road. Anything short of a major fire in one of these buildings would go unnoticed unless a close inspection took place.

Averell positioned his van on a side street and waited. Marlene usually passed here about this time of day and Averell allowed a thirty-minute window for her arrival. It was almost 7:30am when Marlene rounded the corner wearing a dark blue sweatsuit and carrying a water bottle. She had already given up running and wore a frown as she came up behind Averell's van. He saw her as she approached and waited until she was a few feet past the van when he jumped out and hurried up behind her with his sap in hand. She quickly became aware of the stranger directly behind her and turned to challenge him, that's when he hit her on the head with his sap. She went down on one knee and was immediately given another hit on the back of her neck. Unconscious, she fell facedown to the pavement. Averell went back to the van and pulled it up a foot past Marlene's outstretched frame. He opened the rear door, put on a pair of rubber gloves, placed a bag over her head and wrestled her into the van onto a plastic painters drop-cloth. She was heavier than she appeared, but he managed to get her inside.

"Damn, she's heavy." he muttered to himself.

"Sarah's not that heavy, is she?"

"I don't think so, but Ellie may be."

"Naw, she's thinner than this one, maybe twenty pounds lighter."

"I hope," he said as he took his duct tape, bound Marlene securely, placed a cloth wad in her mouth and duct taped over the cloth. With his subject loaded in the van, Averell picked up the water bottle from the pavement, careful to cover his tracks.

Averell quickly drove to the deserted industrial park and pulled into a lot across the street. He waited for an hour when he heard stirring in the back of the van, turned with sap in hand and tapped Marlene on the back of her neck, rendering her unconscious once more. All was quiet until about noon, when a patrol car appeared and made its way to the side gate. Five minutes later the patrol car exited the gate and pushed it back into place. After the police were out of sight, Averell started his engine, proceeded to the same gate and entered the site. He drove around the back of the building and stopped at a recessed truck dock. The van was all but hidden by the recess and the pass door was just a few steps away. He unloaded Marlene and half carried, half dragged her into the building. The open space was cavernous, extending about a hundred feet toward the front office area and about sixty feet wide. The space contained a number of pallets, shelves and shipping crates scattered about. One overturned crate would serve well as a work-table and Averell forced his prize close to it before allowing her to drop to the floor. Marlene was semi-conscious and almost mobile, so he moved quickly to position the crate and stretch her out on it. She tried to speak, but the gag in her mouth prevented her, only guttural groans could be heard.

Averell maneuvered her into a sitting position on the edge of the crate. He removed her jacket and eased her into a prone position. Marlene, still stunned by the two blows to her head, was easily manipulated and all four limbs were soon tied in place. Averell had spread her arms and legs leaving her stretched out and face up. He pulled on a set of surgical scrubs over his street clothes, then removed the bag from her head and saw she was bleeding from the first blow with his sap. He went out to the van and retrieved his tools, a drop cloth and the plastic container.

Marlene was slowly regaining her wits and started thrashing in an attempt to get loose, having no luck. Averell approached with his knife and cut the cord from her waist band. She looked around frantically, attempting to see who else was there, but she could only see Averell. He walked around her prone figure as if studying, thinking.

Then he spoke no one in particular, "You see my friend, what we have here is someone who should not be permitted to live. We shall remedy that soon enough, but first—" Averell turned toward Marlene, "you are a horrible woman, Sarah, ah, excuse me, Marlene, and we are going to see what's inside you. We are going to see if you have a heart."

He opened her blouse and with his knife, cut the sleeves to allow it to be removed. He then gently removed the remainder of her clothing, only using his knife where he had to cut something rather than loosen her bindings. He paced again, walking around the crate and stared at her bound body. She was naked, completely at his mercy and he stared, paced and thought. Averell was not aroused sexually, but he was rather excited in another way. He was going to cut her, to pierce her body with his probes and watch her eyes. He was going to see her pain and when the time was right, he was going to open her chest and see her beating heart. Then he would let her die, slowly as he watched her eyes, watched the life drain out of her body.

As he approached her with his knife, he spoke, "Stelian, would you like the first cut?"

"Why, thank you Averell," replied Stelian, *"but where to cut?"*

"Ah, yes, let me show you," and Averell took a marking pen and drew a line on Marlene's chest from the top of the sternum to her navel. "You see, follow the line, but not too deep, yet." He then turned away from the crate as if addressing someone else and said, "Now watch closely Ellie, you are going to be next."

Marlene was in a complete panic, she knew this was a mad man and she was about to die. Averell placed the knife on her chest and followed the line with the point of the knife making a series of shallow scratches in the skin. "Yes, my friend, now make the final cut and we shall see if this woman has a heart." He repositioned the knife and started to apply pressure and draw the knife toward the navel and stopped just before reaching the base of the sternum. "Have we forgotten to apply the probes?" He seemed to ask the air. "We shall remedy that right now." He took one of his new probes and positioned it on Marlene's bicep and pushed. The probe passed through her arm. The pain of the probe in her arm and the thought of another probe made Marlene violent. She pitched and thrashed and tried to scream. Averell calmly picked up another probe and positioned it on her belly. Again, he pushed as hard as he could. The probe went in about eight inches and slowed. Averell stopped pushing and looked into Marlene's eyes. Panic, pure panic he thought. He picked up another probe and positioned it precisely on Marlene's neck. Averell recalled his anatomy lessons and held her head still as he pushed the probe slowly into and through her neck.

"Ah, three more to go," said Averell.

"May I do the next one?" asked Stelian.

"Of course, my friend, please."

He picked up another probe and positioned it on Marlene's thigh. He pushed hard and it passed through one leg piercing through to the other.

Averell laughed and said, "Ha, a twofer, you hit both legs my friend."

"Oh, I did, not that I meant to. An accident, it was an accident," replied Stelian.

"Not to worry, we will simply do the other arm next."

Marlene again thrashed and twisted, trying to get free. Her sudden movement knocked the toolbox to the floor.

"Damn it!" said Averell.

"Relax, we are in control here."

He picked up the box and his tools and put them out of her reach and stood holding a knife.

"Now you be still, and this should not hurt at all."

"We shouldn't lie to the woman, Averell, it's not polite."

"Again, you are right, my friend."

Averell looked at Marlene and said, "This is really going to hurt," as he plunged the knife into her chest, between two ribs below her left breast and tried to slice across her chest hitting her sternum. Marlene thrashed, twisted and gulped all at once, then fell absolutely still.

"I think we have lost her, doctor." said Stelian.

"Yes, I believe you're right."

The fun was over. Marlene was dead, and Averell stood silently looking at her body. He had wanted to see her heart beating before he was finished, but she died, *damn it.* Another messy episode with blood everywhere. This time, though, he was more prepared. He picked up all of his tools and set them aside. Those he did not use, he put back into the toolbox and moved it away from Marlene. He then pulled all of the probes out of her body, and with a bottle of water with a straw like drinking nozzle, he rinsed off his tools and probes and put them in a separate plastic bag. Then he stepped out of the scrubs, took off the surgical shoe coverings and placed everything in a plastic garbage bag. He looked at himself and noted some blood had soaked through the layer of scrubs and had stained his shirt and pants.

"Damn it, I thought the scrubs would keep my clothes clean."

"A lesson learned, my friend."

"Indeed, we shall have to make proper adjustments."

"For the next one?"

"Yes, for the next one."

When he was certain the place was clean of any trace of himself and his participation in Marlene's demise, Averell left the building, pulling the door closed. He put his boxes and bags in his van. He checked the toolbox, rubber gloves, garbage bags, sure he had it all, then got in the van and calmly drove away. He went to a small strip mall at a crossroads east of Mentor where there was a coin operated laundry. He took the bag of bloodied clothing to be washed and dried twice with excessive amounts of both detergent and bleach.

As the laundry was going through its first cycle, he rinsed off the bags, removing any obvious trace of blood. Having completed that task, he separated the used clothing into two lots and placed them in clean plastic bags. He left the laundry and drove out of the strip mall. As he was driving on a back road and passing an office park, he noted a trash dumpster where he deposited the old garbage bags, then he headed to the freeway. He was almost to the state line when he spotted a motel and stopped for the night. In his room, Averell checked his mileage and determined that he had put on an additional 573 miles, and he started a new record of miles to be blended into his log to balance with the odometer in his car. He drove something in excess of 50,000 miles each year, so hiding 500 or 600 miles was an easy task. The important thing was balancing his log and odometer. He retrieved his probes and his knife, the only tools that had been used on Marlene and cleaned them as thoroughly as possible then broke the knife and bent the skewers. These parts he would deposit in several trash cans in gas stations as he drove back west on I-90 in the morning.

The next morning Averell drove west again passing Mentor and stopping in Cleveland, Lakewood and North Olmsted. He made it to Toledo that night, and the next morning cleared two appointments before lunch. He had his radio tuned to a local Cleveland news station, the reporter was talking about a meeting at the World Bank when he shifted gears, "This just in: Police have found a woman savagely murdered in a suburb of Toledo, Ohio. The woman was found in an old, abandoned warehouse off Sutter Avenue. The woman's name and the specifics of this murder are being withheld pending notification of the family. We will keep you posted on the progress in this investigation. In other news—" the announcer droned on.

"I am not happy with the way that went. I want to change things," said Averell.

"What sort of changes are we talking about?" inquired Stelian.

"Well, first, Sleepy was big, bulky, you know, hard to move around. Then Marlene was smaller and easier, but still difficult. That leads me to consider only smaller people we can easily lift and carry until we get better at this. We had the right tools, we had a decent place to work in and we planned for the clean-up alright, but—" he hesitated.

"Okay, I can see that, perhaps someone like a younger Sarah or Ellie would be easier," said Stelian.

"Yeah, a younger Sarah. I would enjoy that, the little blond," he paused, staring straight ahead.

"She's not little anymore, my friend, she's grown," replied Stelian.

"You're right, she has grown up. And the both of them are still the objective we are planning for. I hate them, and they will pay, when we are all ready. They had too many laughs at my expense."

"Them and Steve too."

"I told you, I don't care as much about Steve, it's those two I want. Steve would be a bonus, but not a primary target. So, where do we go next? Ellie and Sarah are out of the question, for now. We need to have this procedure down to a science before we do either of them. No, I think we should go for the younger, female, Sarah type. Someone much smaller, easy to handle. A little girl, to start with, then an older one, until we have the process all worked out."

"Yeah, and after a bit we can move on to the real Sarah and Ellie type."

"So, let's make a plan that covers all the bases. We should also hide our work. If we leave any trace, we could be found. We should hide them when we are finished with them."

*   *   *

Fifteen

No, we should follow the plan . . .

As he was driving along Interstate 90 from Rochester toward Buffalo, Averell was thinking he had been lucky as much as clever in the first session with Marlene. He had also been lucky with 'Sleepy', but luck was a gamble, not smart, and he wanted to be smarter and gamble as little as possible.

"Better planning, that's the magic we need," he said aloud, with conviction.

Traffic was light and the conversation with Stelian was relaxed and directed at finding a solution to a few of his greatest concerns. First, a place where they would not be bothered while they did their work and second, a means of disposing of the remains.

"Planning, magic, explain please."

"If we were to find another subject today and do our thing, we know we would not want to leave him, or her, somewhere they can be found."

"So, what do you propose? A river? Bury them?"

"Bury them where? In a field, in the woods, maybe in a cemetery. In a cemetery, yeah, it's a natural."

"Okay, I'll buy that, but how?"

"I'll work on that."

"Well, what about a place to do our thing?"

"We should have a place we can use that is secure and secluded, where no one will interrupt our session."

"Yeah, agreed."

"So, before we do another one, we should take care of those basics.

"Just one of each, in every town from here to Albany?"

"Let's concentrate on one laboratory and at least two cemeteries, around Syracuse to start with."

"Okay, I like that, a laboratory. But why Syracuse, maybe we should look at a site farther away from our home base."

"We'll know the location when we see it. A cemetery that is out of the way, more country than town, maybe we could dig an old grave, make our deposit and fill it up again."

"Or if it's a big enough place, there may be plenty of empty plots." may not be ready to use all the parts of what they have, maybe an acre or two won't be dug up for twenty years or more.

"We could find a grave that has just been filled and the ground is still soft and easy to dig and we come back after hours and dig down to the vault and drop our package in and refill the hole."

"I like that."

"Yeah, it could work."

Averell drove around each city as time allowed, looking for suitable locations. Not much appealed, too many people, fences with locked gates and guard dogs. He looked each weekend and other free days and was getting nowhere. August became September, September became October and his mind drifted to other things. Winter was coming, and several appointments were tightly scheduled. All this time spent searching for a place to hold another session had made him less clock conscious, and that had to change. More discipline in his routine was in order. He began to schedule appointments, two in the morning and two in the afternoon, four per day, minimum, and tried to be fifteen minutes early for each. It sometimes meant spending an extra day somewhere to ensure being on time, but it would set a pattern he could carry through the winter months.

"We could do another one, it's been over two months."

"No, I told you, we need to plan, to take care of some basics."

"When then?"

"Basics first, then fun time."

"Okay, okay."

Averell's routine forced him to work full weeks and travel on weekends, but the job was important, and he was doing fairly well. As a result of this better organization of his time and regularity of appointments, he was increasing his sales and he consistently qualified for his quarterly bonus. A plus for his savings and retirement accounts, while also opening the doors to nicer vacations. Kind of a toss-up for Averell. If he could arrange a two-week vacation in the summer, he might be able to arrange a really good session with two or maybe more subjects.

He continued his search for a laboratory in Syracuse, Buffalo, Cleveland and Toledo and discounted the smaller cities and towns in between. As he narrowed the search, he was honing-in on an industrial park off the Interstate 90 corridor north and east of Buffalo. He still took a side route periodically and in doing so, he found a deserted farmhouse south of Cleveland, almost to Portage County where he could park the van and be undisturbed for days. All planning suddenly concentrated on this remote farmhouse. He decided to check it out. He pulled into the driveway leading to a barn adjacent to the house and surrounded on two sides with overgrown bushes and a thick line of trees. He got out and walked around. If anyone saw him, he'd claim he was in the market for just such a place but wanted to take a closer look.

He surveyed the lot and went over to the barn. The doors opened easily, but with a bit of a squeak. He pulled the van into the barn and dug out a container of motor oil and applied a drop to each hinge. Two or three swings of the doors and the squeaks disappeared. The barn was empty except for a few empty crates, some rusty tools and scattered hay. He then walked to the house, looking toward the neighbors on either side. He couldn't see their houses until he was at the front door, so he slipped around to the side, that door was bolted from the inside. He walked around to the back and tried that door; again, locked, as was the front door.

"Why do they bother locking this place up, it's a wreck?"

"Who knows, why don't we just bust in the door?"

"You are a barbarian."

"Ha, yeah."

Averell returned to the back door and shook it as hard as he could. It started to loosen in its frame, he gave it one more good shake and the door opened.

"So, who's a barbarian now?"

"We're in."

Averell walked from room to empty room. Everything was covered in dust, floorboards creaked, and door hinges squealed for a touch of oil. The windows were surprisingly intact, dirty, but uncracked.

There was no power to the house, thus no lights or any other electrical convenience. He went back out to the barn and sat on a wooden rail thinking. As long as no one noticed his presence, this could serve his purpose.

"I think we have a winner."

"Yes, you may be right, but I think we should watch this for a while, to be sure nobody else comes here."

"Yeah, okay, but how long?"

"For a while, I don't know, but we should go." With that Averell opened the doors and backed the van out. He closed the doors and leaned a long stick against the latch holding both doors closed. Back on the road he decided to check on the place each time he came to the Cleveland area.

Averell drove past the farmhouse and kept an eye peeled for the nearest cemeteries each time he was in the area. The weeks passed, and winter approached, the stick stayed against the barn latch and Averell was convinced no one had been there. He identified three cemeteries within reasonable driving distance of the farmhouse and noted each one was large enough that he could visit in the middle of the night and remain unseen. The rolling landscape, together with the trees and bushes, provided good cover. Thanksgiving was approaching, daylight was diminished and Averell was weighing what time of year would be best suited for his sessions and disposal.

He determined that the bare trees of winter would provide less cover, and shorter days might raise suspicion if he were to use lanterns or flashlights to guide him.

"We may need to rely on the benefit of broad daylight to determine time of day."

"Makes sense, middle of the week so the locals would be busy with work, less likely to nose around."

"Now you're getting it."

"So, when do we do it?"

"Well, we should not be doing it when it could snow, there would be tracks in the driveway, and we might be seen."

"So, now? Before it snows?"

"We have no subject. No, we will wait and be sure about this place and take the time to look around for a couple of routes in and out of here. We should also make the run to the cemeteries and note their routines. Then we can find a subject."

By Christmas, the snow was about a foot deep and the plows had been down the road. The stick was still there and no tracks in the drive. By April, all traces of Winter were gone, and leaves returned to the trees. The farmhouse became more and more attractive to Averell. He'd driven the routes to the cemeteries in the area and established alternate routes between them so that he could adjust his plan on the fly. He began to watch the local obituary notices to find out when a fresh grave might be available.

*   *   *

Sixteen

He ignored her protest . . .

Averell decided the summer of 1991 was the perfect time for his first really controlled session in his newly discovered laboratory. He had decided on a subject type. His intense hatred for both Sarah and Ellie had settled the matter in his mind. He knew what he would look for, he knew what he would settle for.

He was in Erie in mid-August and cleared his last appointment around 1:30pm. He turned his van south and west on Interstate 90 and drove to Cleveland. He was heading for Cleveland Heights, a proper hunting ground for his purposes. Traffic is minimal in these neighborhoods during the bulk of the day and kids play freely in the streets. Baseball and football games use fire hydrants and trees as out of bounds markers and goal lines. Well-trimmed lawns and neatly edged gardens are the norm and fences are almost nonexistent. Boxwoods cut into square-edged barriers follow the property lines, keeping dogs in their own yards. The occasional police cruiser gave this place a level of comfort fully appreciated by the residents.

He pulled into a small strip center on Cedar Road to consider his plan. The streets in the East Side suburban community where he was heading were lined with hundred-year-old trees—oaks and elms primarily. The front yards were not large, and the view from a front window of most homes to the street did not favor his escape. Whatever he was going to do had to happen quickly. He would have to grab his subject, contain them in the rear seat, bind their hands and feet, get a gag in place and drive away. He considered dropping the entire matter when he noticed the gathering clouds.

"An advantage when one considers that people look initially but get quickly involved in an indoor activity; a book, the tube, their phones, but they don't go outside or tend to even look outside." He continued thinking about his hunting ground, where he would go first, then a plan B.

Everything was ready, the farmhouse and the cemeteries. He purchased a newspaper from a coin-operated box at a nearby bus stop and checked the obituaries. There was a scheduled burial at each of his subject cemeteries in the afternoon that day. All the pieces were in place and he had simply to find a proper subject and get to the barn. He knew the chances of finding a subject were good at this time of day, finding one that closely matched his criteria may be a little more challenging.

It was approaching 3:00pm as he pulled out of the strip mall and headed north on Cedar. As he turned off Cedar onto a side street leading into one of the residential neighborhoods, the sky darkened, and clouds began to gather. He continued to drive, and as he drove, he thought about his first two sessions and how he would do better this time. He was pleased it was to be someone like Sarah. Someone who would remind him of the many times Sarah said gleefully, "Mommy hates you," or "I hate you," or "You're a bad boy and we hate you." The memories haunted him.

He wanted to do it right, to prolong the process and see the change in her eyes from the defiant little bitch to a completely submissive little girl. As the life, the light, the very essence drained out of her, he wanted to be looking directly into her eyes. His next subject needed to be easily manipulated, placed where and how he envisioned her. She would be belligerent at first, and sorry in the end. She would be completely in his control, totally dependent on him for the final act of mercy when he would allow her to die.

As he continued down one street and up another, trying not to be obvious, Averell passed through the neighborhoods he had driven many times before, learning the streets, getting comfortable with the turns, traffic lights and alternate routes. Today the more he drove, the more frustrated he became. He saw several young girls, but they weren't quite right. Some were close, but not close enough. He was not seeing what he wanted and the sky was threatening. The change in the weather was causing changes in his plans. Averell was about to abandon his hunt and head for a motel. At the same time, a group of children noted the dark skies were threatening rain and headed for home.

Annette was seven years old and she was alone, walking home when it started to rain. The rain was soaking her pink blouse and denim shorts. Averell was about to turn back toward Cedar and give up as the rain increased in intensity. Then he saw the little blond girl all by herself, the pink blouse, the blue denim shorts and the white shoes. She was perfect, she was better than perfect, she was walking in a hurried sort of way with a determined look on her face. That kind of tough defiant look he had seen in Sarah. She could have been Sarah, as he looked at her, she was Sarah.

It was raining harder now and Annette knew her mom didn't like her walking alone like this, but it was only two blocks and she was a fast walker.

Averell steered his van around the corner directly in front of Annette and stopped. It scared her, she froze and stared at the huge tire about a foot in front of her. She was staring when the man leapt from the van, ran around and said, "Did I hit you?"

"No, I'm okay."

"I'm sorry," he said as he moved closer.

Then, in one movement he opened the sliding door, grabbed the girl and jumped into the van pulling the door closed behind him. He quickly wrapped duct tape around her wrists and buckled her seat belt. He wrapped her ankles with duct tape and pulled her seat belt as tight as possible.

"Nice move, buddy."

"Yeah, now to the place."

"Don't speed, the cops here do not have a sense of humor," he laughed. He was certain that nobody saw the van stop. Sure, that nobody saw a man jump out and grab the girl.

Lightning flashed as if some higher power had witnessed the event and the resulting thunder spoke with great disapproval. Clare went to the window and thought she would go outside and fetch Annette from the impending storm. They would make hot chocolate and watch her favorite TV program. As Clare moved to the front door with umbrella in hand, Averell's van moved down a side street and away from Annette's home. Clare walked out her front door with an umbrella poised above her, an uneasiness in her stomach.

"Let me go!"

"Let me out!"

Averell slowed the van, stopped, put it in park, turned and slapped the little girl, knocking her back into the seat and she started to cry.

"Shut up, Sarah." He grabbed the roll of duct tape and a small piece of cloth. As he was about to shove the cloth in her mouth, she screamed "I'm not Sarah."

He ignored her protest and pushed the cloth into her mouth and wrapped tape around her head and over the cloth in her mouth. Averell did not hear her sobbing, he only heard the engine shift gears as he sped up, staying within the speed limit, and continuing toward Cedar Road.

The rain was heavy now, coming down in sheets that blurred one's vision more than fifty feet away. Clare covered the two blocks in about six minutes, arriving at her neighbor's house soaked through. As she ascended the front stairs, she could see three of Annette's friends in the house, sitting in front of the television. She was relieved, and casually shook the rain off her umbrella, brushed her drenched hair from her face and rang the doorbell.

The van was turning on to Cedar Road and heading south toward the freeway that would take Averell and his prize to the farm. It was nearly 3:30pm. He tuned the local weather station and heard the rain was soaking the Cleveland Heights, University Heights and Shaker Heights areas, but farther south, no rain was falling. "Figures," he muttered, "soak the cities and nothing for the farmers where it was really needed."

Joyce answered the door and invited Clare in. "The rain was awful sudden," said Clare.

"Yeah," said Joyce, "as soon as it started, the kids came running in and went straight for the TV."

They laughed as they crossed the foyer and stepped into the living room.

"But—where's Annette?" puzzled Clare.

"Oh, she went home," said one of the children.

"Yeah, she's a fast walker," said another. The others agreed and turned back to the television.

"I, I didn't see her," said Clare. "I couldn't have missed her. Could I?"

"I'll drive you home and we will keep our eyes open. She may have stopped under a tree or on somebody's porch," said Joyce.

Clare was standing in the rain next to Joyce's car straining her eyes, looking down the street for Annette. "Get in, you're getting soaked," they climbed in and Joyce started the car.

Joyce backed out of the driveway and drove slowly down the street, Clare staring at every tree and porch, but no Annette. Joyce pulled into Clare's driveway and said, "I'll wait here, you check and see if she's in the house."

Clare ran to the front door. She screamed Annette's name inside the door and ran to her bedroom, then to the bathroom, back to the stairs, "ANNETTE!" Down the stairs, "ANNETTE!" Throughout the house Clare called for her daughter, only to be met with stomach-turning silence.

Joyce came in the front door, "Clare, call the police."

Clare fumbled for the phone before surrendering to sobs.
Joyce took the phone and dialed 911. She gave the operator a brief description of Annette and was assured a team of officers would be there soon.

Joyce hung up the phone and turned to Clare, "Call Dave. He should be here." Clare took the phone and dialed, she hesitated on the last number and looked to Joyce, "This makes it real," she whispered. Joyce placed her arm around her friend.

Once the police arrived, Clare stayed close to the phone while Joyce and the officers canvassed the neighborhood door to door for the next hour, asking had anyone seen or heard anything—with every blank stare and shake of the head, they were coming closer to the horrific truth that a young girl was missing, and a terrible monster was on the loose.

* * *

The van pulled into the driveway, Averell jumped out and opened the barn doors. He pulled the van into the barn and closed the doors.

Joyce and the officers continued to come up empty until they tapped on Mrs. Simpson's door. "Why yes, I saw a little girl almost get hit by one of those mini-vans. It was right over there," She pointed to the corner of the only street Annette would have had to cross going home. "A man jumped out and ran around the front, I couldn't see anything else. By the time I came downstairs, the van was gone."

"What color was the van, can you still see it?" the officer quizzed.

"Yes, it was raining pretty heavy, but I'm sure it was a dark blue color."

"Do you remember anything else about the van, like the license plate number, or the state, anything you can remember even any of the numbers? Did you notice any bumper stickers, dents, scratches, window stickers? Anything is more than what we have now."

"Young-man, see these glasses, I could see it was a blue van and the windows were all dark, but I could not see the license plates or any stickers or scratches."

Mrs. Simpson looked a little confused again as she looked at the crowds now in the street. The second officer approached and asked if they had anything, "Yeah, Mrs. Simpson here saw a little girl wearing a pink top and blue shorts talking to a man with a dark blue van with tinted windows. Why don't you start with that house across the street, see if they saw anything," said his partner.

"On it!" With that he jogged across the street to the next house.

"What can you tell me about the man, was he tall?"

"No, he was about average size. Dark jacket, tan pants and short brown hair."

"What kind of jacket was it?"

"You know, a sport coat, a blazer," she said.

"Could you see his face at all? Think carefully on any detail, like glasses or face hair."

"No, I don't think so, but I don't know for sure."

She couldn't recall anything else and the officer thanked her. The next several hours would be spent knocking on doors, interviewing neighbors in and around the neighborhood and searching for clues as to where Annette could possibly be. Clare and Dave were beside themselves, and as would be the case for most any father, Dave just wanted to get his hands on the guy in the blue van.

A local teen thought he saw a blue van leave the neighborhood as he was pulling in from a rained-out baseball practice, but again, no attention to any detail except the vehicle's color and the approximate time, 3:30pm. All anyone could think about was that the unthinkable had become a reality in their little corner of the world.

*   *   *

SEVENTEEN

I wanted her to last longer . . .

Averell looked at the lifeless body of little Annette. He felt a nagging disappointment, he wanted her to be more like Sarah, he wanted to despise her and he wanted her to despise him. Instead, she was terrified, she inspired an odd sort of feeling in him that he'd never experienced before and that actually made him angrier—which was the only reason he could finish the job.

Her tiny screams now haunted him almost as much as Sarah's sneers and snide comments. Initially he wanted her to last longer, but as the minutes ticked on, he felt more and more out of control of his feelings and the situation as a whole, and probably rushed to her demise as a result.

He pretended she was Sarah, hoping to return to a day and time where killing Sarah would be a top priority—he called her names, made threats and even tortured her to the point of making her pass out from the pain. Stelian encouraged him to take it slow, but again, that sublime feeling of being in total control was slipping away.

"You were way too preoccupied—this was a lot less fun than I thought it would be."

"I was. When she'd go limp from the pain, the joy in the process was gone. I can't explain it. What did I do wrong?"

Averell sat in the open panel door of the van, completely exhausted, looking at Annette's body. He remained there for about ten minutes, alone, closed in the barn with Annette. Then he stood and walked over to her lying twisted on the floor in a mass of blood, straw and dirt and nudged her with his foot, but there was no reaction.

"We should clean up and get rid of the evidence," said Stelian.

"Yes, we should," and he slowly turned, surveying the room. "It was not as I expected it would be, I wanted her to feel more."

"We will do better next time. Maybe this one was too little."

He put the probes, the knife and the wire cutters in a pile off to one side and all the rest of his tools in the box. He then removed all of Annette's clothes and placed them in a bag. He put her in a bag also, but it was not working as well as he planned. She was too big, as small as she was, she was too big.

"No problem, we have lotsa' bags."

"Yeah, we do."

He spread her body out on the floor and thought for a minute. Then he took a knife and began to dismember the little girl. After a few minutes he went to his van and retrieved a saw to finish the task. Annette was cut into pieces that fit neatly into three bags. Her head, fingers and arms were placed in one, her legs in another and her torso in a third.

"Almost done."

"What else is there?"

"Well, first, I want to double bag everything, then I will wash off our tools, and I thought about taking a shower in the house. But before I do that, a little clean up," and he used a broom to move the straw and dirt around enough to soak up the blood that was evident on the floor. When mixed with the dirt it was not obvious what it was and he massed it into a single pile, then with the coal shovel he scooped up a load and walked outside and flung the load out across an open field. He repeated the process until the globs of bloodied dirt were gone and the barn looked normal. "Now for a shower."

Averell wiped the exterior of the plastic bags of any blood, double bagged them and placed them in the van. Then he took the tools he used, Annette's clothes and a change of clothes for himself over to the house. He cleaned all the tools, stripped down and rinsed the blood from his and Annette's clothes, soaking them and twisting them to get rid of the excess water and put them in another plastic bag. He stepped into the shower and let the cold-water rinse off his body, rubbing with his hands as if he had soap. He stood in the shower as long as he could tolerate the cold and stepped out.

"Are you finished?"

"No, I am going to do it again." He repeated the process four more times, each time standing in the cold water as long as he could.

"Now, are you finished?"

"Yes, I am," and he dried himself off with paper towels and dressed. He carried his tools and the wet clothes out to the barn. The tools were destined to be destroyed and the clothes were to be given away after a washing at a coin operated laundry. Averell loaded his van and took a final look around, satisfied that all was as it should be, and opened the doors. He backed the van out and turned it around, got out, closed the doors and put the stick back in place. He slowly drove down the driveway to the street, constantly looking around for anybody watching. He did not see anyone, no cars, no people walking about, nobody else was in the area. He was about to turn left and head back into the Heights to the Spring Hill Cemetery when he turned on his radio and heard the end of a report about a kidnapping in Cleveland Heights. He heard the words "blue van with tinted windows." He quickly went to his back-up plan, turned right and drove two miles up the road and turned again. Alton Memorial Park was a small cemetery he had located and designated as his back-up for that day. It did not have a fence and there was only one attendant, an older gentleman, who seemed to handle all the necessary tasks and worked only during the day. He would have probably covered the vault or casket that afternoon with the small tractor-mounted backhoe after the mourners had left and would reset the sod the following day. Averell had selected this cemetery as a back-up for just that reason.

The entry to the cemetery grounds went straight in, passing stone markers, trees and small clusters of bushes. The road was a gradual incline for about one hundred yards and began to slope downward in toward a tee in the road. Averell turned right at the tee and drove along a winding road past small flat open areas on both sides labeled 'Green Pasture', 'Milton's Walk' and 'Rose Garden'. The road wound in a large curving pattern through the cemetery and Averell hoped he would not get lost.

"I have not seen a turn off other than those little openings, I hope we are not lost."

"I think we are okay, the road seems to be curving more to the left than the right and we are probably making a big circle."

"Hey, there we are again, just up ahead, that's where we came in. Alright, now I see," He continued around again, this time making a visit into each named section. As he drove into the 'Rose Garden', he noticed a pile of sod rolled and ready to be placed on a recently filled in grave. Averell looked around, noticing the grave markers were a blend of old and new, Christian and Jewish, large and small. He had checked the newspaper two days earlier for both potential cemeteries and a funeral was scheduled for that afternoon in each. "Planning, detailed planning."

"Yeah, and a little luck goes a long way."

As he approached the gravesite, he looked at the surrounding trees and bushes, the contour of the ground. The description of his van, "blue with tinted windows," heard on the radio was too good and he was very nervous.

"Here we go again, depending on luck."

"We are almost done and it will be dark soon."

"I hope you're right." He looked at the road and it was dry, as if it had not rained here, "Luck, pure luck."

"Yeah, but it is cloudy, we will get it here soon enough."

Averell pulled to the new grave site, "Perfect."

He pointed the van's lights at the grave and got a shovel from the back. He spread a drop cloth next to the grave and removed the dirt down to the vault in a small area and placed the bags in the hole, stepping on them to make them as thin as possible. After getting all three bags in and flattened, he shoveled the dirt back in, stepping on it frequently to compact it. When finished he scratched the top of the grave site so it looked as it did when he arrived. The attendant would probably roll it flat the next day, put down the sod stacked nearby and add some extra grass seed.

As Averell was leaving the cemetery, the rain began, lightly at first, then heavier. Luck was still on his side. He was heading for the rest area on I-90. He took backroads until he was close to the rest area and got on the freeway. Two miles and he turned on the ramp to the parking area. He drove to the end and up over the curb and into a heavily brushed area, not at all visible from the parking lot or the highway. He tuned his radio back to the news station and listened. Usually, pertinent local news is updated every fifteen minutes, and a missing child would be considered pertinent, indeed.

There it was on the radio: "In breaking news, the kidnapping of little Annette Shelton occurred around 3:15 this afternoon in Cleveland Heights, one block from her house. The little girl was walking home in the rain, when a dark blue van with tinted windows almost hit her and stopped. The driver of the van is described by a witness as a Caucasian male, medium height and short, dark hair. He is currently a person of interest. If you have any information about Annette, the van, or the driver, please contact the Cleveland Heights Police department."

"Ah yes, plan B." Averell remained in the Rest Area until well after dark and there were no cars in the parking lot. "Damn it, and I was just getting to like this van." He carefully pulled out and drove north and east toward western New York.

As he was driving on Interstate 90, passing Erie, Pennsylvania a calm came over him like a warm blanket. He was safe, he had gotten away, out of Ohio and he had not been confronted. As far as he knew, nobody knew what had happened in the barn. Nobody knew where she was. With any luck, she would never be found. His plan was almost perfect.

"That was good."

"Yeah, good, but it has to be better."

"Let's do another one and we will do it better."

"No, not yet. We have to finish with this one and then we have to wait a while, let everything settle down. Then, again we have to plan and I think the next one should be a little older, maybe a few years older."

"What else is there to do?"

"We have to get rid of the tools and the clothes."

"Again, with the planning."

"Yeah, planning."

He drove to the last exit on the Pennsylvania part of I-90 and got on to Route 5 to avoid toll booths and cameras on the New York portion of I-90. Another hour and he was approaching Buffalo. He had to decide—would he stop there or go on to Rochester? He knew the packages in the back had to be dealt with soon. Then he saw it, a twenty-four-hour laundry. He drove in and did his two cycles with bleach and packed them in fresh plastic bags. As he drove out, he noted a Salvation Army donation box, "Perfect," he deposited the contents of one bag of Annette's clothing, keeping the bag and driving away. Several miles later, he saw another Salvation Army drop off box in a shopping center. There he unloaded his clothing and drove away. Finally, the tools. This was the last of it. He noted a dumpster in a shopping center and unloaded the probes and after kicking the knife around in the dirt and breaking it, he tossed the knife in another dumpster. The wire cutters were all that remained. No matter how hard he stepped on them, he was not able to break them. He had wiped them clean and put them in a plastic bag. As he was driving, he spotted some water, a small lake. He pulled over on the shoulder of the road, stopped the van, took the plastic bag with the cutters, walked to the guard rail and looked both around. No one was in sight and he threw them as far out toward the middle as he could. The wire cutters hit the surface of the water about fifty feet straight out and sank to whatever depth the water was. He got back in his van and pulled back onto the highway.

"Now that was good," and he laughed to himself, "Next time," he chuckled, "Next time it will be even better." Averell drove for over an hour and found himself starting to pass his Rochester exit.

"Where are we going?"

"Oh sorry, I missed our turn off."

"Where were you heading?"

"I was not thinking, I was just thinking about our next time."

"C'mon Averell, you know where we were going."

"Yeah, we're going home."

"No, no, You want to see Ellie and Sarah. Don't you?"

"I am curious."

"You want to do them."

"Of course, I do, but not now, and yes, I have been thinking about it, frequently, but we can't—not yet. We would be at the top of the suspect list. When we do it, I want the process to be planned, completely figured out and practiced. I want to do it right on them, and remember, there will be no second chances."

Averell turned off at the next exit and turned on a back road that took him west to the exit he missed. "We shouldn't even think about it now, it would be crazy to try it this early, absolutely crazy."

"Yeah, but you do think about it, a lot. We should discuss it so we will be ready when the time comes."

"I wanted to do it before I went in the Army. Now, I can take my time, plan and eliminate any risk, no gambles no depending on luck."

*   *   *

Eighteen

Family, we are part of a very large family . . .

The search for Annette continued throughout the week and into the weekend. As the search moved into its second day, an unusually large number of people from out of the area showed up to help. The neighborhood was searched from top to bottom. Every house was addressed, every backyard was inspected, every car was searched. The ground searchers went as far as a little girl could go and then some. A nearby wooded area was scoured by no less than seventy-five people.

Posters were printed with her picture and circulated throughout the greater Cleveland area. When all the canvassing was done, the out-of-town people who came to help melted away. They'd come from as far away as Ontario, each anxious to take part in a search, and then a celebration when she was found safe. The celebration was not to be. The child was gone.

The police were grateful for all the help, but all the help in the world couldn't take the sting out of every lead turning up nothing. It became personal for many, but especially for Officer Casey who was first on the scene. He had two little sisters growing up, and his protective instincts kicked in early—they would forever be his mission to keep safe, and now he was looking down the barrel of the gun he dreaded his entire childhood, a missing little girl. A missing child, a sick monster wreaking havoc on an innocent family.

Clare and Dave were interviewed on television and their emotional plea for Annette's safe return was broadcast nationwide. Averell caught it on the radio and made a point of watching the news that evening. The tearful plea by Clare made him smile, a little, but the expression on Dave's face scared the living hell out of him.

After the interview, the reporter asked about the people that showed up to help. "Family, we are part of a very large family, you know cousins—and cousins of cousins, like a Clann," said Clare with a glassy stare in her eyes. "My dad and his friends, he's with the highway department, and my cousin, Sean, he's with the CHPD and some of his friends." Clare was exhausted, she hadn't slept a night since Annette disappeared and any brief surrender to sleep only resulted in nightmares and sweat-soaked, breathless wakes in the middle of the night.

Dave was near burnout also, overtired and unable to close his eyes. The two of them were strong together but would crumble when away from each other. Clare's father, Ben Creighton, was another rock she could lean on. He was as hard as the highways he tended and always there for her. He brought several people who worked for him to help in the search and seemed to know lots of others who were from out of town.

The search continued, the police stepped up the neighborhood cruises, dozens of people were questioned, and nothing came of it. Strangers continued to come into town and help distribute posters, knock on doors, do whatever was asked of them. When asked why they were there, they would simply say, "We're family and we want to help." After four weeks, kids were back in school and Annette was a topic of conversation. Dave had to go back to work, but he often found reasons to cut a day short or call in sick. The company was completely on his side and gave him a lot of slack, allowing him a pass on all the time he took. It was booked to overhead, and he did not miss a day's pay. Clare was a complete wreck. She took pills to go to sleep at night and more pills to stay awake during the day.

* * *

Back in Rochester, Averell was thinking about his dark blue van with tinted windows. It had been seen and he may have been seen. This was a problem. He didn't know just how much detail had been noted, color, make, license, driver, he didn't know and that was disconcerting.

"Now what should I do?"

"We could trade this van for something else, even a van of a different color at least."

"I just bought the damn thing."

"We could say that it's not what we expected, can't handle the snow."

"Yeah, that could work."

The next Saturday Averell went back to the dealer and looked for Tom. While waiting, he looked at a four-wheel drive SUV, that probably burned more gas than he wanted, but it would work. Tom came out and greeted him with "Averell, how have you been?" He remembered his name, impressive. He was a good salesman.

"What can I do for you today?"

"Well, the van is a great vehicle, especially in town, but it is not that good in the snow and a little sensitive to wind on the freeway. I am on the road year-round and I can't have a little snow slow me down."

"I see what you mean. So, what would you like to do?"

"Well, I know it has lost some value since I got it, but I feel I have to let it go and get something a little more highway and snow capable."

"Okay, let's look at different machines and get you into a model that works, then we get the right one. You know we have some pre-owned vehicles. They don't cost as much, still have warranties. Something to consider. Let's take a walk."

They went out to the lot behind the main building where the dealer had hundreds of vehicles. They walked through the lot until Averell pointed one out, a green SUV with tinted windows and oversized tires.

"Let's take it for a ride."

"Okay, but I can tell you now, this looks like the one."

An hour later, Averell was in his new pre-owned SUV, driving down the road feeling safe and satisfied.

* * *

September rolled into October, and there was no sign of Annette, the blue van or the man driving. The search had long since taken on the tone of a homicide investigation. No clues, no mention in local or national news, and the prospect of finding Annette alive and well had become only a glimmer of a hope in her parents' minds. With the passing of time, wounds heal, most wounds. Some, like the disappearance of your only child, seem to tear another piece of your heart away every day you wake and realize she is not there.

Winter came, and Averell maintained a low profile. "Let the dust settle." He drove past the farmhouse several times during the winter and noted no marks in the snow. As the winter turned into spring and leaves came back to the trees, the farmhouse and the barn remained untouched. His lab remained ready. All the elements were in place and in June, he began looking for another subject and to check the obituaries and the two cemeteries again.

* * *

Nineteen

Maybe a little shady . . . but not illegal . . .

Jim McClarry was discharged from the Navy in October 1991 and he took the test to join the Cleveland Heights police force that same month. He had earned an associate degree from Cuyahoga Community College before joining the Navy and a career in law enforcement had always been his objective. The fact that his little cousin had gone missing just two months before his discharge, undoubtedly added to the inspiring factors in his becoming a policeman. The thought of possibly being a part of the team that would someday find her kidnapper was another. He passed the test and was one of five people to get the letter inviting him to join the CHPD.

"Here we go again," he said on the first day of training, "back in boot camp." The group around him laughed and they were suddenly introduced to their training officer, a gruff, former drill instructor who came up to Jim's chin in height. After graduation he was assigned to a veteran officer with fourteen years on the job.

"Hi kid, my name is Sean Daugherty, and I'm gonna' show you the ropes."

"Hey Sean, my name is Jim McClarry," he replied with a firm handshake, "not *kid*, you call me that again and I may want to call you old man." Jim stood a solid six feet two and looked Sean straight in the eye and Sean looked back into Jim's dark blue eyes and saw a few more similarities between the two.

"Fair enough, Jimmy."

"And my mom and my girl-friend call me Jimmy, and you ain't that cute."

"Again, fair enough, Jim. Now let's get to work. First, we sit in the call room and see what's happening in our world today. Then we get out there and keep the peace." Sean was impressed with this rookie, partially because he was bright and apparently tough enough for the job, but also because he was family. Jim was not aware of the relationship, but he soon would be.

After roll call, they went down to the parking lot and checked out their cruiser. "Let me drive this first shift and talk as we go, there's a lot to be said and I know where I want to start. You will have the wheel tomorrow. Okay with you?"

"Sure, you're the boss."

"Well good, I was hoping I would not have to explain that to you."

They both laughed and got in the car. "1644 is 10-8 on the road, south on Mayfield," said Sean into the radio.

"10-4"

"Out," Sean drove south for a short distance then pulled into a strip center and parked in a position as if he was watching traffic. He looked at Jim and said, "We have to talk for a minute and then we get back to the job."

Jim looked curious and said "Okay, talk about what?" thinking he was about to be lectured.

"You should know, we are part of a huge family of families. Your uncle and my cousin are married, and there are more of us than you can count. We don't carry cards, have picnics or wear T-shirts bragging about it, but we are family and we look out for one another. Annette was, and still is, one of us and we all want to know what happened to her and where she is. I think we all feel she's dead and the object now is to find the son of a bitch that took her. So, we work together. Don't rock the boat. Don't give whoever it is the opportunity to cry foul and get off. If you or anyone else in our family hears or learns something, we follow the proper procedure and pass the info on to the right people and then back away. Let the guys upstairs at the station handle the case and keep it clean."

"We're related?"

"Sort of, but distantly. We are Annette's family, we are 'Clann'. I would love to find the SOB that took her and have a minute or three in a locked room with him, but—and it is a big but, we want him caught, not just somebody who might have done this, but THE somebody who DID do this. We want him to be tried, convicted and personally, I want him executed."

"I didn't know Annette, not really. I saw her a few times and Dave and I were at Heights High at the same time. Didn't really give him much thought until he married my cousin, Clare. She is really torn up over this, and I would like to see it happen as much as you."

"Okay, let's do our job and not get in the way of the detectives doing theirs. Agreed?"

"Yeah," said Jim, "but I wouldn't mind a minute or two with the SOB myself."

"You'd have to buy a ticket and get in line, Jim, a very long line, there's more of us than anybody ever thought. Family I mean."

Jim mulled this over and said, "I remember stories about the family doing things, like that kid in California about a hundred years ago. Somebody killed him and when the system did not do their job, well, the family did it for them."

"Yeah, his name was Liam Rynne. The guy that killed him was found by the family, the Clann, and dropped in a pit for three years. When they finally told the police where he was, all that was left was his bones. The rest of him, well, food for worms or rats, who knows."

"So is the Clann still active, I mean, are they involved in this case, Annette's disappearance?"

"I have had a few calls from some people asking questions. They are not interfering in the investigation, more like they want to help if they can."

"So, who from the family is involved?"

"Some of us are cops, like you and me, others are lawyers, engineers, doctors, bus drivers, teachers or ditch diggers. We are a little of everything. When a situation has to be addressed, like this case, the ones that could be most effective in helping are invited to do something. Something like you may be asked to shadow someone, because as a cop, you would know how to do it and it would get done right. A lawyer may be asked for a little legal advice, but nobody has to do more than they can without being burdened."

"So, maybe I would be asked to follow somebody for a day when I'm not working?"

"Yeah, that's the idea, and somewhere there is a group of older folks who decide what projects we may get involved in. As I understand it, if you have a problem, a serious problem, that you cannot deal with on your own, then you are eligible for a little assistance. Someone would have to know who to talk to. It's not as easy as putting an ad in a newspaper. The family, or the Clann, keeps an eye on things in general and when something merits the type of help they can provide, they look into it. Annette's case is one of those situations that get a second look and maybe more. They control the money to pay expenses and they pick a team to run an operation. Kinda like when they caught that guy in Oklahoma and dragged his butt back to California and dumped him in the pit."

"They organized that deal?"

"Not really, that one was kind of the kickoff for what we have today. We are not entirely like the Mafia, but we are organized to help family members."

"How do you mean?"

"They may pay a doctor bill here and there or help someone find a job, or like with Annette, help the system find the bad guy."

"And pitch him in a pit?"

"That was a long time ago, today they may put out the word that a search party is being organized and in need of help. They did that when Annette went missing, we had a couple of dozen folks from around the country just show up and help beat the bushes. And if you asked, they'd be back tomorrow to do it again."

"If they found the guy, would they do the pit thing again?"

"Who knows, I guess if the system didn't take care of the guy, the Clann just might. Anyway, the point of my telling you this is that you or I may be asked to do something, something perfectly legal, maybe a little shady, but not illegal."

"Nothing illegal?"

"We can get tough but, we're not gangsters. And I guess we probably would be open to violating a civil right or two, if the need arose and the benefit was obvious. There was a situation in Pennsylvania a couple of years ago where a street gang roughed up an elderly couple. The gang was convinced to leave them alone, forever. It apparently involved a few broken limbs and a car disappearing, but they got the message and now there is peace."

The radio crackled to life, announcing a traffic problem and Sean acknowledged the call and said to Jim, "Think about all this and we should sit down and talk more soon."

"Okay, I am very interested in learning more."

They pulled out of the parking lot and drove for about three minutes in silence. Jim was looking out the window when they passed a doughnut shop. He turned and looked at Sean, but before he could say anything, Sean said, "Don't go there." They both laughed, and Jim's on-the-job training had begun.

*　　*　　*

TWENTY

They had not been to church in a while . . .

On June 14, 1992, Annette would have celebrated her eighth birthday. But there was no celebrating in the Shelton house. By then, she had been missing almost a full year. True grief is not something that goes away, the pain does not diminish, the sadness stays in the heart. The hope that Annette would someday come home is all that kept Dave and Clare from losing what was left of their sanity. Clare had cried herself to sleep many nights over the last year and Dave spent his free time trying to divert her attention from the pain that constantly enveloped both of them. They did not smile, they did not laugh, they did not spend time with friends, they were very much alone.

Clare baked a cake. Annette had loved layer cakes that were chocolate on the top and vanilla on the bottom with chocolate frosting all over. She sliced the cake and put it on the front porch table and sat there looking up and down the street. A group of kids, Annette's friends were playing outside and when they saw Clare, they came over to ask if there was any new leads.

"No, I'm afraid not. Today is her birthday, she's eight and I wish she was here." Clare's eyes were red and swollen and a tear rolled down her cheek.

Danny touched her hand and said, "Maybe she is in heaven, that's what my dad thinks. He said she is too nice to be anywhere else."

Clare almost smiled, "Please have some cake and remember her," and she went in the house. The kids sat down and shared the cake and sang a very subdued Happy Birthday song and then went home.

Dave had gone out to get a few things at the store and he planned on taking Clare to church when he got home. He walked up to the front porch and saw the remains of the cake. Three slices were still there and he was thinking about that when Clare said, "I would like to go to church in a few minutes and then maybe we could walk in the park and talk."

"Sure, I see someone had cake this morning."

"Yeah, some of Annette's friends were here. It was nice, they're good kids."

Dave noted her eyes were not as red as they had been and said, "I'll put this stuff away and we can go."

Clare said, "Okay, I'm ready when you are."

They had not been to church in a while and were greeted by a number of people when they arrived. After the mass, the crowd grew a little larger and Clare felt overwhelmed. Dave was a little curt with the last of the inquiries from friends and they finally escaped, got in their car and drove to the park.

As they walked around, they passed soccer fields and baseball diamonds full of kids, laughing and screaming—having fun. Clare looked a little sad but no tears. She was surfacing, coming to grips with the fact that Annette was gone, and she had to go on. She squeezed Dave's hand and the both of them felt some of the weight lift off their shoulders. When they got home, the rest of the cake had been eaten and there was a birthday card on the porch table signed by the kids. It said "Happy Birthday" on the outside and "We miss you" on the inside, and they had all signed it. Clare cried again, a different cry, a healing cry.

*   *   *

Twenty-One

Don't make me laugh, it hurts . . .

The neighborhood had treelined streets with houses on one acre lots, and bushes and flower beds partially obscuring the view from inside the sprawling colonial homes. This severely hampered the ability to observe activity on the street and sidewalks. As Averell was cruising the streets, he saw a young girl he estimated was at least ten and maybe closer to twelve. She was almost perfect, definitely older than his last subject a year earlier. "I like the way this one looks."

"Very nice, and maybe her name is Sarah. The hair and the eyes are right."

She had blond hair and blue eyes and she was wearing a bright yellow blouse, blue denim shorts and white shoes. Candice Brighton was walking around the block with her dog when he saw her. The time was right for another session in the barn, everything had been made ready for just this sort of encounter. As he watched her walking and talking to her dog, his pulse quickened, his palms moistened and he started to breathe heavier. This one, being older, should be tougher and definitely would last longer.

"She will be harder to control, but I know we can handle her."

"Yeah, she is perfect, how are we going to do this?"

"We will get her at the corner, near those bushes." He drove to the corner and got out of his SUV, leaving the door open. There were several tall trees surrounded by bushes in the middle of a flower bed at the corner, making his SUV barely visible from the immediate homes. He had a piece of note paper in his hand and he was staring at the street signs when Candice approached.

"Excuse me miss, but could you tell me where School Street is?" said Averell.

"Oh, I have seen it, but I don't know where it is." Her little dog was agitated and pulled at his leash. Candice pulled back.

"Perfect," thought Averell, as he approached her. "Do you think it would be that way," as he pointed up the street. That distracted Candice as she looked in the direction Averell was pointing. "Or would you go that way," he said as he was now standing next to Candice.

"I don't know," said Candice.

Averell put his hand on his chest and said, "I have to find my mom's new house, she is expecting me by 4:00 this afternoon and it's already 3:45," and he moved slightly closer to his SUV. Candice moved with him as if magnetized and drawn toward him. Averell mumbled something, and Candice came closer and said, "Pardon me, I didn't hear what you said."

Averell saw that the time was right, and he turned toward Candice, grabbed her arm and dragged her into the SUV. Candice was startled and screamed as she was shoved inside the vehicle. The dog was barking but, posed no threat. Averell ripped the leash from her hand and threw it out of the car.

"Shut up," said Averell as he turned and slapped her across the face. He pulled the door closed, grabbed a tie-wrap and bound her hands behind her and drove down the street slowly with the dog in pursuit. Candice was stunned, crying, but did not scream again. "This will be good, it is going to be better than the last one." He was starting to fantasize about what he could and would do.

As he turned on to West Road and started for the Interstate, the dog was left far behind and Candice started to fuss louder and was kicking the back of Averell's seat. He pulled over, turned with a vicious snarl and slapped her again, then taped her hands and ankles and fastened her seat belt. "Now shut up." He stared at her pushing his face as close to hers as he could. He was breathing hard and drool began to drip from his mouth. He turned and slowly started to move the SUV forward. When he reached the highway, he turned west and headed toward Mentor and the farm beyond.

Candice was being difficult. She cried and would not stop. He slapped her and she cried louder. She would not stop crying. She kicked and cried, he could not control her at all. After getting into the barn, he opened the back of the SUV and pulled out a drop cloth. He placed it over a large crate and returned to the SUV. He grabbed her around the waist and lifted her out of the SUV. She seemed heavier now and he wrestled her over to the large crate and tied her arms down. He cut the binding at her ankle and was removing her left shoe when she kicked as hard as she could with her right foot. The treaded heel caught Averell on the left side of his lower lip. Her kick was well placed and blood spurted across the edge of the drop cloth covering the crate and on to the floor but missed Candice completely. He spun to his right and stepped away from the crate. Blood was dripping on the floor and Averell was furious. He went to his SUV and looked in the side view mirror. His lip throbbed and was bleeding profusely. He had to adapt, to change his plan. He took a piece of cotton and a six-inch piece of duct tape and closed his wound, taping the cotton in place.

Now for the little bitch who had kicked him. His eyes were wild and angry as he picked up his knife and approached Candice. "You little bastard, I'm going to cut you apart, one piece at a time."

She screamed as loud as she could, loud enough to be heard and Averell swung the knife at her face without thought. He caught her across her right eye and nose. He quickly grabbed her right arm and started to cut in a sawing motion trying to cut it off. She screamed again, and Averell slashed at her face again, cutting her through the right cheek and part of the left cheek. Candice fainted, and Averell finished taking off her arm. He cut off her left arm and started to poke her with the knife, making shallow punctures on her chest and stomach. She would not respond, she could not respond, she would not draw another breath. Her remaining eye was open and saw nothing. Averell stood over her staring, panting, not thinking. He was still angry and wanted to hurt her again, but she would not feel it. He wanted to scream at her again, but she would not hear it.

"She's gone, and we are finished here."

"No, no, no, I want to see more, I want to see her heart." Averell fell to his knees with the knife in his hand, staring at Candice partially dismembered in a pool of her own blood. "She's gone." He hung his head and allowed the knife to drop to the floor.

"We should clean up now."

"Yes, yes, yes, we have to clean up, stick to the program, clean up and get rid of her." He raised his head and slowly stood, all of a sudden realizing his lip hurt and was still bleeding. He knew he had to have his lip looked at, probably stitched. He picked up her arms and threw them on top of her and rolled her up in the drop cloth.

"I should throw her away in the trash," he was breathing heavily as he bent and picked up the knife.

"No, no, we should be patient," said Stelian.

"You're right, we will bury her as planned and get back to Buffalo or better yet, to Rochester and get this lip fixed."

Averell scanned the barn and started picking up the tools and put them away. He was still angry. He went into the house to the shower and turned it on. He paced back and forth in front of the shower, cursing under his breath. As he calmed, he stepped into the shower and rinsed the blood off his body and rinsed the clothes. He repeated the process only once and dried himself off. Then he dressed and returned to the barn.

"Damn it, this was no good, the little bitch kicked me, pissed me off, it was over before we had a chance to get started, before we could do it the way we wanted." He was absolutely furious.

"We picked a bad one, didn't we?" said Stelian.

"Yes, we did, this was no fun. Now we have to get rid of her and she wasn't worth it. I just want to throw her in a damn landfill."

"No, Averell, we have to put her where she will not be found."

"The cemetery?"

"Yes, I think the cemetery is the perfect place for her."

He drove out the driveway and started for the Alton Memorial Park, the cemetery he had used for Annette. On the way, he passed a police car on the side of the road, writing a ticket. "Too close to the cemetery," he said.

"You're right," said Stelian, *"but we have an alternate."*

"I know, that's where I am heading now," and he turned at the next light and drove a few miles south. "I'm trying to remember what time the service was scheduled for this one. The other one was at noon, and this one was half past as I recall. So, they should be finished by now or close to it."

Spring Hill Cemetery was his first choice the previous year because of the contour of the land. The other cemetery, Alton Memorial Park, appeared to be smaller and he initially thought it was going to be harder to conceal his activity. As it turned out, Alton was perfect, and he wanted to use it again, but the police vehicle gave him pause and he opted for Spring Hill. This cemetery was spread over about thirty acres of rolling landscape. Like Alton, Spring Hill was not tended on a full-time basis.

He drove in the entrance and roamed around looking for the site where today's funeral had taken place. He saw a man driving a backhoe away from what looked to be a new grave site and heading toward a winding roadway. He saw the small pile of sod, rolled and stacked nearby. The site was in a slight valley between two small hills. He continued past the site and headed back toward the entrance. The backhoe seemed to follow him until it reached the small white building next to the chapel and office complex. The man pulled the backhoe over a gravel driveway and parked it. Averell continued out the entrance and turned right and slowly drove to the intersection about three hundred feet away and turned right again. He drove another hundred feet and parked across from a small office building and watched the cemetery attendant as he hosed down the backhoe. The man went into the main building and a light came on. Averell rolled his tongue across his split lip and winced, "If luck is with us today, this fellow will call it a day and plan to lay the sod tomorrow."

"We should come back in what, about an hour?"

"Yeah, it will be almost dark, just enough light to get this done."

He drove down the road to a fast-food restaurant and turned into the drive-thru where he ordered a milk shake. A straw was about all his lip could handle at this point. At the pick-up window he turned his face to hide the bandage and drove back in the direction of the Cemetery. He parked and after a few minutes he saw the man drive the backhoe into the little white building, lock the doors, then get in a car and drive off. He sipped his milkshake for a few minutes more before deciding the man wasn't coming back. "I think it's safe," he said.

"Yeah, let's get this done and get back to business," said Stelian.

Averell drove into the cemetery, casually drove around the twisting two lane roadway and soon found the fresh grave. He felt a little uneasy because his success thus far had been heavily dependent on luck, and he feared it might run out. He pointed his vehicle toward the gravesite and left the lights on. He then grabbed his shovel and set to work digging.

After a bit, *"I'll take a turn,"* said Stelian.

Averell paused and said, "Okay, your turn." and proceeded to dig with renewed energy until his shovel struck the concrete vault cover. This one was flat and clearing a spot for Candice was easily accomplished. He dragged the bags from the SUV and lowered them into the hole, then he stepped on them to make sure they were as flat as he could make them and returned the dirt to the hole. As he smoothed the top he noted that it was a little higher than when he started. He stepped on the dirt trying to compact it as much as he could then smoothed it out again. "There, done. It's so much easier when you help."

"That's why I'm here."

Finished, Averell packed his shovel and tarp in his SUV and calmly drove out of the cemetery. He headed back toward Erie and then east to Rochester. As he crossed into Pennsylvania, he again felt that warm calm of safeness. He followed his usual pattern, laundromat, Salvation Army drops and a visit to a secluded dumpster.

When he got to his townhouse in the Rochester area, he took a close look at his lip and decided that he had to go to the emergency room and have it properly treated. His concern was that he would be questioned about how it happened, and he wanted his story to be believable. He looked around the house and decided an accident in the kitchen could be easily staged. He opened a kitchen cabinet door and lined himself up with it. Then he turned around and rehearsed turning into an open cabinet door several times. A glass of water in his hand when he hit the door would look convincing. He removed the bandage and peeled away the dried blood and scab starting to form. He squeezed the lip forcing a flow of blood to the wound and positioned himself with water in hand. He turned slowly and let his lip make contact with the door, leaving a trace of blood and dropped the glass. He then tossed his head to the left, throwing a spurt of blood across the counter and another cabinet door. Then grabbing a handful of paper towels, he placed them on his lip encouraging flow. He left a few bloodied paper towels in his kitchen, picked up his keys and drove to the Emergency Room.

A doctor put four stitches in his lip and filled out a required report for all such injuries. The doctor wrote a prescription and gave Averell a few extra bandages and he went home, stopping at the pharmacy to fill the prescription. He sat down in his living room, turned on the television, took out his logbook and started to figure his mileage balance when his doorbell rang. Not surprised, he answered the door and was greeted by a police officer.

"This is a follow up to your hospital visit," said the officer.

"Sure, c'mon in," and he backed up a step.

The officer entered and said, "Tell me what happened, and I can get out of here and you can get some sleep."

"Sure, I was getting a glass of water and I guess that I left the cabinet door open. Turned right into it."

Averell showed the officer to the kitchen and said, "I have to clean up this mess" he said, referring to the broken glass and spilled water, "But I'm not in the mood right now."

The officer grinned, noted the open door and the blood on the edge and on the wall. Everything looked in order, there was no reason to question the events as reported and after taking a few notes, he said, "Drinking and walking around your own kitchen don't mix."

They both laughed, and Averell said, "Don't make me laugh, it hurts," and he half smiled. The officer returned the smile and left. Averell cleaned up his mess, picked up his log and got back to his calculations.

"Another negative 360 miles, damn it."

"Damn it."

* * *

Twenty-Two

What makes a man do this sort of thing . . .

Averell had to withstand several weeks of ribbing from his customers as his lip healed. He kept his story consistent and soon he could barely recall that it wasn't truly what happened. The teasing continued until the scar was nothing more than a rigid line. It wasn't pleasant but much better than being found out and paying the price, and he derived pleasure in knowing he had gotten away with it again.

As time passed, Averell sort of grew to like his scar. It implied some sort of violent encounter during his service in the army or perhaps an impromptu fistfight in a bar.

His need to find another subject and play in the barn grew stronger each day. He was still angry about being kicked, losing his temper and ruining his fun and he wanted to do it again, this time without the kicking. What he really wanted was to have Sarah in the barn. He thought about her and how much he was hurt each time she repeated the words—"She hates you." As they grew up together, his need to make her pay increased. He wanted to open her chest and see if she had a heart, and if it really pulsed blood through her veins. The thought was constantly with him. The vision of blood flowing out her mouth as her heart tried to beat again was his nightly dream. In his dream Ellie watched while sipping her coffee and as he finished with Sarah and approached Ellie with his knife in hand, he would awaken.

- (Break here)

Jim read the newspaper on June 24, 1992, and saw an article describing a missing girl in McKean, Pennsylvania. He read all that there was to read, but as with Annette, there were no witnesses and no body. The disappearance of Candice made the news nationwide and Jim

McClarry, always searching for answers about Annette, collected information from other, similar cases and tried to understand, tried to build a profile of the person who may have taken her. He wanted to know, one way or the other, where she was—could she be saved, could she be found? He hoped for the best and planned for the worst. If she could come home and be with her family again, he wanted to help make it happen. If she was dead, he wanted to find her and give her remains a proper burial, then he wanted to find the person responsible for her disappearance and death. He wanted to be sure they were properly arrested, tried and punished.

Jim started a file in his home computer, where he recorded everything he could about Annette and information on a number of other missing child cases that remained unsolved. It began as a single spreadsheet with columns for age, sex, hair, eyes, height, weight, school, and other items and soon became unwieldy. He found out there are thousands of children that go missing each year across the country. The numbers were staggering. According to the Department of Justice, more than 2,000 kids go missing nationwide every day, that's well over half a million kids each year. Out of those numbers, over one-hundred kids are abducted each year by a stranger for several reasons. Most of these abductions result in abuse, injury or death. Some abductions are for ransom, some are kept for a day and released. The ones that are missing for a long period with no trace are probably dead, adopted by the abductors or trafficked.

As he gathered more information, he added columns until the single spread sheet was more easily divided into two sheets. He recorded information in a uniform way, on each spreadsheet so that he could go back and forth between the two sheets. As he read about a new case and found a new category, he added columns to include the new information. He was getting frustrated by the limiting factors of the spreadsheet and needed a different tool to track the information.

An IT consultant had been brought in to help organize the station's computer system and Jim offered to buy lunch in return for a few helpful hints on his home system. The consultant, Geoff, immediately told him he thought a database was probably best for his analysis.

"You can have as many fields and entries per case as the database will allow. Sorted as you see fit. " After a few more lunches with Geoff, Jim was ready to put together a database to track the information he could and would accumulate. He determined it could serve law enforcement and hopeful loved ones for years to come. He started with what he knew about Annette and added every detail he could think of. Then he looked at the information he had on Candice. She became number two in his database. He continued with every missing child he could identify. Initially the information went in easily as he converted his spreadsheets.

As he progressed with this project, Jim found he had two basic sets of information. One was all based on the victims and the other was based on the predators. He had more on the victims than on the criminals and he had no idea if the predator who took Annette would turn out to be a regional hunter, or possibly a nationwide or even an international mass murderer. It could even be a onetime killer. He had no frame of reference, so he entered everything, even the insignificant information.

Time passed, and Jim scoured the newspapers and paid close attention to the nightly news, constantly increasing his information base. He had also gathered information on a number of other cases surrounding several disappearances over the last ten years and tried to draw parallels between those and Annette's and Candice's cases. There was simply not enough information published to properly evaluate the possible parallels.

His notes showed Annette in Cleveland Heights and Candice in McKean and he pinned these locations on a map. These two were relatively close together and he gave them a little more attention. The other missing children were also tracked, but the next closest one was in Missouri and that seemed outside a reasonable area of consideration. More data was needed to properly profile the predator who took Annette. He researched back one year at a time, intending to go back as far as the records would allow, even though it would become less and less meaningful after an unidentifiable point. He had no fear of ever reaching that point, there was enough data generated each year to keep him busy.

On Thursday, August 13, 1992, in Syracuse, New York, an eight-year old girl, Megan Norris, disappeared sometime between two and four in the afternoon. Megan became number three in Jim's database.

Jim added a pin for Megan in his map. He now had a triangle from Cleveland Heights, Ohio to McKean, Pennsylvania to Syracuse, New York. He still needed more information. No one knew what happened to these three children. Why had they been taken? Had they been sold into some sort of slavery? Had they been abused in some perverse way? Had they been tortured? Were they still alive? The answers to these questions could lead to one or more kidnappers. Jim wanted to understand, as much as possible, the mind of someone who could do these things, someone who could abuse or kill a child.

The Cleveland Heights Police Department had a psychologist that advised them on special cases where the deviant mind-played a significant role. Jim had seen him and attended two 'Lunch and Learn' sessions where he spoke on related topics. Dr. Alexander Robertson was also an instructor at Cleveland State University in the Psychology department. He had written several articles that dealt with child abuse and predatory behaviors and was doing research at a state facility with convicted child molesters. Dr. Robertson was in the station several times a month and usually used an empty office on the second floor. The door was open when he was available and closed when he was not. On August nineteenth, Jim was coming off a night shift when he saw Dr. Robertson drive up and park in the lot.

When he had cleared all his paperwork and was about to change and go home, Jim went to the second floor and saw the door was open. "Good morning Dr. Robertson, could I pester you for a minute?"

"Come in, please. I don't think we've formally met."

"My name is Jim McClarry and I've been on the job a little over a year."

"What can I do for you?"

"Well, I'm a patrolman, not a detective, but I'm very interested in a specific case and I'm trying to understand some things a little better."

"Which case?"

"Annette Shelton."

"Oh yeah, I'm familiar with that one. She is still missing, and there have been no new leads I am aware of. What is your interest?"

"Annette is my cousin."

"Oh, well, that puts a spin on everything, doesn't it? Should you be working on this?"

"I'm not working on it, officially. I want to understand, and yeah, I want to help. I watch the news and read the papers and have started to collect information on a couple of other cases that look similar to Annette's. I do not want to get in the way of what's being done officially, but if I turn up something that might help, I'll just hand it to the guys in the suits and back away."

"You have to be very careful not to cross the line and hurt the investigation. you understand that?"

"Yeah, I do."

"Okay, so you are collecting data, what have you gathered so far?"

"Well, not much. I thought there would be a lot of stuff I could look at, but I don't know what specific information would be significant and where I should concentrate my attention."

"First, there is no such thing as too much information. The key to what will tie one thing to another may be as simple as the color of somebody's hair, or the way they say hello. You don't know until you have collected a lot of data and compared it."

"So, if there are three cases of missing kids, the common factor could be something that is not obvious to you or me at first and we depend on the next victim to add to the data base and open our eyes."

"We have to look pretty hard at everything, and it could be several factors that together flip the switch. Why don't we look at what you have thus far and maybe we'll see something?"

"Okay, I don't have my data with me, it's at home. When will you be here again, Doctor?"

"My name is Alex—I was planning on next Wednesday. Will you be around then?"

"I'll be sure to be here, same time?"

"Okay, next Wednesday, the twenty-sixth, nine sharp," he said as he made a note on his calendar. "See you then."

"Thanks, Alex."

Jim went home, reviewed all his data and was ready the following Wednesday for his meeting with Alex. At 9:00am he was on his way up to the second-floor office with his data. "Good morning Alex."

"Jim, I am anxious to see what you have, come on in."

"What I have are three little girls kidnapped over the last two years between here and Syracuse, New York. They ranged between seven and ten years old at the time of their disappearance. Two are blond, one is a redhead, all three have blue eyes."

"Okay, now what about the insignificant stuff, like what they were wearing, the time of day, day of the week and what they were doing?"

"Yeah, I got some of that, too. They all disappeared in the summer months, mid-week, a Tuesday, a Wednesday and a Thursday, all in the afternoon. These three were taken within a one-year period, two with blue shorts and white shoes, one with pink shoes and a white skirt and they all had different colored shirts."

"What about weather, you know rain, sunshine, cloudy? It may be nothing, it may be something."

"I can dig that up, I think. I do know it was raining when Annette was taken, not sure about the others."

"Anything unusual about the day they were taken?"

"Not that I am aware of."

"Any witnesses?"

"Yeah, with Annette, someone saw a dark blue van with tinted windows. The driver was medium-height, slight build, short dark hair, blue blazer and tan pants."

"Only about half a million people fit that description, but the van, now that's something. What the clothes tell us is that the guy may be a professional of some kind, van hints at a family man. Mid-afternoon indicates that he has some freedom with his time."

"I wish I had more."

"Well, you may have more and not know it yet. Are we sure that the same person is responsible for all three of these abductions?"

"I have no idea, how could we know that?"

"We keep looking at what we have and look for more. We hope for a break, maybe somebody saw something and doesn't realize it. We may have to revisit the neighborhood, talk to the people again and see what pops up."

"How do we make that happen?"

"Let me talk to George, he's a good man, he may already be on it. This is good stuff. I assume the suits already have all this."

"Yeah, I just wanted to know if I was on the right track in collecting data. I will keep looking, if something else turns up, I'd like to do this again."

"Correction—if anything turns up, you damn well better be up here with it."

"Let me ask you a few questions."

"Sure, fire away."

"What makes a man do this sort of thing?"

"Do you want the college version or the simple version?"

"Let's keep it simple for now, and we will build as we go along until I hit overload."

"Okay, there is no stock answer, it's a very individual thing. The exact same things could present to two or more totally different people and the reactions will probably be as varied as the number of people. That said, there are things that tend to elicit a specific response. If I step on your toe, you will probably say ouch, or some variation of ouch. If you did it to a hundred people, you will probably get several phrases that are common to maybe half of the group, then another that are common to about half again."

"That makes sense."

"Okay, now let's complicate the equation and say that someone has a lot of negative experiences. The probability that individual will try to respond to those experiences increases. So, if a man walks to work every day and whenever it rains, he passes a large puddle at a specific spot. If a car passes by, he gets soaked. So, after a while, he finds another route. Another man may respond by screaming at the driver of the car, another may throw a rock at the car. Same experience, different coping mechanism. If I call you an SOB, you might laugh, you might call me a name or you might punch me in the nose."

"Okay, I understand all that, but killing someone, isn't that going to extreme?"

"Sure, it is, now we begin to deal with psychosis, and the equation becomes more complex. We may have to go back in someone's history and piece together a profile. The farther back we go, probably the better the resulting profile."

"So, this predator is reacting to something that happened to him?"

"We don't know. As we gather evidence, something may present itself that stands out as reason. More than likely, it will be a combination of things. Now, our problem is not being able to profile an individual by looking at his past—here we have to develop an identity from the bits and pieces of his actions."

"And that's why there is no such thing as too much information and nothing is left out of our search."

"Right, everything we know today could be a piece of the puzzle. By the same token, a lot of the information may be coincidental or meaningless, but at this point, we don't know."

"So, gather everything and keep it in the mix until it gets ruled out."

"In a matter of speaking, yes, but sometimes the true key is not found until long after a case is closed so, you hang on to everything." Alex's phone rang and he turned to answer it. He indicated that he had to take the call.

"Thanks Alex, I really appreciate this. I can see I have a lot to learn about these kinds of people."

Alex paused his call and said to Jim, "Listen, check in every couple of weeks whether you have something or not."

"Okay, see you in a week or two." Jim went back downstairs and was heading for his car.

Through the rest of the summer and into the fall, Jim stopped in to see Alex every other week at first and by December it was once a month. Their conversations centered on things Jim had found and how they might be used to identify their predator. Over the winter Alex was lecturing at a few other colleges and the visits dwindled to one in January and one in March.

* * *

Twenty-Three

They want to know what we know . . .

In June of 1993, Averell was in Sandusky, about to head to Toledo to finish a westbound trek. He was still checked into a motel and decided to keep the room at least for the night. It was 2:45pm and he thought about getting dinner and perhaps taking in a movie.

"An opportunity to play again, my friend."

"Yes, we could go west and come back here for the night."

"We could do that, easily. And we know a place."

Averell went to the theater and bought a ticket to the evening showing of a film he had seen several times. He made sure his tools were in the car and headed west on I-90. He passed Toledo at 4:00pm and was in Goshen, Indiana at 6:35pm. He had exceeded the speed limit most of the way and had not seen any police. The trip back to Sandusky would be completely within the limits of the law. He wandered a bit through residential areas looking at the children playing in yards. Most of the kids were in groups which was problematic, and he continued on his way. It was almost 7:30pm when he spotted a prime target. Kathy Callen was obviously older than the others, walking alone, carrying a couple of books and daydreaming. She was thin, probably 5'5" tall and maybe a hundred pounds. The attraction, however, was her blond hair, pulled back into a ponytail, her blue eyes, the blue denim skirt and a light blue blouse she was wearing, complete with the white shoes Averell associated with Sarah. She was walking in an area that was shaded by trees, and between two well separated houses. He passed the girl and stopped below a wide spreading oak tree. He got out, opened the back door and paced back and forth next to his car, holding a map and looking very confused. This ploy had worked before and the young girl appeared no wiser than the others he had fooled.

"Excuse me miss, could you tell me how to get to Main Street? I have to pick up my mother."

"Oh, I don't know any of the streets except this one and the one at the corner. That is where I live."

"Are you going home?"

"Yes."

"Could I ask your daddy where Main Street is?"

"No, he is at work until late, but my mom is home."

"Great, I will follow you home and ask your mom."

That seemed to make Kathy relax, and she turned to walk toward her street. As she turned, Averell put one hand over her mouth and the other hand grabbed her around the waist and launched her into the SUV. As he pushed her into the seat he reached back and pulled the door closed. He was on top of her and pushed his hand into her face preventing her from screaming. He had a gag at the ready and stuffed it into her mouth and pulled a piece of pre-cut duct tape off the back of the driver's seat and put it over her mouth. He grabbed a couple of pull ties and secured her hands and ankles, while she thrashed. He buckled the seat belt and used a third pull tie to restrict her hand movement, securing them to the seat belt. He crawled between the front bucket seats and positioned himself behind the wheel. As he started the engine, and slowly drove below the speed limit heading toward the Interstate, he noted that the time was 7:48pm.

"Nicely done."

"Yes, it was," Averell said as his breathing slowed. He was now on the ramp to I-90 East and Kathy's mother was just beginning to wonder what was taking her so long to get home.

An hour later, Averell had reached his wooded area just across the state line in Ohio and Kathy's mom, Dorothy Callen, had called the police and a full-scale search was beginning to unfold. It was almost 9:00pm and daylight was fading, Averell was torturing the little girl and her mother and father were still searching the fields around their home. The police had widened the search area to a 20-mile radius. Averell was about eighty-miles away, taking the girl apart limb by limb as the searchers were still being deployed. The search area covered less than half the distance to the wooded area where Kathy finally and mercifully stopped breathing. Averell was excited and very pleased with the time he spent with Kathy. He had explained to her what he was going to do and as she listened, he started with his probes and she whimpered but stayed quiet. He opened her chest and she passed out, but he did see her heart as it pulsed for the final time. When he finished, Averell dismembered her body and collected all of Kathy's parts, putting them in bags as he had done previously and then following his ritual of rinsing himself off five times in a nearby stream.

Cleansed and collected, Averell drove to Maplewood Memorial Park, a cemetery about 5 miles from the woods, arriving before midnight. He had checked the newspaper and this cemetery had interred a burial that day. The gravesite was easily found and digging was not difficult. Averell placed the three bags containing his latest subject in the hole and replaced the dirt. The sod was destined to be placed the next day and as he was tamping the ground with his feet, he saw a vehicle come in the entrance, moving in his direction. The car dipped between two of the low rolling hills and did not reappear, "A late-night visit to a gravesite?"

"Or a couple of kids who can't afford a motel room?"

He gave the dirt a final brush with his hands, put all his tools away, started the van and drove slowly away with no lights. There was just enough light from the moon to allow him to pull out on a service road away from the cemetery without using his headlights. As soon as he was on a highway, he turned on his headlights and drove directly toward the interstate.

"We're safe."

"Yeah, safe."

At 1:23am, Averell was back in his motel in Sandusky and standing in the shower. He awoke at 7:30am and went down to breakfast where he took the movie theater ticket and tore it in half, putting one piece in his pocket and the other in a trash container. After breakfast, he returned to his room to pack up and get ready to get on the road. He turned on the television and caught a news report. No mention of any girl missing in Indiana. He wondered if she had been missed yet, and he sat on the floor in a corner with his back touching two walls.

"I want to know what they know."

"They want to know what we know."

"We have to be very careful, I think we will be very quiet for a while."

"Yeah, good idea."

"Maybe they saw something, like the SUV, it sticks out, we could be identified."

"Maybe somebody saw your fat lip."

"Not funny."

"Yes, it is."

"We need to look at new cars when we're back in Rochester."

"Another van?"

"We'll see."

"Okay."

He sat in the corner, not saying anything for an hour, until his head drooped, and he fell asleep.

*   *   *

Twenty-Four

The next one, yes, the next one . . .

Averell woke around noon to the sound of the maid rattling the doorknob.

"Still here, but I'll be out in a few minutes."

"It's okay," said the Spanish accent, "checkout was at noon, ten minutes ago, maybe I am not here yet, okay?"

"Thanks, I'll hurry."

"Okay."

Averell had already packed up and simply had to vacate the room. He hurriedly visited the bathroom and was out the door when the maid said, "You just leave me the keys and I will tell them you were gone before noon."

Averell looked at her name tag and said to the stout, middle-aged woman, "Maria, you are a beautiful person."

Maria giggled and said, "Oh Mr. Danker, you are always so nice."

Averell loaded his car and drove out of the lot, heading east.

The trip east was longer than he had anticipated. It seemed as though everyone on his list wanted more of everything in anticipation of the upcoming school year. He decided to violate his rule of two stops per day and was making three most days and staying longer in each town to make sure he hit everybody he could. His normal two-week trek west took over three weeks, but the orders made it worth his while. When he finally made it back to his base in Rochester, he looked at his records and said, "Holy cow, I could take a few months off, I did damn good this trip."

"So, we look at new cars now, right?"

"Right, a new buggy for Averell."

"And me too?"

"Yeah, and you."

Averell made an appointment with Tom Walters and paid him a visit that afternoon. He was comfortable with Tom's friendly, personable nature, his willingness to listen to his preferences with little to no pushback and his ability to offer a fair price.

Within a few short hours, Averell was in a navy sedan with a sizeable back seat and trunk. He was pleased with the smooth ride and his new reduced payment meant a few extra dollars in his pocket every month.

The rest of the summer passed without incident. Averell was doing quite well financially, and the new car was proving to be a wise investment. He paid close attention to the maintenance to ensure repairs would be minimal. On several occasions, Averell passed by Ellie's townhome. He noted her car and Steve's truck frequently. "They must be getting along."

"They deserve each other."

* * *

Jim McClarry scanned the morning newspaper on a daily basis, looking for anything to add to his database. There were several missing children reports each month and he recorded each one in the database as he found them. His sources were limited, but he was persistent, and the database was growing, but still no definitive connecting factors. The missing persons and murder cases were scattered around the country. "Maybe this is a waste of time," he thought. Frustrating, but that's what detective work was—frustrating, until one little piece of something adds to another and then it grows. Like a puzzle, it starts to come together.

The day following her disappearance, Jim found an article about a missing girl in Indiana and added Kathy to the map. He now had a line that went from Goshen Indiana to Cleveland Heights to McKean to Syracuse, New York. Interstate 90, interesting, very interesting. This could be what Alex was talking about. One little piece that ties the others together. He felt it was time for a visit with Dr. Robertson.

He grabbed a notebook and headed out. If he hustled, he wouldn't be late for work. He kept a brisk pace for the two-block walk to the station, making it on time.

Jim pulled Sean aside and told him he might be on to something.

"Let's take a walk upstairs," said Sean.

They went up to the detectives' offices and caught the captain. Sean called across the squad room, "Hey George, you got a minute?"

"For you guys, all day," he said sarcastically, but with a grin. "Come on in. What can I do for you?"

"You guys know Annette Shelton is my cousin?" said Jim.

"Yeah, and Sean is also related. I figured it had to do with Annette when I saw both of you. I've had several conversations with Alex, seems he thinks we should revisit the neighborhood."

Jim stepped closer, "Look, I don't want to screw anything up, so I do my thing just with stuff in the papers and what I catch on the internet. And I may have something."

"Okay, so let's see it," said George.

Jim opened his notebook and flipped a few pages, "I've been tracking any kid gone missing I see in the media. These four kinda' stick out. The interesting thing is I-90. In ninety-one, Annette in Cleveland Heights; in ninety-two, Candice Brighten in McKean, Pennsylvania; in ninety-two again, Megan Norris in Syracuse, New York; and in ninety-three Kathy Callen in Goshen, Indiana. All along Interstate 90. It may be nothing, and you guys may already have noted this but, well, Alex told me the smallest thing could be important, so I had to say something."

"First, never hesitate to bring stuff up here and second, no, we do not have this. You did this at home, from the newspapers and the internet?"

"Yeah."

"Good work, and you're not supposed to be doin' this, but I'm not gonna' tell you to stop. That door is never locked," said George pointing at the squad room door.

"I'm gonna' get outta' the way now," said Jim.

"Okay, when you see something else, you better be back up here. By the way, Alex will be in this afternoon, so why don't you stop back around four?"

"I'll do that."

"We'll do that," added Sean.

Sean and Jim were a little late getting on the road and the sergeant was not happy with that.

"Aw come on Jeff, how many times have I been late? And little Jimmy has never been late even once, so don't push."

"Well, what was that all about?"

"Annette."

"Alright Sean, but let's not make this a habit."

"Okay, but we're meeting with George and Alex at four today and that's it."

"Why, did the D's come up with something?"

"Jim may have something, they're going to see."

"This afternoon, okay. Check in at three-thirty and get your paperwork done and the rest of the day is yours."

They came off at three, did their paperwork and were upstairs by four. Alex was in his office and Jim went directly to him.

"Little pieces, eh Doc. I found something and then I noticed something else."

"Jim, let's get George in here and run the whole thing."

The group assembled in Alex's office, and Jim laid out his papers.

"What I noted today is that the four disappearances have occurred along Interstate 90. If this is one guy, he's a traveler. The four sites are Cleveland Heights, Ohio, McKean, Pennsylvania, Syracuse, New York and now Goshen, Indiana. All along the interstate ninety corridor. Could be a trucker."

"As I recall the description from Mrs. Simpson, he was well dressed, and driving a van," said Alex.

"Right, so the next option is a traveler, like a salesman," said Jim.

"That works," said George. "Now we have to identify a salesman with a blue van, who has been in all four locations on the days in question. Good luck with that."

Alex looked at Jim, "You said you noticed something."

"Three of the girls were blond with blue eyes."

"Interesting," said George.

"All three were wearing white shoes and blue shorts, and all were taken midweek between 3:00pm and 8:00pm."

"Anything else?" asked George.

"No, that's it."

"That's good, now what can we do with this information?"

"I don't know, that's why God made detectives," replied Jim.

"What if there's more than one kidnapper?" offered Alex.

Jim's brow furrowed as he considered the question, "Then, I split the victims three and one. The three with similar traits on one team and the other girl on another team."

"Right, now what does that tell you?"

"His targets are specific, like he sees the same person in each of them."

"That's a strong possibility," said Alex, "but who is the person he sees in each of the girls?" asked Alex.

"I have no idea," said Jim.

"It is hard to say. Getting into the mind of such a monster is no easy task," said Alex shaking his head.

"So, do you think he is constantly killing the same person, or setting the real target up so she fits into a group when he kills her?"

"People do weird things and this bogey is no exception. He could be killing the same person over and over, and I'm going to assume she is still alive because the victims are getting older as he moves along. He may be prepping a kill for her or, he could be doing this and never intending on killing the central person. There is no way of knowing until we get more information."

"Well, we have something we didn't have yesterday, so that's good," said George.

* * *

June passed into July and Averell thought more and more about Sarah and Ellie. He flip-flopped between wanting to do them right away and waiting for the perfect opportunity. His mind changed almost daily—one minute ready to kill them, the next allowing them another day on the planet. Averell was in constant turmoil over his hatred for Sarah and Ellie and his desire to be safe.

"We should have taken her and Ellie."

"If we did, they would suspect us, we can't afford that yet."

"When will we be ready?"

"Not yet, maybe soon, but not yet."

"I want to do them now, how will it get any better than now?"

"We have to perfect our procedure. When we do them, it has to be perfect."

"It will be perfect, the next one will be better, then maybe we'll be ready."

"The next one, yes, the next one."

* * *

In October of that same year, a twelve-year old girl was kidnapped at knife point from her home in California. The search for this girl involved thousands of people and both local and national media coverage and her body was found after about four months. As it happened, the individual eventually captured, tried and convicted of her murder had been sought by the California Highway Patrol for an unrelated parole violation at the time of the abduction.

Even though he was the subject of an APB by the Highway Patrol, he eluded capture for a period long enough for him to commit this act and even walk away from an encounter with a local police group after a minor traffic violation. This case brought to the national stage a problem experienced in this and undoubtedly many other cases. Communication between law enforcement groups needed improvement. Different localities and different agencies were not always in helpful communication with one another.

* * *

Twenty-Five

You mean we need another victim . . .

The summer of 1994 required some changes. Averell drove past the farmhouse hoping it would still be available. As he approached the site, a pick-up truck was pulling out of the driveway with a realtor's name on the side. He approached slowly and saw several people standing in the area outside the barn discussing something. He wondered if it had sold and kept on driving.

"No sense even starting a conversation. If it has sold, then it's gone, if not, it's getting too much attention. Hmmm, I wonder if there are any traces of our activity in the barn."

"May well be, and we were in the house, did we leave anything there?"

"I don't think so, I'm sure we didn't." He continued down the road for a few miles when he noticed a dirt road off to the left. "I wonder what's down there."

"One way to find out."

"Yeah, let's check this out."

He turned onto the dirt road and drove about a quarter mile. The road entered a wooded patch and followed the road for a few hundred yards. He was moving away from the main road and there was nothing but trees and a few open areas. The road ended in an opening where several vehicles had parked recently. He got out and walked around looking at the trees and trying to see what was in the woods and beyond. He walked in a circle around the clearing where there were tire tracks and saw a darkened spot on the ground. A dark brownish color, dried blood. What was this place? He continued looking around for a few minutes when he saw a pick-up pull into the clearing. The driver wheeled his truck around and backed into a position facing the road. He cut the engine and got out of the truck.

"Hey, good mornin'," he said. "You here fer the crows?"

"Ah, well, I was just looking to see what it's like in here."

"Hey, yer from New York, the city?"

"No, closer to Buffalo, near the Pennsylvania border."

"M'name's Phil, pleasure meetin' ya. Some good huntin' up that'a way in New York, what brings you down here?"

"Oh, my name is Al, Al Davis, I'm here on business, and I have family in Cincinnati, so I drive by a lot."

"You got you a Ohio huntin' ticket, Al?"

"Ah, no, no not yet."

"Hell, neither do I," he said with a laugh, "been comin' out here fer more'n twenty years, never had one. Hell, they don't care, long as you bag a bunch o' them crows. Don't have a fishin' ticket neither and that stream yonder has some good eatin' swimmin' aroun' in it."

"Well, I don't want to be in your way, so I'll just be moving on."

"Oh hell, yer not in my way, I'm probably in yer's. I only got an hour or so and I gotta' git a go on, git my butt back home. Live 'bout five mile south down the road."

"How often do you hunt here?"

"Lucky if I make it once a month anymore, safe as hell here, nobody fer miles, I'm the only one comes this time a year, all of them others is only after deer, you know, bow an' arrow stuff, that starts in September some time. That's when I jus' stay away all together. Them bow people is goofy, probably think I got a white tail an' be pitchin' arrows at my butt."

"So, nobody would be here after you leave 'til September?"

"Nope, nobody. You wanna' bag a deer off season, this is the perfect place. I got one last week. Hey, I gotta' go, git me a bunch a them damn crows. See ya," and he disappeared into the woods with his shotgun.

Averell looked around for another few minutes and was getting in his car when he heard Phil get off two rounds. The sound was dulled by the trees. Averell rolled down all his windows and drove to the edge of the woods, still not visible from the road. He listened for twenty minutes and thought he heard a few more shots from Phil's shotgun, but the sound was very faint. He smiled and drove out to the main road and paused. There was no traffic from either direction and he was sure Phil was still shooting at crows, but he heard nothing. Again, he smiled and turned south on the road.

"That was very interesting."

"Yes, it was."

"We could use this place all summer."

"Let's see what happens next time we are here. "

"I'm ready."

"I know you are."

That summer, on Tuesday, July 19, Allison Kinsey, a thirteen-year-old girl, was by herself at a park in Elyria, Ohio. She was sitting on a bench about twenty feet from the street. Averell noticed she was wearing a light blue blouse and denim shorts. She had blond hair and blue eyes and was swinging her feet below the bench seat as if she was waiting for someone. Averell pulled up and parked. He got out and walked past her as if he was looking for somebody. He paced back and forth a number of times and returned to his car, stood there looking around and repeatedly looking at his watch. It was 3:40pm. Allison saw him and wondered to herself what he was looking for. He looked very unhappy. Averell noticed she was watching him and he paced some more. She continued to watch. Averell noted that nobody else was around, there was no traffic, this was his moment. He opened his trunk and took out two tie wraps and a cloth balled up on a piece of tape. He left the trunk partially open and walked quickly toward the girl. There was no preliminary talk, he quickly grabbed her, stuffed the cloth in her mouth and pushed the tape against her cheeks. He grabbed her arms and put the tie wrap over her hands and pulled tight. Then he picked her up and pushed the lurching girl in his trunk where he struggled to grab her ankles and secure them with the other tie wrap.

He slammed the trunk and got behind the wheel and drove away in a very controlled and legal manner. He drove for about an hour, then he saw the dirt road and turned in and went to the clearing. Nobody was there, all the tire tracks were obviously old and the grass was growing straight. He got out of the car, looked around and listened. Satisfied he was completely alone, he walked into the woods a very short distance and found another smaller clearing that would do for his purposes.

Averell returned to the car, looked around and opened the trunk. Allison was red faced with swollen eyes and her hands were almost blue. She looked terrified.

"Oh, did I make the tie too tight?"

"That was very un-thoughtful of you. You should apologize. Now."

"You are right. Young lady, I am so sorry for making the tie too tight."

"Not bad you liar, you'd have made it tighter if you knew it would hurt."

Allison was scared and confused, the man was talking to himself and he was hurting her.

"Now remember, I told you before, we should tell her what was going to happen before we do it and watch her eyes."

"Yes, yes, I remember."

"Well Sarah," he said as he pulled her out of the trunk, "we are going to have some fun with you. You are my little toy and I am going to see what you are like inside. I am going to probe you with my probes and then cut you open with my knife and see your heart while it is still beating."

Allison was screaming into her gag as Averell watched her eyes bulge and tear.

"And then?"

"Oh yes, and then I will cut off your arms."

Allison was in a complete panic and almost swallowed her gag. Averell laughed, "This is great."

"And?"

"And then I will cut off your legs."

Allison was out of control, she was vomiting into her gag and Averell pulled it off. She gagged and vomited more and screamed.

"And?"

"And then, when I am finished, I will kill you."

Allison passed out.

"I may have already killed her."

"Check her pulse."

Averell cut the tie on her wrists and checked for a pulse. Then he checked her neck. She was still alive.

"We may not have a lot of time, we should go for seeing the heart first."

"You're right," and with that Averell laid Allison on the ground and started to remove her blouse. "This is very awkward, I want her to stand. Let's tie her to that tree." He lifted her and held her arms over her head and spread between two branches. She was half suspended with her knees bent about a foot off the ground and her feet dragging in the dirt. He stripped her to the waist and used his box cutter to make an incision starting at her neck and extending down to her navel. He made two more cuts and opened her, exposing her ribs. He saw her heart, beating.

"Do you see that?"

"Yes."

"Is that cool or what?"

"That's cool."

"Now I want to see what happens when I cut her throat."

"Okay."

He took a probe and thrust it through her carotid artery, blood flowed freely for a few seconds and then stopped, the heart muscle stopped pulsing and he lifted her eyelid.

"Aw, nobody's home."

"That was amazing."

Averell was covered in sweat, and he was exhausted. He cut the ties that held Allison in place and placed her on a drop cloth. He proceeded to dismember her body and get ready to bury her at the cemetery. As he cut her apart he envisioned Sarah lying in front of him and he smiled.

He imagined Ellie standing next to him criticizing the way he cut into Sarah's flesh and he thought about cutting Ellie next. He smiled.

"What are you grinning about?"

"Oh, nothing, I'm just enjoying the great outdoors."

"I see, you're thinking about Sarah and Ellie. They could be next, and this place is perfect. I wonder where they are right now, what they are doing?"

Averell seemed to snap out of a daydream, "First things first, we have to get this one to the cemetery."

"What do you think about burying her here in this place? Phil said nobody comes here. No transportation, no risk."

"You know, that may be a good idea."

He went to the trunk, got out the shovel and looked around for a spot to dig. "Here, this could be good." He started to dig. After an hour he had a pit deep enough for the three bags. He put them in and started to fill in the hole.

"Rocks, we should use rocks."

"Yes rocks." He looked around and found a few rocks that he put in the grave. He shoveled more dirt and walked around again looking for rocks. Another hour passed, and the job was done.

Averell completely drained. He sat on the ground and noticed his clothes. Soaked in blood. He stood, stripped and put all his clothes in a plastic bag. He double-bagged everything and put it in his trunk. He was naked standing next to his car, thinking, *Water, I need water.* He put clean clothes in a bag, grabbed a beach towel and walked into the woods, in the direction that Phil had indicated there was a stream.

The water was cold but the air was warm. He waded in a few feet and the bottom was starting to drop off. He dove in and swam for a few minutes and climbed out refreshed. "That was nice, a little chilly, but nice." He waded in again till the water was up to his waist and he squatted down allowing himself to be completely submerged. He stood and took a deep breath, then he squatted again. He stayed under as long as he could and then stood, gulping another large breath. He repeated the process two more times, each time staying under as long as he could. After the fifth full dip, he slowly walked out of the stream and dried himself off, then dressed and made his way back to the car. The only sign of his activity was the blood on the ground. Anybody would assume that a deer was taken here and this is where it bled out. He went to the car and checked for all his tools. He took everything that had mud or blood on it to the stream and washed it off.

After loading the car, he checked his watch, it was 8:36pm. He drove out of the woods and back on the road toward Erie. Once again, he would bury his mileage and come back in this direction the following day as if he had not been there. Everything was working out, he felt very safe, very comfortable, very relaxed—all the tension had left his body.

* * *

Jim McClarry heard a news report that evening about a girl missing in Elyria, Ohio. When he got home, he tuned in the evening news. The information was not complete, and he waited until morning to read about it in the newspaper. He added all the information about Allison into his database and put another pin in his map in Elyria, Ohio. Located on Interstate 90 about thirty-five miles west of Cleveland Heights, the time of day and the girl's description were similar. There were now four cases of interest ranging from Goshen, Indiana to Syracuse, New York and the one odd case in Syracuse. A pattern was emerging. Since it was Wednesday, Alex might be in the station and Jim was anxious to get the newest information on the table. He drove to work and went directly to Alex's office. No luck. He asked George if Alex would be in.

"Not today, out of town. If you have something we can bring him up to speed later."

"Okay, there was another girl taken from Elyria yesterday. She's in tune with the other three blond, blue-eyed victims all the way down to white shoes, blue shorts and within ten miles of the I-90 corridor."

"So, now we have four victims that fit your profile?"

"Yeah, well sort of, there are four plus several others that don't fit, but could all still be the victims of one predator."

"Okay, Jim, are you on the road today?"

"I am, and I better get downstairs before roll call or Jeff will lose his sense of humor."

"Right, when is your next day off?"

"Friday."

"Any plans?"

Jim shrugged, "I guess not, I have a date Friday night, but the day is open."

"Good, I'll see you then, and maybe Alex will be in too. He's due back in town late Thursday afternoon and he usually checks in after a trip."

"Okay, I'll be here."

Friday came and Jim showed up in the detective's area. Alex arrived an hour later and was carrying a box of file folders. "Hey, Jim, I know about Allison and I know you want to talk, but I have another case in Chicago that they need a read on early next week."

Jim was not pleased to be bumped to second place on Alex's priority list, but he said, "Understood, what do you have in the box?"

"If you really want to know, you can help me sort it out," replied Alex.

Jim lifted his eyebrows, "I had to ask, but if I can help, I have the rest of the day open."

"First things first, you get us some coffee and I'll see if we can take over the conference room and spread this mess out," said Alex.

Jim went to the kitchen and loaded up two large coffee mugs with too much sugar and cream and headed back to the conference room. "Just the way you like it, Doc."

Alex took the mug and said, "Okay, let's sort this stuff by date and victim, then we start to read through it."

"Sounds familiar, we've been down this road before."

Alex sipped his coffee, set the mug down and said, "Not all cases are the same, but we seem to do a lot of the same stuff on every one. This time we have a couple of possible suspects. Each one has an alibi of sorts and of course none of these people would ever hurt a kid."

"Have you met each of them?"

"Yeah, two men and a woman."

Jim looked surprised, "A woman?"

"Yes, a woman. She is a piece of work too. So are the two guys. They all have records for molesting children, and she worse than either one of the other two. She liked them both, boys and girls, the younger the better."

Jim shook his head, "I never even considered a woman. Of course, the witness at Annette's nabbing was not all that definitive, but the suspect she described was surely a man. Of course, he could have had an accomplice, maybe a woman—damn."

"Yeah, the other two are no better, all three ought to be locked up forever. I'm a psychologist, supposed to understand people and show compassion, understanding, but these three have busted too many rules."

"What makes a person do this stuff, Alex?"

"Nothing *makes* them do anything, the different psychoses allow them to act out in different ways. Take this one, the woman, her name is Eleanor and she's a sociopath. She has no feelings of guilt for hurting anybody else. To her, whatever works for her at the moment is okay. So, she could be doing something minor, but illegal, like parking in a handicap zone, even though she is perfectly healthy, and if you saw her, she may have no reservations about killing you to keep you quiet. That's extreme but real. There is no balance between cause and effect. There is no conscience, a sociopath has no empathy for others."

Jim hesitated, "Could our predator be in that group? He, or she, may have taken these kids and after they finish with them, they kill them just to keep from getting caught."

"Yes," Alex nodded. "There are no hard and fast rules. Just as easily, he could keep them alive so that he could abuse them again. Then, when he has used them as much as he cares to, he can dispose of them, any way he wishes. Remember, he writes his own rules."

"So, is this Eleanor is like that?"

"Exactly," said Alex. "Then there is this character, Mark, he's psychotic, not living in the real world. He has delusions, hears voices. The voices tell him to do things and he does. So, a voice may say 'Let's kill Joe' and Mark picks up a rock and bashes Joe's head in. Another extreme example, but real none the less."

"Delightful, so who do you trust?"

"Well, there you are, not knowing who can be trusted until they display some symptom of their problem. If we're lucky, we catch it early on and with proper treatment, some of this negative stuff can be avoided. But we are dependent on good diagnoses and proper treatment."

"What kind of treatment?"

"Prescribed medication, psychotropic drugs, the right dose of the right drug can keep some of these characters from doing any damage. Again, it depends on proper treatment, meaning they take their drugs on schedule, see their analyst on a regular basis, usually takes another party to watch over them and keep them in line."

"What about the other one, you only mentioned two?"

"Oh yeah, Paul. This one is a pedophile, a sexual deviant. He has urges he can't control. He sees a kid, boy or girl, and he wants to do things to them that turn your guts. He's been convicted once for molesting a three-year old girl. Can you imagine that—three?"

"What treatment do you have for that kind of person?"

"I never said this, and you never heard it, but I would toss this one in a blender and dump it in the sewer."

"Could our guy be like that?"

"Yeah, he could be."

They finished sorting the files and started reading. By the end of the day, they were not even halfway through the piles. Jim had a date and Alex had a number of calls to make so they made a few final notes and got up to leave.

"Jim, thanks for your help today, I really appreciate this," said Alex.

"I wish I could say it was fun, but that would be a lie. Are you going to save the rest for Monday?"

Alex took a deep breath, "Wish I could, but no, I'll be back here tomorrow morning," he said as he rubbed his eyes.

Jim thought for less than a second and said, "Tell you what Doc, you sleep in 'til noon, buy us some decent coffee and I'll meet you here around one and we can wade through the rest of this stuff."

"You don't have to do that."

"I know," said Jim. "One o'clock, not before."

"No argument," and the two left the station.

A month later, on Tuesday, August 23, 1994, in Utica, New York, a seven-year-old girl disappeared. Her remains were never found, so it cannot be categorically stated that she was murdered. Sandy Furnasco was walking from her home to a park less than two blocks away. She never arrived at the park. At the time of her disappearance, Averell was in Elyria, Ohio meeting with a manager of a distribution center.

Wednesday morning, Jim was reading the Cleveland Plain Dealer and saw the article about Sandy. He immediately added her to his map and the database and noted that he now had a total of six girls along the I-90 corridor that were of interest. Four of them were still alone as a group and the other two, Megan and Sandy unlikely candidates for their predator, but there was nothing concrete to tie these two to the others. As he was thinking about the number of possible scenarios, he realized he was going to be late for roll call. He tossed the rest of his tepid coffee, grabbed a banana and headed out the door.

"You're a little late this morning, Jim," said Jeff as Jim came into the locker room. "Alex is upstairs and asking for you. You go on up and I'll have Tony ride with Sean today."

"Thanks Jeff, I'll see you tomorrow." Jim took two stairs at a time going up and spotted Alex immediately. "Alex, are you looking for me?"

"Jim, did you see the paper this morning?"

"Yeah, the girl in Utica, New York. I saw that. But she is not in line with the profile that we are building. Maybe we are all wrong in our assumptions. This little girl and the others could all be victims of our guy."

"Jim, I have worked with this group of detectives for almost twelve years and I have learned some things. The best cop in all of creation can only know what there is to know. We have looked at everything and we know very little. Hell, the stuff you are pulling together is terrific. Yeah, maybe the team here would have put the same info together in time, but the fact is, they didn't. You have done some fine work, Jim, so hold your head up. You know police work can be very frustrating. We solve many cases because we get a tip from some guy and it proves to be the glue that holds the case together. In this case what we know for sure is very little, what we surmise, well we're going to see today. That's why I wanted you up here today, we are going to do a brain dump from everyone on this case and wade through it again, see what seems to stand out."

"Okay, so where do we begin?"

"First let's grab some coffee and see if George is available."

As they were setting up a large note pad on an easel, George came in with his coffee mug in hand. "What are you two up to today?"

"Rehash—you're just in time," said Alex. George turned and walked out of the room saying, "I'll be right back."

Alex and Jim went to the kitchen and poured themselves some coffee and were on the way back to the conference room when they met Sean.

"George asked me to come up for a few minutes, what's up," said Sean?

"We're going to do a dump and rehash," said Jim.

They went into the conference room and George joined them. "Okay, I have a few minutes. First, I have given this case a lot of time and been pulling away from what I am supposed to be doing, so, I'm going to assign a new set of eyes to your team."

They all turned and listened.

"Sean, Alex you both know Vince Galley?"

"Yeah, we have pulled a few tours together, seems like a good guy," said Sean.

"We have met, but never worked together," said Alex.

"He'll be in around nine this morning, he's the full time D for a while. I have cleared his slate and he is anxious to get at it. Let's give him some time to read the case file and let him ask the questions. Right now, let's start the dump. Sean, you have to hit the road this morning so, you go first."

Sean began with what he knew, followed by what he surmised, and finished with what should be ruled out. As he was winding up, a tall, slender man with half a head of grey hair came through the door.

"Good morning, all."

"Vince, you know Sean, Alex and this is Jim McClarry, he has pulled a lot of this stuff together that we are looking at today."

"Jim, I've seen you around, good to finally meet you," said Vince.

"Vince, my pleasure," and he extended his hand. Vince had a large hand and a firm grip. His rough and hardened calluses betrayed his otherwise gentle appearance, he obviously did something other than shuffle paper.

"Problem is, just like Sean, he's related to Annette," said George. "So, he is in the background. Sean just unloaded, I'm about to put my two cents in and then get out of the way. Jim, Vince will be the lead D from now on, so you talk to him rather than me. I will never be that far away, so I'll know what's happening. Everybody good with that?"

Sean agreed and said he had to get on the road and excused himself. George sat down with his mug and started his piece. Alex took a marker and added notes to the large pad that held the last of Sean's input. As he was finishing, George stood and moved to the door.

"Keep me in the loop, Vince. Jim when you finish up here today catch me in my office. We need to talk," and he walked out of the room.

Alex walked over to Vince and handed him the marker and said, "You're driving this bus, might as well start steering."

Vince took the marker and said, "First, let's hit the head, refill our mugs and get ready to settle in for the next hour or so. I got a bunch of questions."

The team dispersed and regrouped within five minutes. Vince moved to the last of the note sheets to be hung on the tack strip and read a few lines quietly to himself. "You guys have been with this for a while and I'm just coming in. I hope you don't mind my late arrival and probably some dumb questions while I get up to speed."

Alex responded, "Vince, you have been around a while, I am a consultant and Jim is not even officially in this group. He's a uniform on loan because he has studied this case for the last three years. This is now your case, you call the shots."

Vince nodded and turned toward Jim.

Jim looked up and said, "I'm not a D yet and if I was, they would put someone else in charge because Annette is family. As Alex said, this is your case, I just want to help any way I can without hurting the cause. If you think my being here is negative, I'm gone."

"Okay guys, it's my case, but you better believe George will have his nose in whenever he can. He started this before he was put in the boss's office, and he wants results."

Jim gave his input and Alex gave his. There was a lot of duplication of thought and the final list turned out to be rather short. Vince led off with a question: "Let's describe our bad guy. What do we know about him?"

The resulting profile was a middle-aged man, in his thirties or early forties, married, probably divorced, professional type, probably sales, his complexion was dark, mid-European.

"Okay, from what I see, if the blonds are his only targets, he does one each year in summer. None have been found and the other consistencies include age, eye color, shoes and shorts. I think this guy is fixed on an individual that would have been about seven or eight when he started, at least four years ago, probably dressed in that mode during the summer. If he is, as we think, a mid-European, blue eyes and blond hair may indicate a different family. Could also be a neighbor, classmate, cousin, adopted sibling, or a girlfriend. I think we should narrow the focus and see if anything pops. Trouble is, he could live anywhere over the fifty-miles north and south of I-90. So, about four hundred miles east and west and one hundred miles north and south, that's about forty thousand square miles of turf around Toledo, Cleveland, Erie, Buffalo. A lot of area to search for something as common as this guy appears to be."

"We need more information," said Alex.

"You mean we need another victim," said Jim.

"I was hoping for some piece of info we have overlooked. We have to go over everything again. We should go back before the first one, before Annette Shelton. If she was the first, what made this guy start? If not, then we need the additional data about whoever came before her."

"Okay, let's say Annette was the first," said Alex, "where does that put us?"

"That was in 1991, so our guy has been traveling the road up and down I-90 for the last four or five years. Smells like a salesman of some kind."

Vince went back over the list of information hanging on the walls. "Here, it says he was in a dark blue van with tinted windows. A traveling salesman would tend to have a more economical vehicle, unless he has bulky materials he carries with him."

Alex added, "He could be one of those guys that goes from store to store and takes the orders for his wares and never touches the product itself. That could be anything from ballpoint pens to snow tires."

"Yeah, so why the van?" asked Vince.

"Samples, catalogs—just tools of the trade."

"So, do salesmen buy or lease vehicles?" asked Alex, "I lease my car because most of the driving I do is business related and it's better tax-wise. I would guess if he is in sales, he probably leases his vehicle."

"If his turf goes from Cleveland to Buffalo or a little beyond in each direction, he probably puts a lot of highway mileage on whatever he drives and would probably trade it in every year or two. So today, four years after Annette, he might have a different vehicle, may have gone through two or three by now," said Jim. "He could be driving a Cadillac today."

"Well, let's check with the lease places locally and see if anyone leased a dark blue van in '91. It's a start." Vince put the marker down and sat in a chair facing the notes hanging from the tack strip. "That was the only visual. Damn. Let's keep going. Have you guys looked at the known pedophiles in the area and their vehicles?"

"I don't know if anyone has, but I will now," said Jim.

"No, make a note of that and I will do it in the morning. That will take some time and we want to get through this process first," said Vince.

"You're the boss," agreed Jim.

"Let's talk about where the bodies are. None have been recovered. Where does he put them, or are they even dead?" Vince slumped in his chair. "Let's kick that around a while."

The group spent the remainder of the day talking through scenarios of what might be and tried to reduce them to the several most likely ones. They ended up with little more than where they had started.

"Whoever this guy is, he is smart. He leaves no trace, gives us nothing to go on." Vince sipped his coffee and made a face, "Cold. Okay, let's call it a day. There's a lot for me to digest and I have a few items to check out in the morning. We'll get there, guys, it's just a matter of time. He has left a clue somewhere and we will find it."

The group broke up and Jim walked over to George's office. "Hey boss, you wanted to see me."

"Yeah, c'mon in and close the door."

"That doesn't sound good."

"No, nothing like that. Listen, Ken is going to retire soon, like in a month and the slot he is holding is going to be open. I have watched you and your work and I like what I see. Talked to Jeff and he's with me on this. So, are you intending to sit for the next exam? Because if you are, you have to get the paperwork in, like yesterday."

"Oh, I meant to do that."

"This may be the only break I'll ever give you. Here's a package. Fill it out and get it to me before you leave today. Not a word to anyone."

"When's the exam?"

"In two weeks, And be sure to read everything in the folder, it will be on the exam."

"Thanks George, I really appreciate this."

"Yeah, now get outta' here and fill out the forms."

"Aye-aye, sir," Jim said with a salute and a smile.

He filled out the paperwork and turned it in to George before heading home. He was tired from the all-day brainstorm session, but he gave his girl Margo a call and suggested dinner and a movie.

Jim washed his face and stared in the mirror for a few seconds, smiled, went to his bedroom and took a small box out of his dresser drawer. Margo was ready when he arrived. "Where would you like to go to dinner?" he asked.

"Anywhere is good, I'll get my purse." Margo turned back toward her bedroom when Jim took her hand.

"Let's sit down for a minute."

They never made it to the restaurant or the movie that night. In the morning Margo was making coffee and singing when Jim came into the kitchen. She looked at him with a big smile and held up her hand to show him, "See how it sparkles in the sunlight?"

"It's kinda small," said Jim. "Yeah, but it worked," she smiled.

* * *

Twenty-Six

Tell her the rest . . .

Winter came and went, spring followed and summer was just getting started. Jim passed the test and placed high enough to get him a gold shield and a desk on the second floor. Margo was now Mrs. James McClarry and Jim was settling into the routine of a detective's life. He was assigned as Vince's partner and the two worked well together. Cleveland Heights was large enough to experience its fair share of major league crime but the borders between the several east side communities were such that most cases were cooperative efforts. They involved several individual police departments and Jim proved to be an asset in coordinating activities between them. He was becoming well known in the area amongst law enforcement agencies and it was obvious he was going to be more than a detective someday.

On Thursday June 22, 1995, Linda Young, an eight-year-old girl living in Northeast, Pennsylvania was seen being dragged into a silver mini-van at 12:20pm. Her abductor, a man in a light blue shirt, dark baseball cap and blue jeans was described as being about 5'10" tall and heavy set. His hair was short and dark, and he was clean shaven. The van had white license plates with blue lettering. Linda's remains were found four weeks later in a ditch beside a country road. She had been violated, beaten and murdered. Death was determined to have been by strangulation.

At the time of her abduction Averell was in Toledo, Ohio, over three hundred miles away in a meeting with a store manager discussing a special deal on marking pens. Jim McClarry expanded his database to include Linda and searched the newspapers for additional information. He learned that she had brown hair and blue eyes and that she was wearing a sun dress and flip flops. Everything that he read about the girl was copied and put in a file or entered into the database. Linda was the number seven possibility attributable to Annette's abductor. Once again,

Jim studied the information available and Linda did not exactly fit the profile of the victim their predator sought. Linda was found, unlike the others, and her hair and clothing did not match the developing profile. Even though the predator's description was close, and the van was in line, Linda was given a lower probability of being one of the group.

Jim rated the potential cases with respect to each being the work of the same predator on a one to ten scale giving Annette a ten. Candice, Kathy and Allison were given eights, Linda got a seven and Megan and Sandy were given fives. It was not as definitive as he wanted it to be, but he was not about to abandon this record keeping.

* * *

On Monday, August 14th, Averell took several meetings between Toledo and Cleveland. His logbook indicated that he then drove to Erie, Pennsylvania where he visited another two clients, spent the night and drove to Buffalo on Thursday.

Actually, Averell filled his tank in Erie and back tracked into Ohio past Cleveland that Wednesday around noon. Before beginning his search, he readied a gag with a ball of cloth and duct tape and placed several tie wraps in the passenger pocket, behind the driver's seat. He also had a large blanket folded on the rear seat. He was ready. He drove to a residential section outside Sandusky proper and began to cruise the streets early in the afternoon. He spotted a very cute young lady with blond hair and blue eyes and he estimated she was about fourteen. She was wearing a red top, blue denim shorts and white shoes. It could be better, but she would do. He noted that she was heading across an open park toward a housing development. Averell quickly drove around the park and stopped directly in her path. She was about fifty-yards away when he got out of his car and stood looking off to the right. When she was about to divert around Averell's car, he turned and acted surprised.

"Oh, excuse me, did I bump into you?"

"No, you didn't bump me," replied Rebecca.

"Well, could you tell me where Main Street is, I'm afraid I'm lost," he said.

"Sure, is that your car?" she asked looking at Averell's car.

"Yes, it is."

"Well, go straight the way you are pointed and in about three blocks, turn right, then the next street is Main. I think a right will head north and a left will head south, I think."

He stepped toward the car and muttered something that Rebecca could not hear. She took a step in his direction saying, "Excuse me."

Averell half turned still muttering and making Rebecca lean in his direction to hear what he said. She took another step, getting a little closer to him and started to say something when he grabbed her, turned and pulled her into the car. The next few minutes would mirror his past experiences with his subjects; tie wraps, duct tape, the gag—it was all becoming quite routine. He pushed her to the floor, pulled the blanket over her, closed the door and quickly got behind the wheel.

The trip to the Portage County site was uneventful. Rebecca was cowering in the back seat on the floor, unable to get up to a sitting position and too scared to do anything but cry. Averell pulled into the wooded area and parked in the clearing. Again, nobody was around. He pulled Rebecca out of the back seat and stood her next to a tree. "I'm going to stretch you between these two trees, okay."

"Tell her the rest."

"I am going to check your insides with my new probes."

"And then?"

"Yes, then, I am going to open you up and see your beating heart."

"There's more."

"Oh, and then, we will remove your arms and legs."

"And finally?"

"Yes, well, finally we will kill you. Isn't that absolutely exciting?" he said as he broke into a sweat. He reached up and grabbed a branch of a tree, pulled it toward Rebecca's hands and with another pull tie, he bound her right arm to the branch. As he started to cut the binding between her arms, he positioned another tie to bind her left arm to another tree. With both of her arms bound to the trees and her ankles still secured together, Rebecca was unable to defend herself. She was completely at his mercy and she was terrified. He was breathing hard almost to a point of collapsing and sweating profusely.

"Calm down, Averell. You have to be in control. Take a deep breath and relax. We have things to do."

"Yes, I have to calm down."

Averell paced for a minute until he was able to gain control of himself again. "Now, to work." He picked up a probe and approached Rebecca. As he placed the probe against her midsection, she tried to scream but inhaled the cloth gag. She choked and was dead before Averell realized she was in difficulty.

"Damn it, I wanted to see her heart."

He was furious and took his larger knife and hacked her apart. When finished, he stood over her remains sweating and soaked in blood.

"That was exciting, not very profitable, but exciting. We should find another subject to examine."

"I'm very tired right now and all I want to do is sleep." He sat down and hung his head.

"C'mon Averell, Let's finish what we started and get out of here, we can sleep when we are home, or in Erie."

"Yes, you're right, Let's finish up here." With that Averell stood and walked to the car, took the shovel out of the trunk and found a spot to dig. The finished hole was about five feet deep and Averell placed the three bags evenly at the bottom. He threw in some leaves and rocks and filled the hole. He put more rocks at the top of the hole and covered the entire site with heavy brush. A trip to the stream and a thorough washing was all that he needed to reinvigorate himself for the trip to Erie, his motel room and bed.

* * *

Jim read the article about Rebecca in the Cleveland newspaper and noted the similarities: her hair, eyes, shorts and shoes all lined up. The mid-week, afternoon timing also fit and finally, the interstate corridor. He made a few quick notes, sent an e-mail to Alex, and Sean listing all the similarities and was leaving for the station when the phone rang. He answered.

"Jim, it's Vince, come into the conference room when you get in. I have already contacted Alex and Sean. Also talked to Jeff and cleared it for Sean to join us today."

"Okay, I was just about to head out, so I'll be there in a few minutes," and he hung up, picked up his notes and hustled down to his car. Sean was in the parking lot, talking to Jeff, when Jim pulled in.

"I'll see you tomorrow Sean, don't get used to wearing a suit, you're still on my crew," said Jeff and he went back into the building.

"We have to get upstairs. Are you ready?"

Sean grinned, "Hell, yes, I'm ready!" They went up to the second floor and met Vince in the conference room.

"Good-morning guys, come on in and sit down. I think Alex will be in a little later and we'll brief him then. Okay, now we have identified another incident that ties into the Shelton case and we want to revisit the neighborhood and run a new set of interviews. The two of you will have to hang back for the most part, but I would like you to talk to the family. Are you good with that?"

Both nodded and Jim said, "Yeah, sure, we can do that today."

"I added Rebecca Markum to the list. She lives in Sandusky. That puts her in the interstate corridor I initially thought was a common factor for the first few and she is the eighth since Annette, that's now eight in a four-year span between Utica, New York and Goshen, Indiana. That's less than seven hundred miles of Interstate. Now of those eight all are Caucasian, disappeared in the summer months of June, July or August, on a Tuesday, Wednesday or Thursday and all in the afternoon between noon and 8:00pm. When I figure in the physical characteristics, five are blond with blue eyes, similar clothing and footwear. If I tighten the times based on these five, the range reduces to 2:45pm to 7:30pm, just under a five-hour span, with Goshen being the farthest west at 7:30pm. We had a description of Annette's abductor as a man about 5'8", one fifty and dark hair. Linda's abductor is about 5'10", two hundred and dark hair. Both drove vans, different colors and four years apart."

"If we continue to concentrate on these four similar cases, we may be dealing with the same predator. The Linda Young case could be our guy, so I think we should start with contacting the other shops again and share what we have. They may be able to add something to our database, just as we add to theirs. Jim, this is yours to set up, you know some of these guys and might as well meet the others."

Alex came in about the same time and joined the group. They decided to start with redoing the interviews in the neighborhood after contacting the other shops in New York, Pennsylvania, Ohio and Indiana as well as the FBI. If correct, this predator had crossed state lines when taking his victims, whether he transported any of them across a state line was still an open question. Vince let Sean and Jim talk to the Shelton's. Clare was home and Dave was at work. Clare was obviously still shaken by the whole thing, but much more communicative than she had been four years earlier. They learned nothing new from her and determined they would come back that evening to talk to Dave. Vince left for Elyria and Sandusky to interview the Kinsey and Markum parents.

It was an exhaustive day, and in the end, they didn't learn as much as they'd hoped. "We know five of the girls are enough alike to have been sisters," said Jim.

"And if the Linda Young case is also our guy, we have to be aware of what he did," said Alex.

Sean was pacing back and forth, "She was raped and strangled, then tossed aside. That does not fit our guy. He has yet to let us find any of the four victims that we feel are similar. I really think Linda is not one of his."

Jim cleared his throat and said, "I'm with you on that Sean, it just doesn't fit."

"Is someone else pursuing this from a 'Linda' perspective?" asked Alex. "I mean, each one of these little girls deserve the same kind of attention we are giving Annette."

Jim looked at Sean with a tilt to his head and answered, "It's time for another visit to the other cop shops in those towns. I think we start with phone calls, get what we can and give them what we have, then, if face time is needed, we hit the road."

The three of them looked at each other and Sean said, "Let's divvy 'em up and make the calls."

* * *

In January of the following year, 1996, a nine-year-old girl was abducted in Arlington, Texas. Her kidnapping was witnessed and the local police were notified almost immediately. Her body was found less than a week later, but the predator who took her was never found. The girl's family formed an organization that worked to convince the state legislature to write tougher laws to protect children. Through hard work and the assistance of individuals and businesses, the local congressional representative was able to put proposed legislation in front of the Congress. This resulted in the signing into law of the Amber Hagerman Child Protection Act in October of 1996. The outcome of this was the eventual establishment of a national alert system directed at finding missing children called the "Amber Alert." Progress in this arena has been slow and establishing a national database to identify the numerous pedophiles and other predators that prey on children, and even young adults is an ongoing, constant process. One that demands care and attention on a daily basis.

The database Jim started is but a small and brief exercise in the overall computerized network of information that exists today. It was useful in his hunt for that unknown predator who took Annette, but its useful life was just that, the duration of this specific case.

* * *

Twenty-Seven

Procedure, follow the procedure . . .

Barbara Harkin, 16, of Auburn, New York was taken on Thursday July 11, 1996. Averell took her to a heavily wooded area near one of the Finger Lakes where he found seclusion and privacy. He realized that his victims were increasing in age, but so was Sarah, so it just felt right to him.

He proceeded to describe his intentions and observe her eyes. He was obsessed with the eyes as he described what he intended to do. Barbara was frightened but did not initially believe him. She learned as he pushed a probe into her side, and another through her arm. She felt the pain but did not scream. Her eyes were wide and tears were spilling down her face as he penetrated her flesh with his probes, but still, she did not scream. He remained calm as he pierced her slight body and watched her deep blue eyes lose their fire and life. He had four probes in her when she quietly stopped breathing and her heart no longer pumped blood. Averell maintained his composure this time, though she died too quickly. This was very different than his reaction with Rebecca when she died too early. He never cut her living body with his knife and now he did not want to see her heart.

"You seem well contained, my friend."

"Yes, well this one was almost like a religious ceremony," said Averell.

"She was fascinating, amazing, I just wish she could have stayed with us a little longer, until we could look at her heart." He slowly and deliberately dismembered her body and gently placed the pieces in the three plastic bags. Averell very deliberately dug a hole for her remains, humming as he worked. It seemed effortless as he moved shovel after shovel of dirt. "This one was at a proper six feet," he muttered.

"Very nicely done."

After placing the three bags in the hole, Averell stood at the grave and bowed his head as if in prayer. After about five minutes, he took the shovel and gently started to cover her remains. As the hole became filled, his shovel took larger and larger amounts of dirt and when he finished, he placed as many rocks as he could find on top of the grave. Finished, he began to undress for his cleansing in the water. He removed his shirt and noticed very little blood. He thought about not going in the water, about not changing his clothes.

"Procedure, follow the procedure."

"You are right my friend, little mistakes can be very expensive." He took his clothes off and walked into the water until it was waist deep, then he submerged and stayed under as long as he could. He repeated this dip five times and walked out of the stream, dried off with a towel and dressed. As he finished loading all his tools and his bag of clothes into the car, he stopped and looked out through the trees over the lake. "It is beautiful here, why has it taken us so long to find this place?"

"Would you like to come here again?"

"Yes, very much."

"Then we shall, next time."

"Yes, next time," He started the car and drove slowly out of the wooded area and turned toward Buffalo.

The next day as Averell was driving through town, he spotted a car wash. He turned in and had the car cleaned thoroughly, "We should do this more often, I like the way it looks when they finish. It shines, like it was new."

"Yes, it is nice."

* * *

Jim McClarry added Barbara to his database, making it six girls who met the victim profile. The fact that Auburn is about twenty-five or thirty miles east of Syracuse, stretched the range to match an earlier estimate. Jim wrote an email to Alex and Sean and spelled out the similarities. The problem continued to be the lack of evidence, and therefore the lack of suspects. The crimes were unclassified. Were they kidnappings? Were they murders? Molestations? Runaways? There was no evidence to indicate what had happened to all those little girls. None had been found, no evidence and no real information on the predator's identity. The team was discouraged but undeterred. Some of these people would never give up.

A month later, on Tuesday, August 13, 1996, Janet Tyler, a six-year-old girl who lived in Toledo, Ohio, disappeared. Her remains were never found, so it cannot be categorically stated that she was murdered. She was walking home from school with a group of other children when the group stopped to watch a fight between two older boys. Janet was frightened by the hitting and kept on walking. She was approximately four blocks from her home when she disappeared. Jim McClarry added her to his database and looked up a newspaper article to gain some more particulars. Janet was a brunette with brown eyes and unlike the group of six in denim, she wore a dress and sandals. Jim gave her a rating of five, talked to Vince and updated the team.

*　　*　　*

Twenty-Eight

He is just as lucky as he is smart . . .

Darlene Skinner lived with her parents and two older brothers in Jamestown, New York. On Wednesday, June 25, 1997, this seven-year-old girl was abducted by two people from her front yard at 7:30pm. When found about five weeks later, it was determined she had been raped multiple times by at least two people and beaten to death. At the time of her abduction, Averell was preparing to head west from Sandusky, Ohio to his next stop in Toledo.

Jim read about Darlene in the newspapers and added her to his database. She lived in the interstate corridor around I-90, and that fit his initial profile. Her age of seven-years was younger than he would have expected, especially since she was shorter than the last two victims and her black hair and brown eyes were in conflict with the continuation of the profile. Nevertheless, she was retained in Jim's database. Her clothing also was not consistent with the others and finally, the two abductors discarded her body in a ditch and she was easily found. All of this was so unlike the other victims and Jim felt unsettled.

On July 8th of that same summer, Averell took another subject, this time in Schenectady, New York. Her name was Emily Molin, she was sixteen-years-old and she was coming home from a summer school session. It was just before 2:30pm, she was walking a little behind a gaggle of children. She was moving very slowly, not paying attention to the others and she presented an irresistible target to Averell. Emily was tall, slender and looked older than her years, she could have passed for twenty-one. He took a chance in grabbing this girl while there were so many witnesses only a block away. He took her from behind, clasping his hand with the gag and tape over her mouth and forcing her into his car. The abduction was almost silent, and he had the tie wraps in place in no time. She was quickly covered with a blanket and Averell was behind the wheel and around the corner before the other children realized Emily was no longer there.

The children were confused but sensed nothing sinister. They assumed she had stopped at one of the houses they had already passed. When Emily did not come home and her mother began to look for her, Averell already had her on the road to the wooded Finger Lakes area where his last session with Barbara had been the year before. His session with Emily did not go as he envisioned it. Emily was not complying with Averell, she was terrified and in a state of shock. One of the probes entered a main artery in her arm and this, combined with the sheer terror she was experiencing, caused her heart to fail. She, like Rebecca before her, mercifully died before Averell could induce the pain he had planned.

Her disappearance was reported in the local news that evening and an "Amber Alert" was issued. Her parents were dragged in front of the camera to make pleas for her safe return. People lit candles and sang songs. They made signs and gave speeches. Averell did not notice, he did not have the news turned on, his car CD player was playing one of his favorite CDs. The music was soft and soothing.

Emily was another, almost religious experience for Averell. As he dismembered her body and placed the pieces in the usual three bags, Averell thought about Sarah. He wondered if she would die as well. "Soon we will know, we are almost ready for them."

As he worked digging her grave, Averell thought about Sarah and Ellie, "Yes, almost ready for both of them." The grave for Emily was near Barbara's, the process of putting her in the grave and using stones near the top was intended to discourage animals from digging her up and spreading her bones around the neighborhood. After completing his task and swimming in the stream to cleanse himself, he packed all the bloodied clothes he had rinsed in the stream and drove to a nearby coin operated laundry. After conducting his usual ritual of two cycles, he loaded the clothes into several plastic bags and started for home. Each Salvation army drop off box that he passed was a receptacle for a portion of the clothes. By the time he reached his town house, there was no trace of Emily or his session with her.

Averell had wanted Emily to go further in this session than she did and he was disappointed, but he remained very controlled, very calm, as if nothing had happened. He was planning for Sarah and Ellie, and this was another step in that direction. While watching the television and thumbing through the newspaper that evening, he paid no attention to the coverage of Emily's disappearance. Stelian was unusually quiet, Averell was unusually controlled. He fell asleep for the night, sitting in a chair in front of his television.

* * *

On Wednesday, Jim McClarry added Emily and her information to his growing database. She, like the others before her simply disappeared. No witnesses, no trace. The difference was the location. Averell had redefined the territory he used to hunt his prey. It now extended from Goshen, Indiana to Schenectady, New York. There had been one abduction each summer since Annette initially disappeared and now there were seven. He talked to Vince about it every day, constantly revisiting the information.

"Damn it, Vince why doesn't this guy leave a clue?"

"He is just as lucky as he is smart," said Vince "and he is very lucky."

"What if he stops, I mean just stops and never does it again? How will we find him?"

"We probably won't, you have to be ready for that. Right now, as far as we know, he does one girl every summer. So, he struck again this year and we now have to wait until next year for the next bit of information and if he moves on, away from here, how would we know?"

"That's not what I wanted to hear."

"I know Jim, why don't you go on home and I'll finish up our report. Take your wife to dinner, enjoy the evening and we'll hit it again in the morning."

"Yeah, I'm gonna' do that." Jim went back to his desk and picked up the phone, "Hey babe, don't start dinner, I want to take you out tonight. Okay, I'll see you soon."

"See you in the morning, Vince." As Jim was walking toward the stairs, George came around the corner from the kitchen with a fresh cup of coffee, "Half day, eh McClarry?"

"Hey boss, I'm takin' my wife to dinner, gonna' get a good night's sleep and be back here, refreshed, in the morning."

Vince called out to George, "In here George, I'll give you the latest."

George turned and went into the conference room. Jim went down the stairs and out to his car.

*　　　*　　　*

Twenty-Nine

Do you care as long as we get to see her die . . .?

A year passed and Averell remained very calm, controlled and quiet during that time. He went about his business, visiting his clients and expanding his contacts. Stelian remained similarly subdued and Averell did not visit any residential neighborhoods.

Then on a Wednesday in July, before the holiday in 1998, a six-year-old girl was abducted from her neighborhood in Findlay, Ohio. Carol Denton's body was found by a search dog on the Sunday following her disappearance. Her little body had been senselessly abused by someone and she had been strangled and deposited in a field several miles from her home.

At the time of Carol's abduction, Averell was in Albany closing a deal with an old client and ready to drive back to Rochester for the holiday weekend. He did not hear about this incident until he read a brief article in the Rochester newspaper on Monday detailing the discovery of her body the day before. It did not interest him. He read the article and moved on to the sports page. Jim also read an article about Carol and he added her to the database. Her hair, eyes and clothing separated her from the prime group, but as he well knew, she could still be one of the predator's victims.

A week later, Averell was in the Syracuse area visiting a client in a mall when he noticed a woman with blond hair walking with a little girl, perhaps two years old. As he watched her, he was reminded of Sarah. He paused and thought for a moment and realized that Sarah would be about twenty-five now and could well be married and a mother. He looked again at the young woman as she held on to the child and walked away from him. His mind began to work, "Was that Sarah, did she have a baby, where was Ellie, who was the father, where was Steve, I have a lot of questions."

"What's the problem?"

"Not now," and Averell walked out of the mall and to his car.

"So, what's wrong? Do you think that was Sarah, with a baby?"

"I don't know." Averell started the car and drove out of the parking lot. He turned north and started to accelerate.

"Whoa, slow down buddy, we don't want to get a ticket or worse, crash."

Averell slowed and continued down the street. He turned into another lot and stopped. "Gotta' think."

"Just where are we going? This is the way to Ellie's place. We haven't been there in a long time, about a year. Is it time to check on her again?"

"Yeah, let's just drive by and then we will go home."

"Okay, but maybe we don't just drive by. Maybe we hang around and see what's going on."

"Yeah, maybe we do just that." Averell drove to Ellie's townhome and stopped across the street and down a few houses. He waited. He waited for two hours when a silver coupe pulled into the driveway. It was Ellie, she went into the house and Averell was thinking about what he would do next when a pick-up truck pulled up in front of the house. Steve got out and jogged up the stairs and went in.

"Still together, that's amazing."

"Yeah, amazing, I wonder where Sarah is, if she is still with them."

"We should go now, been sitting here for a couple of hours and that could draw attention."

Averell started the car and drove away, passing the house and continuing down the street. "Maybe we'll come back later and see if anybody else shows up."

"Like Sarah?"

"Yeah, like Sarah." He went about four blocks and pulled into a small strip center and entered a coffee shop. A few minutes later he was back in the car with a cup of overpriced coffee and a muffin. He sat there for an hour sipping the coffee and picking at the muffin.

"Well, what do you want to do now buddy?"

"I want to push a probe through her throat and watch her eyes as the blood comes out of her mouth and she dies."

"Okay, let's do it."

"Could we do it and not be suspected?"

"Do you really care if we are suspected? Do you care if we are caught? Do you care as long as we get to see her die?"

"See them die, both of them."

"And Steve, what about Steve?"

"I don't care about him anymore, but I want them to die."

"Let's check on them again and then we should start planning."

Averell started the car and drove to Ellie's house. There was another silver coupe in the driveway. He stopped the car and watched for about an hour when a young woman came out and got in the second coupe and drove away.

"That's her, that's Sarah."

"She still looks the same. Let's follow her see where she goes."

She drove about fifteen minutes and pulled into an apartment building lot, got out and went in the main entrance. Averell watched for a minute and was about to get out and check when Sarah came out and got in her car. She pulled out of the lot.

"We should follow her."

"No, we should check the mailboxes, see if she lives here."

"Yeah, you're right, "Averell got out of the car and walked to the entrance. He looked at the mailboxes, there she was, S. Danker, Apartment 205.

He noted the address and went back to his car, "Got it, now let's go."

"Let's go home and figure this thing out."

"Yeah," he started the car and drove away.

* * *

Thirty

They will find her . . .

The next few weeks were busy for Averell. September meant a new school year and that meant a huge demand for supplies. On Tuesday, August 11, 1998, Averell was once again passing through Cleveland Heights and the memory of his encounter with the little girl in the pink shirt seven years earlier, stirred within him. He wanted to find another subject.

"Are we ready for this?"

"I think we are, don't you?"

"Let's be sure, are the woods still safe?"

"We should go and check it out. We could find a site and dig a hole."

"Okay, I see, then what?"

"Then I want to get a newspaper and check the obituaries, we need a plan B, just in case something goes awry, then we go back to Cleveland Heights. I really like that neighborhood."

"Are we house hunting?"

"Maybe we are, I haven't decided. But it would be great."

He was driving south and east and looked at the sky, "What a beautiful day."

"Not a cloud to be seen, will it last for a few days?"

Averell tuned his radio to the local news station for the Cleveland area. The reporter said that the weather for the next three days was going to be clear and warm with temperatures reaching rising into the low 80s and cooling to the low seventies at night.

"It doesn't get much better than that."

He took 480 east through Twinsburg toward Portage County. He got off at state Route 44 and turned toward the wooded area where he would dig a hole in preparation for the subject of the day. When he arrived, nobody was in sight, "Perfect, absolutely perfect."

Averell dug a hole, keeping the removed dirt close and covered it with brush just in case someone else showed up. Finished, he was wiping his hands clean and walking toward his car when he remembered his shovel. As he turned and looked back, his eyes scanned the area and finally caught the orange paint on the shovel handle. It was leaning against a tree next to the pit. "Ah, well now it's a marker for me when I come back, soon." He laughed and turned toward his car again.

"Hey, the shovel ."

"Leave it, we will be right back." He got into his car and drove out to the roadway. As he was about to head back into Cleveland Heights, Averell stopped for a fast-food dinner. A burger, fries and a milkshake. He also bought a local paper from a newsstand outside the restaurant. As he sat in his car starting his dinner and browsing the obituaries he muttered, "Nutritious."

"And the other thing?"

"Delicious." Then he saw what he was looking for, a funeral being held at St. Michaels Church, today, "Cool, now then," he read on, "the internment will be at Alton Memorial Park, hey we have been there, that is where we put the first one, what was her name? That is a perfect plan B." He was excited, everything was coming together, the day was beautiful, the site was prepared, the alternate route was defined, now all he needed was a subject.

Along with his delicious and nutritious meal came a bumper sticker that, if read by the right observer, could earn him one-hundred dollars. He found this amusing and while sitting in the parking lot, it occurred to him that his car could be identified as a blue sedan, 4 years old, and other specifics. If, however, he had a huge dent in his rear bumper, that may be the main identifier. He thought about putting several loud bumper stickers on his bumper now and he would remove them after he was clear of his abduction site.

"A test, we need a test."

"Yes, why?"

"We will try it with this sticker and if it works well, we will get more stickers."

He peeled the backing off of the ends of the sticker exposing only about a quarter of an inch of adhesive at each end. "This will hold till we get free and then the sticker comes off."

"I like that, we give them something to look at, then take it away."

He adhered the sticker to his bumper, drove back to Cleveland Heights and slowly cruised the streets in a neighborhood near the one he had visited in 1991.

As he rounded a corner, he saw a perfect target. Melissa Winton had blond hair and blue eyes. She was wearing a pink t-shirt, blue denim shorts and white tennis shoes. She was with several other people and Averell drove as far away as he could and still see the group of teenagers. He parked and waited and watched. He sat in his car for an hour when finally, the group broke up and dispersed. Averell planned on using the "I'm looking for my mom's new house" approach and he had a piece of paper with some writing on it. He noted that Melissa was turning on a street two blocks away. He started his car and drove around the block so he would intercept her at an intersection a block from where she turned.

He drove toward that intersection and parked about two houses away, got out and with paper in hand he approached the corner.

Melissa turned the corner and was coming in his direction. He turned and walked slowly toward his car. Nobody was in sight except Melissa. This was working perfectly. He paused next to his car and turned. Again, perfect, he bumped into Melissa.

"Oh, please excuse me, I am so lost. I didn't mean to bump you, are you okay?"

"I'm fine, are you okay?"

"No, I can't find my mom's new house. Do you know what street this is?"

"Yes, this is Calverton, and up there …" as Melissa turned to point toward the street where she had just turned, Averell quickly opened the back door of his car, grabbed Melissa and threw her in. He was instantly on top of her, with the gag and the tie wraps.

Once secured, he closed the door, got in the front seat and drove around the corner. As he turned, two people passed him and waved. Averell returned the wave with a smile and kept on driving.

"Nicely done, Mr. Danker."

"Why, thank you my friend."

Fred turned and looked after the passing car and said to his wife, "Who was that?"

Angie replied, "I have no idea," and she also turned and looked at the car.

They both saw the car, it drove right past them, but later they would not be able to agree on the color, make, model or license plates—just that it had "One of those WJ… something stickers that'll win ya a hundred bucks."

Averell stopped at the next corner and turned to look at Melissa. She was struggling to get up on the seat, he turned, slapped her hard and said, "Stay down or I will hurt you."

"You should be nice to our guest."

"I'll be nice when we get there."

"Ah, yes, that will be good."

Averell got out of the car and walked to the rear bumper and pulled the sticker off and got back in. He drove toward Cedar Road and said, "Yes. I really do like this neighborhood. Maybe we should move here in a few months."

"That would be very interesting, we could observe the people as they try to figure out who we are. Ha, I love it."

Averell laughed and drove out to the freeway.

Melissa was going to be another success for Averell. He had had two reasonably successful sessions and he was sure that he had the right ingredients this time. "She will be quiet, respectful of the work that we are doing here. She will show me her heart as it beats."

"We must be very careful to keep her calm and quiet. We will tell her what we are doing and what we will do."

"Yes, we will tell her everything before we begin. We can even show her the grave that we dug yesterday, just for her when we are finished." As he pulled into the open area and parked his car, Averell spotted his shovel. He dragged Melissa out of the car and over to a tree near the pit.

"Should we be taking photographs of this, I mean, we are getting better at this and there are just so many opportunities for us to do it right. This one is just right, the only other one we had that was just right was the first one. Remember?"

"Yeah, but I can't remember her name?"

"I don't think we ever knew."

"What is this one's name?"

"I don't know."

"Let's ask her."

"Yeah, we'll ask her."

Averell stood Melissa next to a tree and used another tie wrap to secure her to a branch. He did the same to another tree and removed her gag. "Hello little girl, what's your name?"

Melissa screamed and cried. She was near hysteria but managed to say, "Let me go, I wanna' go home."

"First you tell me your name."

"No, you're hurting me, I wanna' go home." and she started to sob, uncontrollably.

"No cooperation, just like Sarah, let's get to the probes."

"Ask her one more time."

"Okay, okay, I will."

"Are you going to tell me your name."

Melissa was not hearing his question, she was aware of the sharpened probes in his right hand and the knife in his other hand. She knew what that meant, she knew she was going to get hurt, but she didn't know how badly. The mind of a young girl who hasn't hurt anyone was going to be tortured for being blond, having blue eyes and her choice of wardrobe. She had experienced bumps and bruises, little cuts and scratches, but there was nothing in her frame of reference to prepare her for what came next. This would bring pain that would make full grown men cry and scream for mercy. She was as pure and innocent as any human being could be, and she was about to be butchered to satisfy one man's perverted sense of pleasure. He wanted to see her heart beating and see her eyes as she died. This was his afternoon of pleasure. This was the end of her very brief life.

"Do you see that hole in the ground? We dug it for you. That's where you will be put when we are finished, in that hole and then we will put all that dirt on top of you." He smiled and held the probes up in front of her eyes, "These are for you too. We are going to put them into you and it is going to hurt." He smiled again and touched the sharp end of a probe to her skin. She was as frightened as anyone he had ever seen. Her eyes, Sarah's eyes were full of tears, reddening, wide and terrified. Averell placed the first probe against her side just above the hip and pushed it into her. Melissa screamed and choked while trying to inhale. She vomited and coughed, choked again and gasped for air. The probe went in about four inches and slowed. He took another probe, waved it before her eyes and placed it opposite the first and pushed it into her body. Her screams were exquisite, her pain was greater than anything she had ever felt. Averell picked up his knife and started to make an incision just below her throat, when she let out a final blood curdling scream and fell limp, dead. Nature was merciful, she would not suffer any more of the pain of being torn apart while she was still alive.

Averell was dismayed, he did not see her heart and he only briefly watched her eyes. He remained calm, composed, and concluded that the next time, he would have to get someone a bit older, perhaps it was time for a woman. Someone who could better understand what was happening, someone who could last longer. A woman like Sarah. "This is not working. I want them to last longer, I want to see the heart beating, then, and only then, I want to see their eyes as they die."

"Do you think we are ready for Sarah?"

"I think we may be, she should be able to last longer, and if she lasts long enough, we will see her heart beating when I kill her."

As he dismembered her body and placed her parts in the three bags, Averell thought more and more about Sarah and Ellie. "Yes, we are ready. But what will we do, and where?"

"This is a good place."

"No, too far to travel. We need something near Syracuse."

"The Finger Lakes."

"Yeah, but I had wanted to bury them in the woods near the old house where I grew up."

"We could do that."

"No, too risky, they can just disappear. We can put them near the others up there."

"What do you want to do to them?"

"I'd like to string them both up like this one," he said pointing at Melissa. "Facing each other, then put a probe in one, then the other. Then watch them watch each other, watch their eyes as they die. I want it to last a long time, I want it to be perfect." As he spoke, his eyes widened, his voice became deeper and sweat appeared on his brow.

"Do you think they will cry or complain when we do them?"

"Probably both." Averell laughed aloud. "Both!" and he laughed again.

"We have to work this out, Averell. Right now, we should clean everything up and get back on schedule."

"Yeah, we are ready." Averell had packed the customary three bags with Melissa and put them in his trunk, then he went to the stream for his ritual of rinsing his body five times. When finished, he dried off, dressed and was walking back to his car when he noticed a pick-up truck coming into the clearing. He was completely surprised by this and quickly put the bag of his soiled clothes in the trunk and closed it. He looked around to be sure that he had everything and noted his shovel next to the hole intended for Melissa.

"Phil, what a surprise. I was just going to take another look around, though about bringing my shotgun on this trip, but left in a bit of a hurry."

Phil was out of his truck and walking in Averell's direction when he said, "Good to see you, Al. What's that over there?"

"What, where?"

"There, it's a shovel. What the hell?" as he walked past Averell and toward the shovel, "Is that yers?"

"What, that shovel, no, what's it doing there?"

"Somebody's figurin' on buryin' somethin', I reckon," said Phil.

As they approached the hole, Averell said, "Hey, lookout, there's a hole there."

Phil stopped and looked down, "damn, could'a fell in there, thanks Al."

"Sure Phil, you know what that may be?"

"Yeah, coulda' almost been my damn grave."

They both laughed and Averell said, "No, no I mean that might be a boar trap. Are there any boar in this area?"

"I don't think so, never seen 'em 'roun here," said Phil. "Som bitch dug this coulda killed someone."

"Maybe we should fill it up so nobody falls in," said Averell.

"You should fill it, you dug it, dummy."

"Yer probably right, damn I wanted to nail me some crows."

Averell grabbed the shovel and said, "How long would it take to dig this thing?"

"'Bout an hour, give 'er take."

"Hmmm, let's see how long it takes to fill 'er up," and he started to shovel the loose dirt back into the hole.

Phil stood and watched for a minute then walked back to his truck. Averell thought "Serves me right, never should have dug this thing."

"Putz, he's leaving."

Phil put his shotgun on the rack in the cab, took off his coat and walked around to the back of the truck.

"Guess again," said Averell as he looked toward Phil. He was heading back with another shovel.

"Can't let you have all the fun," said Phil, and he started to help fill the hole.

After about twenty minutes of shoveling loose dirt, the two men both leaned on their shovels and looked at each other. Almost at the same instant they both said, "Good enough."

As they walked back to their vehicles, Averell banged his shovel against a tree to shake off the dirt and set it next to Phil's shovel in his truck.

"That one's not mine," said Phil.

"Well, it sure ain't mine," said Averell, "wouldn't know where to keep it or use it."

"Ha, I go through these damn things, maybe two a year, so it'll get used proper good."

"Deal," said Averell, "Oh my goodness, I'm going to be late, gotta' run. Phil, I'll be seein' you."

"Okay Al, hey if yer headin south, drive slow, there's a cop about a mile down the road, gotta' make his quota."

"Thanks, Phil," and he got in his car and drove out to the main road. He turned left and headed north this time aiming for the cemetery about ten miles away.

"We going to the cemetery?"

"Yeah, not a matter of choice now."

"Understood."

"If there was one cop."

"There are probably others."

Twenty minutes later, he was pulling into Alton Memorial Park, the cemetery where he had buried Annette. He drove around looking for the fresh grave that he knew was there. He spotted it near the tree line and not visible from the highway. He parked the car, opened the trunk pulled out the three bags and took them one at a time into the woods. He had all three bags ready to drop into a hole and it occurred to him, "I gave my shovel to Phil."

"That was stupid."

"I know, I know."

"So now what?"

"I have to think."

"Well think fast, there's a cop."

"I see that."

Averell walked to the front of the grave and knelt down and read the headstone. He bowed his head as if he were praying and waited for the police to approach him. They drove past and kept going.

"Respectful, nice."

Averell thought for a moment and walked up to the bags. The cop was gone, he had no other obvious options. He dragged the three bags about twenty feet into the woods and said, "I have to take the bags, they are covered with fingerprints, but our little friend is going to stay here."

"They will find her."

"I know, but they will not be able to tie her to us. We'll spread her around and cover her as much as we can, then we have to get outta' here." He scattered her body parts and covered each part with leaves and branches. Then took the plastic bags back to his car and put all six in another clean bag and put it in his trunk. As he was thinking about his next step, the police car was coming in the cemetery again.

"We should leave."

"Yes, now."

He got in his car and slowly drove out of the cemetery and turned toward the freeway. In an hour he was on I-90 heading toward Erie.

"New car time?"

"Good thought."

"No more Portage County."

"Another good thought. We have work to do. We are going home for a few days."

"The car …"

"Yes, the car will be first."

*　　　*　　　*

Thirty-One

I like it, nicer than the one we used to have . . .

The dismembered body in the woods next to the cemetery drew the attention of crows and other critters, which, in turn, attracted the police. Melissa was identified almost immediately and Josh Dembro, the officer who drove through the cemetery the previous night, was being questioned about his near encounter with the kneeling man. All he could remember was that the man was rather slight in build, with dark hair. He was kneeling when Josh saw him, so the man's height was only a guess. He figured no more than five foot ten and no less than five foot six. He drove a dark blue sedan, probably four or five years old, with out of state plates, probably New York. Josh made a second pass through the cemetery because, as he thought about it, it was a bit strange for a mourner to be kneeling at a grave that late. He just wanted a second look. When he got there, the man was gone.

The detective in charge learned that the person buried in that grave had a number of family and friends in attendance, some from New York and yes, the kneeling man fit the description of several people who did or may have attended the funeral or come late. That little bit of information never made it to the media.

As all of this was unfolding, Averell was back in Rochester and ready to visit Tom Walters again. His car was now four-years-old and it was fitting that he make a change. He drove to the dealership where Tom was working and approached the receptionist. "Hi, I'm looking for Tom Walters. He has helped me in the past and I thought …"

"Mr. Walters has moved on to our main office and no longer is involved in the sales efforts. He's in charge of our fleet department. Can I get another salesman to help you?"

Averell thought for a minute and said, "There was a fellow, I think his name was Dave that helped out."

"When was that?"

"About four years ago."

"That may have been Dave Martell, let me give him a ring."

A minute later, the young salesman that had helped out four years earlier came out of the office and with extended hand said, "Mr. Danker?"

"Yes, good memory."

"Tom was the best, he could remember everybody's name and I am trying to do the same, but it is difficult, so I cheat."

"How's that?"

"Same way Tom did, I go over the list of people that I have met weekly and recall as much as I can, then I imagine a conversation with them and see their faces. Now I have to update my info on you," he said with a smile.

"I like this guy."

"So, what can I do for you today?"

"Well, I think I'm ready to retire old blue here and get something new," said Averell pointing at his car in the front lot.

"Anything specific in mind, another sedan, or something different?" asked Dave.

"I think I want to see the SUVs again. I really liked the one I had before the sedan."

"Okay, we can look at the new ones or start with the pre-owned vehicles in the lot. I know you're aware these things can be a little expensive, so you tell me where you want to start."

Averell thought for a second and said, "Let's start with the new ones, get a feel for what I could get and go from there."

"Okay," said Dave as he turned and pointed out a new SUV in the showroom, "Now this baby is loaded, and as you can see, it leaves nothing to the imagination, except a chauffeur."

Averell opened the door and climbed in, "This is very nice. Is that a six-disc changer?"

"Yep, and you get the premium speaker package in this one."

Averell stepped out and walked around the back and opened the rear door, "Nice storage space, that's a plus."

"That's a big plus."

As he was coming around the side, Dave said, "Full size spare tire, large gas tank, big eight-cylinder engine, great for towing a boat or trailer. All leather interior, all power windows, seats, tilt wheel." He opened the hood and they examined the engine, "The bad thing is that if you work on your own car, this requires some help from a mechanic with all the right tools."

"I wouldn't even try, that's why you guys have service departments, so I won't put a wrench in there," said Averell with a laugh. "Okay, I saw the sticker and it is quite expensive, nice but expensive. What do you have in the pre-owned area?"

"Let's walk out there, I think you will be pleasantly surprised at the choices," said Dave.

They walked out to the side lot and there were about twelve new looking SUVs in a row. "There you go, these are all less than three-years

-old and all are very low mileage. Some folks buy these things and find out after a little while they are more expensive to operate and maintain than they thought."

"Well, I do a lot of highway driving and these buggies are pretty good if you drive at or a little over the limit and give them proper care and feeding. Let's see inside this one, with the tinted windows."

"I'll get the keys, be right back," and Dave checked the number on that one and as he passed another one with tinted windows, he checked its number.

"I like it, nicer than the one we used to have."

"Yeah, looks nicer and the price is in the ballpark," Averell said as he looked at the sticker.

"We should get a gun rack and a shotgun."

"I don't think we will be back in Phil's playground anytime soon, too risky, best we move on."

"Yeah, damn it, I liked that spot and I liked Phil."

"Me too."

"Excuse me," said Dave as he walked up to Averell.

"Just thinking out loud, I like this one."

"Well, here's the key, let's open her up," said Dave as he unlocked the door, "hop in, what do you think?"

Averell climbed in and sat behind the wheel looking over the buttons and dials. "Looks like the cockpit of a fighter jet. Let's see the engine." Averell stepped out and walked to the front.

Dave reached in and pulled a lever that unlocked the hood and came around front and opened it. "There it is," the engine was clean, no rust, no grease or oil spatter, no dirt. "We steam clean these babies for display purposes of course, but this one was very clean when it came in, didn't need a lot of help to look good."

"Looks good, and the sticker price?"

"If I may," said Dave, "let's look at this other one, then we will talk dollars."

"Okay, which one?"

"Right here," said Dave and he walked over to the other one with tinted windows. This one was a deep blue, full tinted windows and clean looking. He opened the door and Averell looked in.

"Cloth seats, I really do like the leather."

"I understand, but you do visit a lot of different locations in both the summer and winter. These seats are never hot on a summer day and never cold on a winter day. They are also a little softer and on a long trip, well, you should get in, sit and feel."

Averell got in, Dave was right, it was more comfortable, softer than he would have guessed, "I am surprised, this is nice."

"Now, the rest of this is the same as the other one, except it has about five thousand miles more on it but look at the price."

Averell got out, looked at the price, smiled, "Well it passed the butt test." An hour later, he was driving his new pre-owned SUV home.

"What do you think?"

"Very nice. Is it time to go hunting?"

"No, not yet. This last one was a problem and it could be risky to do another one now."

"Yeah, in Ohio maybe, but we have other places we could use."

"True, true, true. Okay, we will look around for a new place to play, but we'll go very slowly and be sure of things, remember—planning."

"Yeah, magic."

"Exactly, and…"

"And what?"

"And maybe we can do someone a little older."

"Are we ready to take Sarah for a ride?"

"We may be, but first let's find a place, and I did like the Finger Lakes."

"Me too, I liked the Finger Lakes, and I liked Phil's farm."

"Phil's place is out of the question, we pushed our luck by going back there. What if Phil had come in while we were busy?"

"The Finger Lakes it is, then?"

"Yeah, let's go back there and look around, we should find a very special place for her."

"For them?"

"Yeah, for them."

*   *   *

Thirty-Two

And I have a couple of answers . . .

This latest victim proved to be that little slip in Averell's very well thought out plans that would prove to be expensive, very expensive. This was where he had been able to thank "luck" over the last several years, when a little glitch had crept into his organized plans and an old lady's eyes, a policeman's slow uptake in a cemetery, a witnesses description seeing a bumper sticker rather than his license plates had failed to open the door to Averell himself. He didn't know how many times he had almost been seen, how many times he had been a second or a minute from being interrupted and being caught in the act. This time, his curiosity had brought him back to a scene he should have avoided, but he had to see.

Jim McClarry had more information for his database. Melissa Winton was the fifteenth victim he recorded that fit the broader limitations he was using. She was the second little girl taken from Cleveland Heights. She was also the eighth that fit his tighter parameters. She was a blue-eyed blond with a pink top, blue denim shorts and white shoes. But her body had been found. On top of that, her picture in the newspaper looked like Annette. He gave her a 10 on his rating scale.

"Sean, this is Jim, listen, I got something with this latest victim, why don't you come upstairs when you have a few minutes today?"

"I assume you are ready to run out the door, right?"

"Yeah, as soon as pack my briefcase."

"I'll be out front in five minutes, I'm driving."

"Okay, see you in five."

Jim packed his briefcase, gave Margo a hug and said, "I may be a little late tonight, Babe, we may have something with this latest victim." He ran down the stairs. Sean was just pulling up and Jim got in. "The Winton girl taken yesterday is almost a twin for Annette, it was scary."

Sean drove to the station and pulled into the lot. They went up to the detective's office.

"Good morning Vince, Jim has something for you."

"I figured he would, I read the newspaper too, let's see it."

Jim spread out his materials including a picture of Annette and one of Melissa. They could have been twin sisters, seven years apart but they looked very much the same.

"Do we have photos of the others that are on the list?" asked Jim.

"No, but we will in a few hours. George is on his way in, he'll open the doors for us at the stations we have not talked to yet."

"Okay," said Sean.

"Is Alex around?" asked Jim.

"He's not in today," said George. "Vince look at these pictures, what does it look like to you?"

"They could be the same girl or related, like sisters?"

"Neither, this is Annette Shelton and this other one is Melissa Winton. These pictures were taken seven years apart and Melissa is a little older than Annette was then."

"What else you got?" asked Vince.

Jim sat down and reviewed the entire file with him. "Something else we should be aware of."

"What's that?"

"Whoever the ultimate target is, assuming she is still alive, she'd be older now, possibly even in her twenties.

"Okay, so what do we do with this new information?" asked Vince.

"How about getting one of those aging programs that show what someone would look like when they grow up."

"Then what?" asked George.

"Then we do the aging thing to each of the girls, see what they might look like today and search for this person along the I-90 corridor. We might get zero response and we might get a hundred responses, only one way to find out. Keep in mind that a hundred maybes may be exactly what we need."

"We're listening," said Vince.

"This Melissa was taken apart, legs, arms, head, torso and scattered in the woods at a cemetery. The question in my mind is, Why? We have not found any of the other seven, so why this one?" quizzed Jim.

"You have a theory?" asked George.

"It can be answered in several ways. First, maybe he has reached his goal. I don't like this answer, but we have to consider it."

Vince looked at George and said, "We should give Alex a call, this is his turf."

George looked over his shoulder and said, "Janice, can you hunt down Alex, see if he can join us?"

Jim cleared his throat and spoke up, "Second answer is, he intended to put this body where it could be eaten by the wildlife, but that is not very likely."

"Agreed."

"Third, he may have been in the process of hiding the body. In a cemetery. It's a natural—and he was seen. Someone was seen kneeling next to a fresh gravesite the night before her body was found. I think he may have intended to re-dig the same site and deposit the body, then cover it up. But the patrol car upset his plan, made him improvise, scatter the body in the woods and get outta' there."

Jim gave his fellow detectives a moment to consider.

"The officer that drove through the cemetery and saw a man kneeling at the grave said the plates on his vehicle were from New York."

"What else you got, Jim?" asked Vince.

"Well, when I add it up, we had a man seven years ago that could be the same man in the cemetery, the descriptions are close. We have a blue van seven years ago that he could have traded for the sedan that was seen in the cemetery yesterday. The plates were from New York, so, I think that we should look for the possible target, the current version of what these little girls could grow into, in New York rather than Indiana, Ohio and Pennsylvania."

"Sounds reasonable." George saw Janice and asked, "Is Alex around?"

"Can't find him, boss."

"Okay, we'll catch him later," George came back into the conference room and sat down. "Jim, this is good, and I want to run with it, what are you going to do next?"

"I got this far but now we have some more work to do. If you give a go ahead, I'll get one of those aged pictures generated and try to get them circulated in New York State along the I-90 corridor. And I know you won't let me forget the other three files on my desk."

"Okay, let's reconvene when Alex is available and maybe you guys will have more to add at that point."

"We may, let's get at it," and the meeting was over. Jim went back to his desk and wrote up a summary of what was just covered in the meeting and put it together with a cover note stating that the psych evaluation should be attached. He then filled out a requisition for a forensic artist to do an age progression sketch.

When Alex came in and reviewed the package, he made a few notes and the information was forwarded to the FBI for their review. They already had that and a little additional information from local police, about the location of the cemetery. Still, no one had enough to focus in on any one individual.

Averell was very uncomfortable and needed to know he was safe from any suspicion by the police. He drove back to the cemetery and drove past, straining to see if there was still activity at the gravesite. He drove around the block several times, trying to see and finally drove into the cemetery. He drove slowly around and past the site, looking for activity.

There was yellow tape around several trees in the woods and two men slowly walking through the wooded area, looking down. As he continued on the road, he passed a police car coming the other way.

Josh was given the task of looking at anyone and everyone who came near the site in an effort to try to find the kneeling man. The car was all wrong, but the guy was close enough for a second look. He noted the license plates were from New York, so he called it in. "47 to base, I got a maybe on the kneeling man. It's kind of thin, but a maybe nonetheless."

"Keep an eye on him and we are sending back up."

"Roger that, he's pulling out and heading east on Derby. I'm on him."

"47, this is 23, We are close, on the way, Josh, hang with 'em."

Within five minutes there were three black and whites closing on Averell. He saw them and calmly pulled into a shopping center with an office supply store. He had never been to this store but he did deal with the distribution center that supplied this store. His ploy was to claim that he was looking at different stores where he could run a promotion for the up-coming school season. As he stepped out of his vehicle, an officer approached him. "Mr. Danker, you are Averell Danker, correct?"

"Yes, is there a problem?" Averell feigned calm, but he suddenly felt sick to his stomach.

"We would like to ask you a few questions, do you have a minute?"

"For you guys, absolutely. What can I do for you?" Averell surprised himself at his ability to hold it together.

"Where were you on Tuesday the eleventh?"

"Ah, you mean two days ago?"

"Yes, Tuesday."

"Well, I'm not sure, I had an appointment in Erie at ten in the morning and ..."

"You were in Erie, Pennsylvania?"

"Yes, in the morning, then I went back to Rochester to get more materials for this trip."

"So, you were not here in Ohio on Tuesday?"

"Oh, no, I drove down this morning. What's this about?"

"We noticed you at the cemetery and thought if you had been here on Tuesday, you might have seen something. Thanks for your time," and the police let him go.

"I don't know about this guy. We should let the Feds know about him and follow their lead."

Averell was watched very closely by the local police as he went into the store and as he stayed in their jurisdiction. The Feds were notified and picked up the observation as he headed north toward Interstate 90. For the next several weeks Averell was observed, closely. He was extremely careful and stayed close to his work routine, taking in a movie periodically and stopping at the library to exchange books and book tapes.

Alex Robertson had developed a preliminary profile of the predator with all the information that the team had assembled. When Averell Danker showed up on their radar, he drew as many parallels as possible. The problems were many and not all resolvable. Danker was a possible suspect, but the proof was not there. Both Vince and Jim were in agreement, he could be the one, but could was not good enough. They wanted to be absolutely certain. The only case of the eight missing girls that matched the profile that could be considered was the Melissa Winton case. There was a body and a connection to Danker, a very weak connection—but a connection, nonetheless. Meetings with the district attorney were held and even several trial scenarios were put on the table. Each one assumed they had more evidence to effect an arrest than they actually had, but in the end, they had nothing. If Danker was the best they could do, then they failed. So, as time passed and the case against Averell Danker could not be built, the team on his case was diverted to other things. Averell was beginning to feel as though he had dodged a very large bullet.

"Gotta' stay clean," he mumbled.

"Speak up, my man, we are home."

"They could be listening, bugs."

"Naw, they got zip, nada, nothing."

"Still, careful is best."

"Okay, we can still talk if you think loud enough."

Averell paused and thought, "Can you hear me now?"

"Why yes—yes, I can good buddy."

* * *

Thirty-Three

But I really do understand . . .

Jim McClarry was coming in when he ran into Vince Galley in the parking lot. "How are you doing this morning?" asked Jim.

"C'mon upstairs and let's get Alex and George, we should talk," said Vince.

They went into the captain's office, "Afternoon Vince, Jim," said George, "sit down."

Jim sat and Alex came into the office.

George started the session saying, "Listen guys, I know how you all feel about this case around the Shelton girl. The good news is we have a way outside, maybe, with this character in up-state New York, a traveling salesman. The downside is we have nothing that we can arrest him on. Nothing that even points directly at him, he became a person of interest when he possibly showed interest in the Melissa Winton crime scene, the cemetery. Then he looks kinda like the guy from 1991, and the kneeling man, kinda, nobody could possibly make a positive ID in either case. He has been interviewed twice, and we even went over some of his travel logs that show him somewhere else when each of our fifteen cases went down. We looked at his family, he was adopted from Europe, has one sister, his mother and father split up, his mother remarried and the new father adopted him and his sister. We got nothing on them, they still live in the Syracuse area, except the first father, he moved to California when the kid was five-years-old. He does not have a juvenile record sealed or otherwise, did a stint in the Army, nothing there and now does this salesman routine from Albany to Toledo, all along the I-90 corridor. That's it, we got nothing to put him into any of the cases except Melissa's, and that's as thin as it gets. All things added up, I think this could be our guy. The feds will never give up and they'll stay on him forever. They will watch him 'til he makes a mistake. For now, that's it, we got other things to do and I want you guys to understand, we are not shutting it down, it's on the shelf and not in cold storage."

Alex looked at George, "You know the way these cases have gone, the guy who did it is no dummy. If he has any inkling we suspect this Danker character, he will hole up and convince us it must be Danker. If it is Danker, and he knows we suspect him, then he also knows we don't have enough to arrest him. All he has to do is sit tight, do nothing and sooner or later we will go away, and he will be free to do as he pleases again."

Neither Vince nor Jim was pleased with the status, but they were frozen. If they acted out in some way, the case, slim as it may be, could be blown away.

George continued, "Jim, you did some damn good cop work without all the advantages of the upstairs facilities before you earned your gold shield and became one of us. I like the way you work and want you to know you will do better on some cases and some will go completely south. I don't want you to be discouraged and give up. Remember there is no statute of limitations when it comes to murder and if he did kill Annette, or any of the others, he will make a mistake sooner or later and we will be right there. We will get him, just a matter of time. Now, I have to trust you guys will take this the right way and let the feds do their thing. Are we on the same page?"

Sean was not smiling, "George, you've known me a long time. I understand, and Jimmy is going to be a good little boy." As he said that Jim looked at Sean and did not challenge his use of 'Jimmy' or 'boy'. Sean was not happy and Jim knew that now was not the time to rebuke him.

Jim did not like this either, but he understood, "I hear you Captain, I do not want this screwed up either."

George looked at each of his men and caught a knowing look in each pair of eyes. "Now, we all have put time and effort into this and you can feel good about what you've done, a lot has been accomplished and things will move at a snail's pace until we get something else, so, y'all have things to do, right?"

"Okay, guys, now I have to get back to keepin' the peace and writing tickets," said Sean. He walked toward the stairs and Jim caught up to him.

Hey, I know this is not going to be easy, but I really do understand."

"I'm with you, Jim." his voice trailed off as if he wanted to say something else.

"What, what is it?"

"Nothing, I am pissed and feel like a drink. Wanna' stop and have one after I get my paperwork done?"

"Margo and I have plans tonight, she probably wouldn't appreciate my hanging around a pub drinking when I should be home," said Jim.

"Yeah, okay, hey, why don't you guys come over to the house this weekend and we will burn some steaks and have a drink then," offered Sean.

"Works for me, I'll check with Margo and you clear it on your end." Jim went back and did his last batch of paperwork, said good night to his comrades and left the building. As he walked home, every other step was accompanied with another four-letter word expressing his frustration.

*　　*　　*

THIRTY-FOUR

Do you know this Aaron . . .?

That weekend, Jim and Margo went to Sean's house and they charcoal broiled steaks, drank a few beers and told some stories. Neither Sean nor Jim was pleased with the situation and they let out their pent-up frustration by splitting firewood from Sean's woodpile. After a few beers each, a couple of nicely done steaks and stacking about a half of a cord of firewood, they were both ready for a good night's sleep.

Sean took Jim aside and said, "We have to talk about the family." The two went into the den and closed the door. Jim sat in an easy chair and Sean pulled a footstool close and sat facing Jim. "Jim, you heard the boss, time for us to back away, let it be handled by somebody else. I know you don't want to let go, but trust me, at this point, we let go. The department here in Cleveland Heights is stuck, not enough to arrest, not enough to bring to a Grand Jury, not enough, not enough, not enough. It pisses me off, but it also opens another door."

"What door, what are you talking about?"

"What I am saying is…well—we are family, you remember our conversation a few years back, we are part of a Clann, cousins everywhere."

"Yeah, I remember."

"Well, that bit we all heard about way back a hundred years ago, that was not just a story, it really happened. The family found the guy and put him in the pit to die. They did it then and they have settled other accounts since then that don't get talked about. Remember, if you know something, don't talk about it, if you don't know, don't ask and what you don't know you can't tell. It's kind of simple, but it works, at least so far."

"So, where are you going with this?"

"I'm sure the Clann has already made some contingency plans for our friend."

"Such as . . . ?"

"Such as, make sure he did do it, first, at least Annette, then figure how many of the others he did. Second, find the evidence that confirms as much of the suspicions as we can, everything if possible. Then third, well, then he will be punished."

"You mean pitted. We can't do that, it's not legal, it's not ethical or moral or right. We can't fall to that level, become gangsters and write our own rules," Jim demanded.

"I'm not saying we will, I'm saying the Clann will probably look very hard at this whole thing and then, they may act, they may wind up running him over with a truck—or even shooting him. Hell, I don't know what they will do, more than likely they would gather the information and go through some legal channel, local or state or federal and get the guy locked up. You know prison is not exactly the safest place for guys who murder little girls, no matter who puts him away. Someone inside will feel entitled to put him down and say he gives regular murderers and rapists a bad name."

"Yeah, bad guys have daughters too."

"Exactly, anyway, just be aware this thing will not fall through the cracks. If the first try doesn't get him—a second, third and even fourth will. Sooner or later, Averell Danker will pay the price for what he did."

"Yeah, I guess if I heard somebody ran him down with a truck, I wouldn't feel bad about it." Confessed Jim.

"I didn't want you to think we had to just accept a possible 'Cold Case' stamp on the file," said Sean

"Understood, but now I am concerned about how the family is going to mete out justice. I'm not comfortable with leaving him in a pit."

"Just be aware that someone may ask you to be involved in some way, and you may have to make a choice. Think about it for a few days and let's revisit the possibility."

"Okay, I hear you, it's a lot to process, but I will give it thought. You think someone will ask me for something—like what?"

"Like the information you gathered, that was a lot of work. I know it was sent to the feds, and we shared it with other departments, so, maybe someone in the family may want to read it over. I really don't know, just be ready for someone to contact you."

"What would you do if they asked you for the information?"

"Jimmy, I would do whatever it takes to get this son-of-a-bitch and hurt him. Assuming he is the guy that did take Annette."

"But that's just it, we don't know for sure."

"They would make absolutely sure, before doing anything to hurt him. In fact, they would probably try to use the legal system to its max, collect the information, hand it over and let the system work."

"Maybe. Thanks for the heads up."

When Jim and Margo got back to their apartment, Jim turned on the television and went into the kitchen to open another beer, when the phone rang. Margo answered it and handed it to Jim with a shrug of her shoulders. The voice on the phone was a deep authoritative sounding man with a slight brogue, "Good evening Jimmy m'boy. My name is Aaron and we have a few things to discuss."

"Yeah, sure—not a great time, just turned on the game. Can you call back tomorrow?" asked Jim, trying to hide his annoyance.

"Allow me a minute and you'll see the importance of this call," said Aaron.

"Okay—but only a minute."

"Annette Shelton."

Jim turned toward the television and pushed the mute button on the remote. "Alright, you have my attention." Margo sat up straight and looked quizzically at Jim. He responded by holding up a finger and listening to the caller.

"You've been collecting information on a number of missing children, including Annette."

"Yes, and . . . ," said Jim.

"And we are in a position to do something with it," said Aaron.

"Does it involve this Danker character?" asked Jim.

"That it might lad, but the less I tell you, the less you can tell someone else. We work behind a curtain of sorts, no names, no questions and no answers to the wrong people."

"So, what do you want from me?"

"Two things. First, have you added anything new to your files the Feds don't have?"

"No, what I have, was sent to them by the department."

"And second, could we discuss several points you made in these files?"

"Okay, now it's my turn. First who are you?"

"If I said that I was a friend, and I'm trying to help, would that answer the question?"

"No, you have to do better than that."

"Well now Jimmy-boy, I think you may have guessed who I am. But if that is not enough, I'll tell you that, in a long-distance sort of way, you and I are related and we are both closer to Annette than to each other. You are an officer of the law and I'm also a part of that same profession, but I can tell you no more than that. I can say we have the same objective in mind, but you have to follow the rules, and I do not. It is because the investigation is stalled and there is no possibility of an arrest at this point that I am involved. I will try to keep this entire process legal, but if I have to cross a line, I will. Now I already have a copy of your files, but it may help if we could go over each item and be sure that we have a firm grip on everything."

"You want me to help you?"

"Yes, and your involvement would be between us. Nobody else would even know we have spoken."

"I can't do that, it's not the way it's supposed to happen. I may want to do something, but you have to understand, we have a process, slow and plodding, but it is the process that continues to protect us all and I can't go against that."

"Understood, Jimmy-boy, and I respect your conviction, but I may still call you with questions. I already know the answer to many of them may be confidential, but I may still call."

"You know, I have to report this conversation."

"You do what you have to and I will too. You might want to talk to your cousin and your wife about this, see what they suggest you do. Now go watch your ballgame, we'll be talking again soon." The line went silent.

"Wait! Aaron…?" But he was already gone. Jim stood looking at the phone.

Margo looked at him and said, "What was that all about?"

"This guy, says his name is Aaron, says he wants me to review my files with him."

"Is that good or bad? I mean, who is Aaron?"

"That's just it, I really don't know. He said, talk to your wife, talk to your cousin."

"So?"

Jim dialed Sean's number, "Sean, it's Jim, I just got a call from a guy . . . ."

Sean cut him off, "Aaron?"

"Yeah, who is he?"

"That's hard to explain. He is one of us, family, or more appropriately, Clann. Aaron is not his real name. I didn't think they would contact us so quickly and I wanted you to be ready when they did."

"Sean, this sounds a little off. Aaron already had the FBI files."

"Yeah, a little strange, but I think you should give him some leeway. He is going to try to address a situation that we can't, like we were talking about earlier. What did he want from you?"

"He wants to review my files with me."

"Jimmy, if I was in your shoes right now, I'd do it."

"You think I should, I mean . . . ."

"Jim, you built a couple of files that are all public knowledge, there are no secrets buried in there. This guy, Aaron, is one of us, he is on the team that represents the Shelton's interests. You will do nothing wrong. There may be a piece or two they have, or could find, when added to your data. It could open a big door, you're helping them do their jobs. Jim, these guys have contacts everywhere, no telling what they may find."

"Yeah, but no telling what they could do with all that info."

"Well, at some point, we may have to trust somebody."

"Okay, do you know this Aaron?"

"No, we've never met, do you have a problem with that?"

"Well, not totally.

"Then I would do it, and don't tell anyone unless you are directly asked about it. Then be perfectly honest."

"I need a little time to think, and I have to tell George," said Jim.

"You can probably wait on telling George."

"Sean, I have to."

"Jimmy, that's what makes you a good cop. I'll see you tomorrow."

Jim went back to the living room and pushed the power button on the TV remote. Second inning, no score, and he sat down next to Margo. She poked him in the ribs and said, "Well, are you okay?"

"Yeah, I don't know, sort of, thinking about what this guy thinks I can give that he doesn't already have." They watched the game, but Jim's mind was on Annette and Aaron. All of a sudden it was the 8th inning and Cleveland was ahead by one run.

* * *

Thirty-Five

Yeah, planning . . . that was a good move . . .

Aaron tossed the cellphone he had just used into a briefcase and picked up a second one. He checked his notes and placed another call. This call was to a man he knew only as 'Adam'. As he was known only as Aaron to all but the very few at the top of the pyramid. At the end of this project all cellphones and e-mail addresses would be abandoned and/or destroyed. There would be no trail to follow, no name to match—nothing. These men understood they could be closely related, or they could be distant cousins, many times removed. It was important that each individual maintain a wall of secrecy around himself. "The less you know, the less you can tell." It had worked before and it would continue to work here .

"Adam, this is Aaron, I've sent the files to you already and had a brief conversation with our friend in Cleveland Heights. I think he wants to help, but his ethics are keeping him from jumping in. I respect the guy for that and assume you do as well. I told him I will probably call him if we feel the need for clarification, so he may change his mind. You have a number to reach me, anytime. Good luck."

The man listened and did not speak, avoiding as much conversation as possible. After he hung up he shuffled a few papers on his desk and found what he was after, picked up his cellphone and dialed a number, "We have a go, files will be in place in the morning. Meeting in two days at the prime location, time as set up," and he hung up. He took his wallet out and placed it in his desk drawer and took out a different wallet, checked the contents and put it in his pocket. He removed his ring and watch and put on others from the same drawer, packed a few papers in his briefcase and walked out of his office. As he passed an administrative aide, he said "Marcy, you are looking fantastic today. I will be out for the rest of the week, got some family business to take care of, everything is in order, if you need me for anything, my cell will be on constantly. I hope to clean this up within a week—give or take a day."

Marcy smiled, "Okay, Jake. Is Paul aware of this one, or do you want me to advise him?"

"He knew it was coming, but yeah, let him know I had to move on this now, and again I have my cell always."

Marcy was used to this sudden shifting of gears, it's what they did, constantly adjust, adapt, address whatever pops up. She nodded and scribbled a note and put it in an envelope. She put the envelope in a mailbox behind her and got back to her file searching. As Jake, or Adam as he would be known for the next week or so, walked out of the building, he hit a number on his speed dial and spoke into the phone, "Yes, I need a flight to Buffalo, New York as soon as possible. I can be there in about thirty-minutes. Put it on my Amex," and he rattled off the numbers as if he did this every day. He got in his car and drove out through the security gate. Adam, or Jake, was a veteran spook with almost twenty years of varied experience. He looked young for his age, able to pass for late twenties when he was actually forty-two. Jake stood a full 6'3" and tipped the scales a little over two-hundred-forty pounds about fifteen pounds more than his ideal, but it was mostly muscle he had gained playing hockey in a local men's league and lifting weights.

He was beginning to lose his hair at an alarming rate, but what remained was still dark brown. He had a fist full of medals from his tours in Viet Nam, including a Purple Heart for a bullet that made a mess of his left thigh. A year of rehab had gotten him over the hump and he passed a physical allowing him to return to active duty in the Marine Corps. His duty, however, was destined to be pushing papers and that was not what he signed on to do. So, he resigned his commission, went back to school for a semester of post-grad work and found a job with an engineering firm in Cleveland, Ohio. Design engineering and construction was an interesting field and he was good at what he did, but he missed the excitement he saw in the corps and found designing air conditioning systems got a little routine. When an old friend approached him about an opportunity with an agency where he could use his many skills, including his engineering talents, he was ready to sign up without any persuasion on the part of the agency. A few years into his new life as an agent with the CIA, Jake was again shot in the left leg, this time by an overanxious East German border guard who mistook him for someone else. This time the resulting hitch in his stride was a little more defined and made his participation in covert activities less likely. He spent the next several years in several departments back in McLean, working at various times on identifications, disbursing, weapons testing, and special equipment development. He, his wife Kate and their two sons lived in a newer suburb of Fairfax County, Virginia in a contemporary home. The boys were both approaching high school age and would be off, altogether too soon, to college and their own lives. For that reason, Jake was glad he wasn't traveling around the world in the field. He was happy to be behind a desk and home almost every night. These last five years of his career had been spent analyzing information gathered in the field and preparing analyses of potential operations.

This was truly family business, as he stated to Marcy, even though she could tell there was something else in the background. Jake was related to Jim McClarry, Sean Daugherty, Aaron and the Shelton's. Each was a distant relationship, but all part of the Clann, all part of the family. This time out of the office was going to use up a week or two of his accumulated vacation time. No problem there either, he had accumulated lots of hours with late nights and weekends in the office.

Jake arrived in Buffalo and went to a motel near his final destination. He was now Adam and the name would be used throughout this specific operation and then discarded, only to be resurrected when and if any activity on this project came up in future. He took out a new cell phone, inserted a battery and browsed the speed dial options. He went back to number one and pushed, "Hey, it's Adam, I'm here and ready to receive the data." He closed his phone and opened his computer, made the appropriate connections between his cell phone and his computer and started to dial a number. The system was up and running and he watched the traffic coming in. His files were there, ready to be accessed. He sat on the edge of the bed, going over them.

Without an admission of some complicity on Averell's part, there was no way he could be arrested and tried for any of the fifteen children that had disappeared or been murdered. It had been three days since Jim McClarry spoke to Aaron and his files had been distributed to the FBI's offices at Quantico. Their review sparked a few phone calls to Jim at the office and at home. Even though the callers always identified themselves as being with the FBI, Jim was not certain just who was calling with the questions but answered as best he could, thinking at times it may well have been Aaron's people and not the FBI. Then again, they could well be the same people, Jim didn't know. Nobody knew.

Over the years since the Liam Rynne incident in California, the Clann had amassed a sizable source of money from donations here and there to the proceeds of an operation where money was recovered and could be disbursed back to its rightful owners. Often there was a bit more than had to be sent back and an operating fund was established. There was enough money to run this level of operation and more. The Clann elders had to approve the use of money, but this project was considered a priority.

Through "Clann" connections, the family had access to a number of buildings of various descriptions around the country. In an industrial park in suburban Buffalo, New York, currently a vacant building, originally designed as a light manufacturing plant, was made available for Adam to conduct the proceedings. It was estimated it would take no more than two weeks to get everything they needed from Averell, and the building would be secured for that period.

Adam now had everything he and his team needed, except their guest. A separate two-man team would be responsible for acquiring Averell and delivering him to Adam's team. This team would restrict their activities to that one task and they were done. The four men, including Adam, who would conduct the interrogation would be on the job the longest, perhaps as long as one full week. Except Adam, who would ride this out until the end. A third team would take Averell, after he was interrogated, to his final destination. Adam would remain involved until he was sure the process was complete and their tracks were properly covered.

The interrogation team assembled in Buffalo at a motel near the interstate. As lead interrogator, Adam would be the prime and possibly only contact with Averell. Andrew was the backup for interrogation if absolutely necessary and split duty at the recording station with Bart. Bart's strength was IT, but its use was limited. The team had the database which Bart could manipulate and he was the primary on recording the sessions and making the edited tapes. In their first meeting, the target, Averell, was identified, everything they knew about him was put on the table and added to the database. Then, the eight specific cases the team assumed were Averell's work were reviewed and the task of obtaining information was clarified. In each case they wanted to know how, when and where he took each girl. Exactly what he did with each girl and where they were today. The assumption was that they were all dead and Averell was the only one who knew where to look for them.

The family had contacts in every city where each incident had occurred and they were alerted to be ready if assistance was needed. Adam had already requested as much information as possible on each specific case from the local police departments. A little additional information on four of the cases was tacked on to their files and all was coordinated through the database Jim McClarry had assembled.

Adam and Andrew well versed in the art of questioning difficult criminals. Each had been through sessions with enemy combatants who had to be broken quickly, while in the military. The information was needed to save lives, while information they were seeking from Averell was about people who were already dead. The task was not perceived to be difficult. It was simply a matter of time before Averell would tell them everything and they wanted to be done with him and get back to their lives and their families. Averell's well-being was not a prime consideration, but an accurate accounting was important. As Sean said to Jim on their first day as a team, "We want him caught, not just somebody who might have done this, but THE somebody who DID do this." The first order of business was to determine a questioning procedure. They decided to do a sleep deprivation process and confuse the time element. Averell would not be aware of the time of day or the day of the week. After being in their custody for a day, he might believe a week had passed. If a week was required, then it may seem like a month to Averell. The net effect was a combination of needing sleep and thinking he had held out for a long time and that the process would continue until he gave in. This technique had worked on some pretty hardened and well-trained people and should work easily on Averell.

The team had reviewed the fifteen possible cases attributable to an I-90 predator and reduced the list to the same eight the Heights detectives had been focusing on. The limited information on the eight victims they were going to pursue was reviewed and a circle of possible candidates for Averell's focus was assembled. It did not take long to reduce that list to Sarah. The specifics behind his desire to kill his sister were not yet understood and may never be determined. It was sufficient for this investigation to know she was the prime target. The similarities between Sarah and the eight victims is what led Averell to select each one. Their objective was to establish Averell as the predator who took Annette and get him to disclose the location of her remains. Everything else, all the other victims, were secondary to this objective. Secondary, but somehow just as important. The more the team, including the Heights people, dug into these cases, the more each one of the victims became important to them. They wanted to find each one of them and give closure, such as it was, to each of the families.

Coincidence is a real thing. There are cases where the occurrence of two similar events are related and others where there is no connection at all. The team did not know if the eight cases were related, but it was a logical assumption and they followed that lead. The known, or the best of the assumptions at this point was restricted to the Melissa Winton case. They intended to build backwards from these and hopefully reach Annette. The similarities were enumerated and were going to be used in questioning Averell. They would look to see how he would respond to these and which would trigger a rapid response. They had eight victims— but did not know if there had been others they did not know about. The list of cases Adam's team would concentrate on was finalize. Averell Danker was a suspect and only a suspect until he confessed to one or more of these disappearances. Then, it would be a matter of eliciting as many details about each abduction as possible. Everything he admitted would be documented and given to the FBI and the local authorities when the team had completed their task. The difference being, this team, the Clann, was not hampered by rules and regulations. They would use any means necessary to question a suspect without reservation. They would bribe, tempt or torture to achieve their goal. The objective was getting the truth from beginning to end. An admission to a crime because of fear of torture was no good. They needed a confession with proof. That proof would come in the form of a full description of the event and locating the remains of the victim. They had to be absolutely sure they had the right guy. Ideally this could be obtained without too much out-of-bounds questioning techniques, but all options were on the table.

When Averell was questioned initially by the authorities in Cleveland Heights, he stated he would like to refer to the personnel log he kept, for a number of reasons, "I track my expenses in this notebook, and other things that help me with my job." When questioned further, he stated he had been keeping these records since he started his job and was sure the old notebooks were all in a box back in Syracuse.

"We would like to look at them if you don't mind," George said in an interview with Averell. "What do you write in them?"

"Well, they are kind of personal, I mean, I wrote a lot of things as I met people and took notes. It helps me keep a lot of the customers I visit straight in my mind. You know, like Bob in the Cleveland Heights distribution center is a bit of a jerk, likes hockey and his wife just had a baby, I think about a week ago."

"You seem to remember that alright," said George as he watched Averell's expression.

"Yeah," said Averell, "that's the point, I read my last notes for Cleveland Heights last night and again this morning, before coming to town, learned that from a car salesman."

"So, could you bring them in, let us look at them?"

"If you really want to see them, but again, a lot of the stuff in there is very personal, I wouldn't want it to get back to any of my customers, or my boss. I think I said some things about him, too."

"Please, Mr. Danker, seeing these logs could help us rule you out as a possible suspect and as a possible witness. Just how many books are there?" asked Vince.

"Oh, I really don't know, I just toss them into a box in my garage when I have a new one well along the way. There may be fifteen, or twenty, I really don't know, but I will put them in my car and have them with me on my next trip this way."

"When do you think that would be?" asked George.

"Oh, I could be back here in about two weeks with them."

"Or, you could have someone pick them up and take them to the local police station. They could ship them here, today."

"Well, they are in my garage, and it is not locked, they are in a box labeled "Logbooks," on a shelf. As you go into the garage, on the right-hand side, maybe the second shelf up."

"So, you give us permission to get them?"

"Oh, sure, no problem. Just don't mind the mess, I have been making Bird Houses for my deck out back."

"Thanks, we will be careful to not disturb anything else."

When the interview was over, Averell thought that he had won that encounter. "You see," he said to himself, "planning."

"Yeah, planning, that was a good move."

"My logs, well they are a bit personal, but if they can be of assistance, well then, I suppose it would be okay." He found it amusing to pretend the material would be embarrassing. He laughed to himself as he told them how to retrieve the logbooks, all twenty-seven of them. He knew exactly how many there were.

When the police received the shipment, they counted out all twenty-seven. The logs were labeled with beginning and ending dates. The first six were numbered 1 through 6 with a marker pen. The oldest ones were well-worn, some were coming apart at the sewn binding. The books were fulfilling their purpose, they were demonstrating his alibi, his continuous alibi for over nine years, from August 1989 to November 1998, all the time since he started his job. The logbooks showed his travel miles, gas purchases, meals, appointments and comments. As the team reviewed each case and compared the timing with the logbooks, they noted that Averell seemed to be more than 100 miles away from the scene of each abduction every time.

"It doesn't fit," said Bart.

"If he was thinking about being caught some day, he could have doctored the logs," said Adam.

"That would take some planning," said Andy. "Is he that bright?"

"I think he is," said Adam, "and in each case he would use an extra 300 to 500 miles. With his travel schedule, that would be easy to bury."

"I suppose," said Bart, "but like Andy said, that takes planning. Look at the book, it looks like a log and diary all in one. He would have to do this sneaky accounting every day until he had covered his tracks."

"Yeah," said Bart, "a clever little bastard."

"Exactly, " said Adam, "I think he was solidifying his alibi from day one. This guy has to feel as though he is untouchable. He figures if he cleans up all trace of his actions, develops an alibi, records it in a way that looks innocent, if the day ever comes that he is caught, he can bring these logs out and say, 'see here, I was nowhere near that place on that date.' But what actually happened, the Heights police requesting the books; that worked for Danker, He *reluctantly* allowed them to read them."

"Crafty," Bart leaned back in his chair and looked at Adam, "but we can use that. Once he sees this ruse is not working, his little brick house will start to fall apart."

"Yeah, I think you're right. Now I want another stick to beat him with, what else do we have?"

Averell's history from Bucharest to Syracuse and Rochester was studied. His name changes and his parent changes were identified. The team had people in Syracuse photograph the house where he grew up, the house where Ellie lived today, his high school, neighbors, stores, and of course Sarah, Ellie and Steve. They also had people in California photograph Allen and his new family. There were also photos of the alleged victims and the areas from which they were taken. As they examined the current photos, Bart asked if there were any photos of Sarah when she was between six and nine-years-old. Adam placed a request for additional information and within a few hours, a photo from a school yearbook in 1981, when she was eight-years-old was e-mailed to the team. Bart took the photos of Sarah, and each of the victims and stepped back. "Bingo, looky here, y'all," he said as he pointed at the photos. "These eight and Sarah could be sisters, they could be nine-uplets or whatever it is for nine that look alike, well—almost alike."

They stared at the board for a few minutes and Adam said, "Well, we do have our link. Just as we thought, he's been killing his sister over and over. Should we contact her and see what we can find out?"

Aaron looked at the pictures of Sarah and said, "No, we do not want any contact outside our circle of people. If we get what we want, we won't need anyone else, if we don't, we do not want any loose ends. So, no contact, especially with his family. We don't want to scare them unnecessarily."

Andy was poring over the paperwork when the team sat down and the discussion continued with Bart saying, "So, this guy hates his sister, wants to kill her and is taking it out on the rest of the world. Nice."

The team spent all day reviewing the information they had on the eight prime cases and even though the others were discounted as Averell's victims more heavily now, they kept them at the ready. As the interrogation team was preparing for Averell, they built a series of rooms in the industrial building as a stage for the interrogation. Averell would be contained in a large square cell, ten-feet on each side. The walls were twelve-feet-high and four large, bright light fixtures were suspended at the twelve-foot level. The door into the cell had no knob on the inside and the hinges were not visible from the inside. A second small door about two-feet-high and one-foot-wide opening to a small cubby hole was next to the door. A corridor was constructed outside leading to two doors. One door led to a bathroom with a shower, the other was for the team to gain entrance to this small layout. There was no view of the outside world from inside the suite and all was painted a bright white. Four cameras were installed high enough so they could not be reached standing on the floor. There was one in each wall and the monitors and recording equipment were controlled by Bart outside the suite. A microphone was in front of the monitors and Adam wore an earpiece. The team was busy preparing the building and rehearsing the procedure to be used in questioning Averell. They wanted to avoid physical force, depending on his own mind to manipulate him into compliance. He would be deprived of any view outside his cell, and they would withhold the time of day. His food would be limited, keeping him hungry at all times and he would not be told his whereabouts or the identity of his captors.

"The cleaner the confession, the better, and we want this to be rock solid. We want to be absolutely sure we have the right guy. No questions, no maybes," said Adam as the team was ready to begin the interrogation.

On Thursday, September 23, 1999, at approximately 8:15pm, Averell Danker was confronted in front of his townhouse in Rochester, New York by two men in dark suits and dark glasses.

"Excuse me, are you Mr. Danker, Mr. Averell Danker?"

"Yes, what is this about, and who are you?"

"We have a few questions for you."

The first man took hold of Averell's right arm and the second man grabbed his left arm. The first man then pulled a hypodermic needle from his pocket, pulled the needle cover off with his teeth and injected the full syringe into Averell's upper arm through his shirt.

Averell twisted and looked at the man with the needle, "I have nothing to say to you guys," and he went completely limp.

The two men "assisted" him into a black Chevrolet Suburban with tinted windows, not unlike Averell had "assisted" his multiple victims into the backseat and trunk of his many vehicles. A bag was placed over his head and handcuffs were snapped on his wrists and ankles. He was then driven to the suburbs outside Buffalo, New York and handed over to the interrogation team at the industrial park, in the middle of the night. The driver and his partner were relieved of any further responsibility and were driven to a nearby motel where they went their separate ways with the simple direction, "What you don't know, you cannot tell, so say nothing, ask nothing and enjoy the rest of your life." The men shook hands and went their separate ways, never knowing the other's names and never intending to see one another again.

Averell was given another shot to wake him up, taken to the central room and stripped of all his clothes, watch, rings and glasses. He was handed an orange jumpsuit and placed in the cell. The cuffs and hood were removed and he was left alone for a few hours. He paced back and forth, knocking on the walls and the doors, checking for an escape route. The room was cold and he put on the jumpsuit and continued pacing. The team watched on a closed-circuit television as he paced, pounded on the walls and finally called out, "Hey! Where am I—what is happening?"

"He's getting tired," said Bart, "it won't be long now."

"Good," said Adam, who had taken a nap and was ready for the first encounter. "So far, so good." He went back to checking his notes and discussing alternative questioning strategies with the team.

Averell paced for a few more minutes and finally crouched in a corner and fell asleep.

"I think he's out," said Andy. "How long should we give him?"

"Let's start with about fifteen minutes," said Adam, "it's now 1:15am, so at about 1:30am we wake him up."

Fifteen minutes later, Adam walked into the cell wearing a dark suit and sunglasses and said, "Averell, wake up."

Averell raised his head and opened his eyes. Still very tired, he was about to say something when Adam spoke.

"First, let me explain the rules: Rule number one, we ask the questions and you answer the questions. Rule number two—ah, there is no number two. Refer to rule one. Do you know why you are here?"

"No."

"Come on, Averell, you know why, you killed a little girl named Melissa."

"No, I didn't."

"Yes, you did, we know you did and you are going to tell us all about it. You will also tell us about the others. Averell, we are not here to find justice. That's not possible. Justice would be for you to experience all the pain and suffering you inflicted on those girls. Justice would mean those little girls never met you. Justice would mean those little girls grow up and become valuable assets to society. No, Averell, justice has passed for them, and for you. What we are left with is punishment. The big question is, what punishment is fair and equitable. We know what you did, at least some of what you did, and we want you to fill in the gaps. So, here's what we are going to do. We will ask you questions and you will answer. As soon as you tell us everything we want to know, and we confirm several facts, you will be imprisoned for the rest of your natural life. It's that simple. Now, we ask and you answer, understand?"

Averell looked confused, "No—and what others?"

"Didn't you get the memo? We ask the questions, not you. All you get to do is answer. Understand?"

"No."

"You will. Now, as I was saying, you killed . . . ."

Averell interrupted Adam, "Who are you?"

"Okay, we'll be back tomorrow," and Adam walked out of the room.

Averell called after him, "You can't do this to me. I know my rights. You didn't read me my Miranda rights. You have to charge me or let me go. I want an attorney!"

There was no answer. Time passed, but Averell had no sense of how much. Over the next hour, nobody came in the room, nobody talked to him. He called for someone, for anyone, nobody responded. Then the small door opened and he saw a bottle of water and a piece of bread.

"Hey, this isn't food. I want food, damn it!" He wedged himself into a corner.

"Are they the Rochester police or the State cops?"

"I don't know, maybe the FBI," said Stelian.

"Shut up!"

"Who is he talking to?" asked Bart.

"I don't know, let me know if he does it again," said Adam.

Averell drank his water and ate the bread. The small door opened again and a plastic wash pail was put in the doorway. Averell walked over to the door and took the pail and the door closed.

"What's this for?"

There was no answer. After another hour, Averell used the pail and put the bottle in it. He paced the cell for a few minutes and sat in the corner again. After a few minutes he fell asleep. It was now 3:55am. The team watched as he dozed for thirty-minutes and Adam entered the room again. Bart came in with him and took the pail out and closed the door. It was 4:25am Friday.

"Wake up Averell," demanded Adam.

Averell stirred. He was still tired, and now a little stressed. He noticed that Adam had on a different tie and shirt and figured it was the next day.

"Who are you?"

"Okay Averell, we are not the police, we are not the FBI, we are from a family—a large family, and we have an interest in what you have been doing for a number of years. Now are you ready to tell us about Melissa?"

"I don't know what you're talking about."

"We'll be back tomorrow." Adam walked out and closed the door.

"Hey, I have some questions. Come back here!"

There was no reply. Averell sat in the corner, "Why don't they answer me?"

"They don't like us," said Stelian.

"Who are they? What do they want from me?"

"You know what they want. They want to know everything," said Stelian.

Averell called out again, "Who are you?"

No reply.

After a few minutes, he fell asleep again. This time they let him sleep for twenty minutes. It was 4:50am. "Averell, wake up, we have things to discuss."

Averell lifted his head, his eyes were red and watery, he had a dull headache, his voice was thick and cracking, "What time is it?"

"We will let that one slide Averell. Now, as I was saying yesterday, you took Melissa and killed her. I want to know when you took her, where you took her and what you did to her ."

Averell's eyes conveyed nothing. There was a blank stare. Adam raised his voice, "Damn it, Averell! I asked you a question, now you answer me!"

Averell started to speak, "I don't, we didn't kill."

"Okay Averell, I will be back tomorrow."

"No, wait!"

The door closed behind Adam.

Averell sat in the corner and repeated the name, "Melissa" and "damn it" several times. He was still tired and soon fell asleep.

"Damn it, Melissa. Tell him about Melissa, and maybe we'll get out of here," said Stelian.

"Yeah, you're right."

Bart noted that he was once again talking to himself. Within the next twenty-minutes, Averell was asleep again.

"He said, 'We didn't.'," said Bart.

"Yeah, I caught that," said Adam, "let's give him fifteen-minutes, I gotta' change."

Adam walked back into the room, it was nearly 5:30am on Friday.

"Averell, get up, now you are going to talk to me. Melissa, what did you do with her?"

Averell was sitting up, trying unsuccessfully to wake himself up. "I didn't do anything."

"Come on Averell, we know what you did, we looked at your logbooks and know exactly where you hid your mileage, we know you were thinking about Sarah when you killed Melissa. Now, tell me everything about Melissa, I want you to say it, I want to hear your words Averell. Start talking."

Averell looked very confused. They knew about Sarah, they knew about the logbooks, what else did they know, "I don't remember."

"Come on Averell, you took her while she was walking home through a park and dumped her in the woods at the cemetery. Why didn't you bury her?"

Averell was in a place between sleep and full consciousness. Not sure what he had divulged up until now. He didn't know what to say.

"Averell, damn it! Why didn't you bury her?"

"No time, cops were there."

"So, you knelt down and pretended to be there for Mrs. Garver's funeral saying a prayer?"

"Yeah, a prayer."

"Who was with you?"

"With me, nobody was with me."

"Yesterday you said, 'We didn't kill her.' who is *we*?"

"I was alone, that was a mistake—it was just me."

"Okay Averell, now where did you take Melissa after you took her from the park?"

"We drove to the farm."

"Where is the farm, Averell?"

"What farm? Which farm?" asked Averell, now confused.

"The farm where you took Melissa."

"Portage County," and he dozed off.

"Averell, when we talk again, you tell me everything I want to know, and I will let you sleep, okay."

Averell muttered, "Okay."

It was now 5:35am. The team allowed him a twenty-minute nap this time. "Averell, time to wake up, we have to talk."

Averell again raised his head and tried to focus on Adam. "Good morning Averell, time for our daily chat, are you ready?" asked Adam.

"No, sleepy, let me sleep."

"You've had all night to sleep, Averell, now we talk. I want you to tell me everything about Melissa, you can start from the beginning."

"Melissa, I told you, Melissa."

"Tell me why you chose Melissa."

"Why? She was perfect, she was Sarah."

Bart spoke into a microphone, "Sarah, his sister, she's in her mid-twenties now."

Adam's earpiece delivered the message.

"Sarah, you mean your sister?"

"I hate her."

"Me too."

"Yeah, we both hate her."

"Averell, you and who else?"

Averell looked at Adam and his bloodshot eyes went from very tired to a hateful stare, "And me," said Averell in a firm, authoritative voice.

"And who are you?"

Averell straightened his back, "Stelian," he replied again in a firm voice.

"Well, Stelian, what can you tell me about Sarah?" asked Adam.

"We hate her—her and Ellie both," he said.

Bart spoke into the microphone, "Ellie is the mother."

"You hate his sister and his mother?" asked Adam.

"Our sister and mother, yeah, both of them," answered Averell.

Again, Bart chimed in, "Stelian was his name before he was adopted."

"When can we eat something, I'm hungry?" Averell asked in his new voice.

"Rule number one, Stelian, we ask, you only answer," and Adam walked out of the room.

Bart looked at Adam and said, "Do we have a schizophrenic, like two guys in one head?"

"There's undoubtedly more to it than what we see at this point, but, yeah, it looks like we have a double of some sort." said Adam. "His name was Stelian Lupasco when he was born and immediately put in an orphanage. His inside friend uses Stelian for his name. Is he psychotic, or does he just want us to think he is? I don't know, but we are not here to analyze this guy, just get some answers. Psychotic, schizophrenic, no matter, so let's get back at it," said Adam. "We will keep the notes and everything gets turned over to the Feds, but we are only seeking the answers discussed initially."

* * *

Thirty-Six

I meant me, I picked her . . .

The FBI had decided to observe Averell on a limited basis for an extended period. They assumed each of his supposed attacks were not 'spur of the moment' actions. They were planned over a period of days or weeks. The cases Jim McClarry had identified as fitting the profile of this specific predator had all occurred in the summer, and there was only one each year. Averell could be checked on periodically and followed closely occasionally. When the Federal agents were about to begin a programmed two-week close surveillance, Averell was nowhere to be found. Jim McClarry was contacted and asked if he knew Averell's location.

"No, as a matter of fact we have been told to stand down and allow you guys to run with this investigation. Has he intentionally disappeared or has someone run him over with a truck?"

As soon as he said that, he regretted it. If the Clann had done something and his tread imprinted corpse was found, Jim could be in for some difficult questioning. But that was not the case, nobody knew where he was or why he had disappeared. What the FBI did know was that Averell's car was still at his home in Rochester, his personal belongings were not disturbed and everything seemed to be present, including his passport, money and wallet. Cleveland Heights police as well as several other interested police departments, launched an investigation looking for him in the areas where each had jurisdiction. Each returned the same results, no sign of Averell. He was off the grid.

Jim's curiosity was stirred, so he called Sean, "We have to check this out. Does the family have Averell? And if they do, what are they doing with him?"

Sean appeared stunned, “Hell, I don’t know. Maybe he went fishing, maybe he tried to do the wrong lady and lost, maybe he’s on the run.” Sean shrugged, “What can I tell you?”

“Okay, let’s assume a couple of possible avenues. First, Averell changed his identity and disappeared, second, he is innocently someplace else and will turn up and third, the Clann has him.”

“Well, I think we can rule out the innocent bit, his wallet was left behind. If he did change his identity, then he is gone and we may as well forget him, not our problem. Third, the Clann, I guess I would go with that, they could have him and we wouldn’t know until they’re done with him, until they wanted us to know where he is.”

“So how do we check with the Clann and find out if he is their guest?”

“We don’t, it’s that simple, if they have him we’ll know what they want us to know, and we can’t change that.”

“So, we’re stuck with nothing?”

“That’s about it.”

*   *   *

Adam walked back into the room and Averell was asleep again. “Wakeup, Averell,” and Adam nudged him with his foot. Not a kick, but a nudge. “Come on, we have to talk.” It was now almost 7:00am and Averell had only had about two hours of sleep in the last twenty-four. He had lost all sense of time and as far as he knew, it could have been five days or more since he had been “arrested”.

“Don’t kick me.”

“That was not a kick, you’ll know when I kick you. If I had you would have bounced off the wall, now wake up. We have to do this one more time. Now, from the beginning, tell me about Melissa. Tell me everything or we will do this all over again and again until you do."

Averell looked almost dead, his voice was raspy and he was starting to cough, "You want me to say it again?"

"Yeah, from the top." Adam stepped aside out of camera range. Bart told him through the earpiece when he was clear.

Averell tried to clear his throat and started, "We were in Cleveland Heights again."

Bart and Andy looked at each other and said in unison, "Again."

Averell continued, "We were driving and I saw her, she was just right, not as old as I wanted, but he didn't care."

"Who didn't care?"

"You know, Stelian. Anyway, we took her to the farm in Portage County." He continued through the entire story.

When he was finished Adam said, "Okay Averell, you can get some sleep now." He walked out of the room and back to the control area. "Did we get it all?"

"Oh yeah, and did you catch the 'in Cleveland Heights again' bit?" Adam smiled, "Yeah, this is looking good." He sat down, "We'll give him about twenty-minutes and wake him up again."

"You are just pure nasty," Bart said with a smile.

Adam waited about ten minutes, changed his shirt and walked back into the cell.

"Averell, time to get up and tell me about the others," demanded Adam.

"I, I don't know what to say."

"This is taking altogether too long, Averell. I have wasted a week getting you to tell me things I already knew. Should I be talking to Stelian instead?" asked Adam.

"No, no I can tell you what you want," said Averell.

"Okay then, let's talk about Emily, you remember Emily, don't you? She lived in Schenectady, remember her?"

"Yeah, she was too weak."

"Why did you kill her?"

"She was supposed to stay with me for some time, but she was not very strong."

"Yeah, you said that. What do you mean by not very strong?"

"She left too early, we didn't have a chance to, to do anything, you know."

"Tell me what happened."

Adam stepped to one side allowing a frontal view of Averell to a camera and a little green light came on next to the lens. Averell began to talk about Emily in detail, describing the probes and his knife.

When he finished his description, Adam allowed him to fall asleep. "Let's wake him at nine and do the next one, Harkin, Barbara Harkin, right?"

Bart suggested that Adam take a quick nap to keep his head clear.

"I'll do that, thanks." Adam wondered what Bart's real name was and what he did for a living. He was pretty good at this interrogation work.

"Adam, it's almost nine, I'll give Averell a kick in the butt," said Bart with an evil grin.

"No, I got him," Adam stood and took a cup of coffee to the room.

"Averell get up, it's time for us to talk again, now, tell me about Barbara."

"Who?"

Barbara Harkin, Auburn, New York, July 11th, 1996. Come on, you are starting to waste my time and I am becoming impatient. Now, Barbara Harkin?"

"I remember Auburn and the Finger Lakes" and Averell began to talk about Barbara. He finished with, "I gave her a nice spot where she could see the lake and marked her with some stones. She was very good, she was almost perfect." He smiled as he remembered. His eyes seemed to glass over.

Adam let him drift into sleep.

"We will do this again at ten. Rebecca Markum is next."

"We only have him figured for one a year, could he have done others as well?" asked Andy.

"I suppose, we'll start the next session with that question and work up to Rebecca." said Adam.

At ten o'clock Adam entered the room. "Averell, get up, let's get through this so you can be returned."

"Returned, I don't understand," said Averell.

"Hell, I don't know, if you tell us everything, then you get the clean cell in a segregated wing. If you don't, you get put in with the general population. They don't like your kind, so no tellin' what will happen there. One guy lasted a year, but he had to work for it. Anyway, you were about to tell me if there were any others I missed. I want everything. So, go ahead."

"I don't remember all the names, only some, some I never knew."

"Okay, give me something, a place, a date. Where else did you find someone in '96?"

"In 1996 she was the only one, Barbara."

"So, what about '95?"

"We were in Sandusky, Ohio, found someone who did not cooperate at all," as he spoke, he was becoming agitated.

"Do you remember her name?"

"No, I don't."

"Rebecca Markum, August 16, 1995. Ring any bells?"

"Yeah, I remember her, she really pissed me off."

"Averell, you better tell me everything, understand?"

"Yeah," and he started into a tirade about wanting to see her heart, but she died before he could, followed by a detailed description of the butchery that followed. Andy and Bart got everything on tape and Adam walked out of the room feeling sick to his stomach.

"I need a break, guys."

"Understood, Adam," said Bart, "we all do."

Fifteen-minutes later, Bart checked the cameras. Averell was pacing, sweating and muttering to himself.

"Adam, I think our friend is going to explode. Take a look."

"Okay, go time, let's see where this takes us," Adam went back into the room.

"Averell, stop pacing and sit down." Red-faced and panting, Averell complied.

"Now Averell, let us continue. What else did you do in '95?"

"Nothing."

"We'll see. I hope you're telling me the truth. So, we move on to '94, tell me about Allison."

"I saw her heart beating, she was great." Averell was beginning to perspire. Within a minute he was soaked with sweat as he spoke about seeing Allison's heart and watching it stop. Again, a full-detailed description and the team pushed for another before taking a break.

"In 1993, you took Kathy Callen from Goshen Indiana."

"Yeah."

"Where did you take her?"

"Same place as we took Allison," he once again gave a detailed description of what happened.

"He must relive this stuff frequently to remember this amount of detail," said Andy.

Averell completed his description of Kathy, then Candice. Finally, Adam was going to hear about Annette.

"So, in '91 you took a little girl from Cleveland Heights."

"We—I had to plan, needed a place where I would not be disturbed. So, I found a farmhouse out on Barkham Lane about four miles from the freeway. I watched the place for a few weeks and nobody came around. Used the barn and cleaned up in the house. Used it three times, then somebody started to work on the place and I had to find something else."

"Okay, so who was the first one in the barn?"

"The woman was difficult to handle and she was a lot bigger than I wanted. So, I had to get someone smaller. I looked at a few of those punk teenage girls, but they were still too big. Then I found this little girl. She was walking in the rain and I almost hit her with my car." He laughed, "She might have liked that better."

Right there Adam knew it was Annette, "What was her name?"

"I don't remember."

"Where was this almost accident?"

"In Cleveland Heights, on Ashton, I think."

"You're not sure? What was she wearing?" asked Adam.

"I remember, it was a pink shirt, blue denim shorts and white shoes. Yeah, she was a blond with blue eyes."

"And where did you put her?"

"What about what I did to her?" Averell asked, breathing hard and looking excited.

"Okay, what did you do to her?"

Averell described the process from his perspective. As he talked, he became very agitated and somewhat confused. He clearly did do what he claimed, but the sequence could be off. As he was talking, Adam noticed Averell sweating, his muscles were tensed, the veins bulged on his neck and head. The description was more than Adam wanted to hear, but he had to get it all. Adam was a pro, he could do this sort of thing with any other psycho, but he was now talking about his own little cousin. He wanted so much to punch Averell, to grab a knife and slit his throat, but he controlled himself. Now came the last question, "Where did you put Annette?"

"Annette, that's her name, I remember that now."

"Averell, where is she?"

"Oh, she's gone, I buried her."

"Where?"

"In the cemetery, where they found Melissa. I used it a couple of times."

"The same cemetery?"

"No, a couple of different ones."

"But Annette is in the same one Melissa was found in?"

"Yeah, yeah, that one."

"Where in that cemetery, it's a big place?"

"Oh, I don't remember. A fresh grave that day."

Adam knew that should be enough to find Annette and said, "Okay Averell, who was next?"

Averell wanted to talk about Annette, now that he remembered her name and was seeing her more clearly. "What about Annette, there's more."

Adam needed a break and doubted there was any more he wanted to hear and replied, "What have I told you, Averell, I ask, you answer." With that he turned and walked out of the cell.

"Hey, come back, there's more."

The team had a hard time listening to the discussion about Annette, but all sessions were taped and copies of each session were made onto DVDs.

Averell was pushed for more and he opened up about Marlene and Sleepy. Adam called a timeout and left the building, phoning his contact. He told him everything was going well and he would be emailing the electronic files of Averell's statements. He asked for an identification of 'Sleepy'. It looks like he was probably the first victim. Marlene was probably killed in the same timeframe, and both, he surmised were probably before Annette. He drove out of the parking area and was turning on the highway when a police cruiser pulled up next to him. He rolled down his window and said, "Is there a problem, officer?"

"No. Are you Adam?"

"Yes, what's happening?"

"Nothing, I was told to contact you as soon as I could and let you know I am running security on this site. My name is Sam," and he handed Adam a piece of paper. "This is my cell number for this project. You need, you call. If I am not on, I'll contact the man in place."

"Thanks, we're in good shape, probably finish early at this rate. I'm heading out to dinner, are you hungry?"

"Thanks, but this may be our only face-to-face. We're family, not Friends," Sam laughed.

"It works for all of us, Sam. Take care."

"Will do," and Sam continued his patrol.

Adam drove down the road about a mile and pulled into a fast-food restaurant. He bought four meals with drinks and headed back to the building.

"Hey guys, my treat, got you some fine dining here."

"Adam, your timing is great, Averell is talking in his sleep," said Andy.

The four of them sat around the monitor and watched, listened and ate their 'gourmet' grub as they listened for anything intelligible.

"A lot of nonsense, but you never know," said Bart.

"Let's help him out," said Andy.

Adam took the microphone and spoke in a low easy voice, "Averell, why did you hurt Sleepy?"

"Drunk, sloppy, drunk," he muttered.

"Where did you put him?"

"Didn't put him, left in bushes—drunk," he said.

"Tell Adam everything, okay?"

"Everything, okay," Adam turned off the microphone. "Keep listening, we will wake him in about an hour."

The group finished eating and cleaned up. Adam changed his Shirt and checked his messages. After an hour, Adam went into the cell and said "Averell, time to talk. We have another question for you. Wake up."

Averell moved, they had let him sleep almost three hours, now he was sitting up on the floor. He looked around the room and noted the table and chair were gone, his pail was on the floor and a bottle of water was next to it.

"So, Averell we want to know about the others," said Adam. "Let's start with Sleepy, tell me about him."

"Sleepy, he…"

A beeping sound caught Adam's attention and he turned and walked out of the room, "What's the problem?"

"No problem, Adam, you have an email," said Andy.

Adam came out and opened the message. "What do we have?" asked Bart.

"Sleepy may be a guy named George Deitz, his body was found in a rest area in Ohio in July of 1990. He was stabbed and left in the bushes."

"That fits," said Andy, "what else?"

"There was a Marlene Fielding, murdered in Toledo that same year. They are both kind of on his sales route," said Adam.

He read through the rest of the message and went back into the cell, saying, "We have a winner." He entered the cell and said to Averell, "We have to talk about George, or as you called him, Sleepy."

Averell thought for a moment, trying to remember the name in 'Sleepy's' wallet. "I don't know his name. It was an accident."

"No, no Averell, an accident is when you trip into him and he is cut, this was a knife being jammed into his guts and the killer tried to split him open. That was not an accident, and the second cut was from ear to ear, that was no accident either. The two together spell m-u-r-d-e-r and you did it."

Averell looked defeated, beaten, wanting to go to sleep. "Yeah, he came at me and I stuck him in the guts. Then I made sure he was dead."

"You mean you cut his throat?"

"Yeah."

"You see Averell, that was easy, now tell me about Marlene."

"Marlene, was . . . she was a bitch. She needed to die. I did the world a favor."

"Tell me about it."

"We picked her because she was not a nice person, she was screwing over an ex-husband and did not respect anybody else, she needed to go away."

"Who is 'we' that you refer to?" asked Adam, "You mean Stelian?"

"I meant me, I picked her."

"Okay, so you did this by yourself, you decided, and Stelian didn't help."

"Yes, by myself."

"How did you get her to come into the building with you, where you killed her?" asked Adam.

"I hit her on the head with a sap and put her in the back of my van."

"Your dark blue van?"

"Yeah."

"It had tinted windows, right?"

"Yeah."

Averell was starting to enjoy talking about doing Marlene. This was the first one he had selected and planned out. He continued, "She was heavy, hard to move around, but I got her in the van and took her to the building. Then when she was starting to come around, the dizzy bitch walked from the van to the table we used."

Averell grinned, thinking about it. Over the next hour, he went into detail about how he set Marlene up to be played with and how it ended. When finished, Averell was tired and starting to slur his words. Adam figured enough had been accomplished for this session and allowed Averell to have a Happy Meal and be allowed to fall asleep.

The team assembled the taping of Averell's monologue and added some notes. It was electronically stored and copied to the legal contact in Boston. He would gather all the information and be prepared to release it to the authorities when the interrogation was complete.

After an hour of sleep, Adam once again woke Averell and said, "We would like to hear about the next one. Who did you kill next?" He had a listing of a number of people that had disappeared and were still missing. Marlene was killed in August 1990 and none of those listed seemed to be in the right geographic area until Annette in August of 1991, but that did not mean one of the unlikely ones had not fallen prey to Averell.

Averell looked confused, "Marlene was messy."

"You and Stelian had to plan better?"

"Yeah."

* * *

Thirty-Seven

There should be two grave sites here . . .

Sean knew more than he allowed Jim to see. A word in the right ear brought a response from the same source that had contacted Jim previously with another phone call to his home.

Once again, Margo answered the phone and handed it to Jim with that same quizzical look, "It sounds like that Irish guy again."

Jim took the phone, "Hello, this is Jim. "

"Jimmy boy, you've lost our favorite suspect, have ya' now?"

"I haven't lost anybody, but I think you may have abducted someone."

"Remember the rules, Jimmy boy, ask me no questions and I'll tell you no lies."

"So, you do have him."

"That's a question and no matter what the truth is, the response would be the same, I don't want you even thinking I might lie, so I won't answer you."

Jim knew this was going nowhere and any information would have to come from a civil conversation. "Okay, I give up. I suppose I will assume if you do have him, he is being treated with the respect a human being deserves, and if you learn anything, you will share it with me?"

"Jimmy, you're a fine young man. I will say this, whatever we learn in our investigation, wherever it comes from, and from whomever, you will be completely informed. As far as treatment of Mr. Danker, I have never met the man, but I can assure you that we have not harmed a hair on his head."

"So, you would turn him over to us?"

"You're assumin' we have him."

*　　　*　　　*

The team's work was almost done. Averell was fed and allowed to sleep for a full eight hours. The team had assembled the information into two identical packages and sent them to a contact in Boston. One package was to be delivered anonymously to James O'Leary at the O'Leary Law Firm in Boston and the other was to be sent via FedEx to Jim McClarry in Cleveland Heights, Ohio. The O'Leary Law Firm was founded over a hundred years ago and had been the prime family business all that time. The Clann had used this firm on several occasions and this was no exception. The story of Carl Mason was well known to the firm's attorneys and the thought that this may happen again someday was joked about, but never seriously considered. It took on the magnitude of an urban legend. So, when the youngest Mr. O'Leary received a call from a man with a slight brogue and the name Aaron, he was stunned, and a bit apprehensive.

"You'll be receivin' a package this afternoon, lad," said Aaron, "open it and that'll be our line for communication."

Puzzled, Jimmy O'Leary agreed and went immediately to the firm's senior partner and told him about the call. Thomas O'Leary told Jimmy to wait for the delivery. He called in the other partners and they discussed the situation.

"Not a lot of choice here, is there, Tom?" said his brother Al, "If it's the same deal, we say what we know, tell them everything, cooperate as much as we can."

"It has to be about the little Shelton girl. That was a tough one on her family. Must be seven or eight years ago now. Don't think her mom has had a peaceful day since."

"I don't know the family, but I remember the story," said another partner.

Tom's secretary came in with an envelope and handed it to Jimmy. "Thanks, Emmy," said Tom.

Jimmy opened the envelope and poured the contents on Tom's desk. There was a prepaid cell phone and a battery. Jimmy assembled the phone, turned it on and set it back on the desk. After five minutes the phone finally rang. Jimmy picked it up, pushed the speaker button and said "Hello." Al had a small tape recorder at the ready and turned it on.

"Good afternoon, gentlemen, my name is Aaron, at least for today," said the caller. "I assume you have gathered all the senior partners for this call, Jimmy boy."

"Ah, yes, I did."

"That's a good lad. Now then gentlemen, this will be a very brief call and you'll never hear from me again. The kidnapping and murder of little Melissa Winton a year or so ago caught our attention and we were able to build a connection with the kidnapping and murder of our own Annette Shelton. The authorities were restricted in their investigation and one of their suspects, a Mr. Averell Danker, was questioned. Now then, a lacking of hard evidence allowed Mr. Danker to be walking about free as you please. No evidence, no arrest and certainly no justice. Well now, that'll just not do. I know what we did was not strictly within the limits of the law, but we did get results, and Mr. Danker will be severely dealt with. The evidence, even though gained in an illegal manner, will be sent to your office by courier within the next day. There is a separate, duplicate package being sent to a Detective in Cleveland Heights, Ohio, one James McClarry. This information includes the locations of some of the children Mr. Danker murdered and best guesses as to several other locations. We could not keep this questioning up any longer as our teams have lives to live and they had to get back to home and hearth."

Aaron continued, "Now then, we intended for Detective McClarry to be informin' the authorities and we will, of course, let both you and Detective McClarry know the whereabouts of Mr. Danker all in good time. I expect someone else will be makin' that call. Now, I have a plane to catch and a little bit of livin' to do before my time is up. Jimmy, you can tell the authorities everything you know, and I recommend you try to keep the envelope and the phone out of everybody's hands. The boys at the FBI will be wantin' it. Well, that's everything I know, so I hope you don't have any questions. Good luck to you, and good day."

With that, Aaron's phone went silent. Jimmy reached over and was about to push the disconnect button when Al said, "No don't touch. Let's leave that to the police."

The package addressed to Jim McClarry was placed in a FedEx box on the first floor of the firm's office building.

*　　*　　*

Several packages were labeled and sent to Jim McClarry at CHPD. These included the recordings of Averell discussing George Deitz and Marlene Fielding.

Jim received the FedEx delivery and after ripping the pull string to open the package and dumping the contents on his desk, he froze. "Nobody touch anything," he said to Vince as he practically ran the three steps to George's office door. "George, you gotta' see this."

The entire squad room stood surrounding Jim's desk as he and George discussed touching the individually wrapped packages labeled "George," "Marlene," "Candice," "Kathy," "Allison," "Rebecca," "Barbara," "Emily," "Melissa" and "Annette". Each package was a zip lock storage bag with a video cassette and folded paper.

Jim looked at George and said, "I don't want to touch anything until it has been checked for prints, and whatever other trace may be present." Jim's phone rang and he answered, "CHPD, Detective McClarry."

"Jim, this is Sean, you are going to receive a package any minute now."

"I already have."

"Okay, nothing to be afraid of. In fact, I was just informed the contents are completely clean, you will not find any prints or other trace on anything, so you can go ahead and touch whatever you want, but I know you will wait for clearance from George."

"He's right here," and Jim handed the phone to George.

"George, Sean, this is awkward."

"You best get in here," said George, "I don't think there is any rush to open these packages."

Sean arrived within twenty minutes and the packages had been relocated to the conference room. The CSI guys were present and the package labeled "George" was being inspected.

"Good morning, all," said Sean as he walked into the room. "I got a call this morning from a man named Aaron. Said Jim here was going to get a package this morning and it would answer a bunch of questions that have come up over the last few years. Asked me to call Jim and let him know it was due by 10:00 this morning and he could open it and share with everyone else. Said that there were ten small packages in all and Jim could send them to the proper folks at the other PD's."

The CSI team found nothing of any use and opened the first bag. The film was the type that could be fit into a special video tape cassette and played in a cassette player. The television was ready and the tape was placed in the slot and turned on. The screen came to life with Averell Danker's face. He looked exhausted, his eyes bloodshot, with dark circles. As the camera panned out, he was seen to be barefoot, wearing an orange jumpsuit and seated in a folding chair. The room was obviously a concrete floor and the walls were all white. There were no windows or doors visible and the camera angle was from above. No other person was in the picture, but it was obvious that Averell was not alone. As if being directed, Averell looked at the camera and began to talk.

"My name is Averell Danker, and I killed George Deitz on July 10th, 1990 in Mentor, Ohio."

There was a "Blip" in the film, obviously, the camera was turned off for a minute or so and Averell spoke again. "George was drunk and asked me to buy him some wine. I said okay and hoped to just drive away, but he followed me to the rest area on I-90. He wouldn't leave me alone and so I stabbed him. Then, I finished him."

Blip

"Yeah, I cut his throat."

The recitation of facts, complete with periodic "Blips," continued for about fifteen minutes, giving details not given out to the press and correcting the misunderstanding of the evidence found at the scene. When the recitation was over, there was another "Blip" and the screen showed the time and date of the confession. The tape had no further images and no erased images.

The room was buzzing with low conversation. George tapped on the conference table, "Does anybody think that this would stand up in court? Who got this confession? More important, how did they elicit the information? What happened between shots?"

The response was a room full of blank stares.

"Who did this, I mean, who recorded it?"

"It's a long story," said Sean.

"Are we ready for the next one?"

"If we take them in order, that would be the one labeled 'Marlene'," said Jim. He looked around the room and asked where Alex was.

"Not in yet," said one of the admins.

"Maybe we should let him review these before we watch any more," Jim suggested.

George agreed and the first tape was placed back in the bag. Jim picked up Annette's bag and said, "I want to read the piece of paper in this one," as he looked at George.

"Okay, kinda' curious myself."

He opened the bag, removed the paper and unfolded it. "This is where she is buried. It's a cemetery. George?"

George immediately told Jim, "Check 'em all, see if they are the same. Then we go back to work, Jim you handle notifying the other PDs then get hold of that cemetery and the local law and set up a visit to check it out." George turned and looked at Sean, "We have to talk, in my office."

Jim started opening the other bags and reading the notes. Each one described where the remains of the victim were to be found and he dug into the file to get the contact information for each PD. They would all go through the same process of contacting the cemetery and arranging to investigate the burial sites.

George closed the door to his office and stared at Sean, "Okay, give me the short version."

Sean began with the story of Liam and quickly jumped to today. "Look George, I have no idea who they are or what they've been doing, they act on their own without me. I have no contact info or control and not even a way to offer input, I have no idea who is running this operation. I am not in the loop at all."

"Okay, but if you do catch wind of anything, I mean anything at all, you come to me. This is not how we function and their involvement is completely unacceptable. Are you getting all this?"

"I hear you loud and clear, if anything comes up, I will bring it directly to you. You do understand that I don't have any control over these people."

"Yeah, I know, Sean, but damn it, you knew something and I gotta' yell at somebody. "

"Okay then, are we are good, or what?"

"Yeah, we're good, now get outta' here. Go write some tickets."

Jim finished notifying the other PDs and was looking up the information on the cemetery. He contacted the cemetery's office and spoke to the director. The director checked the records for the days around Annette's disappearance. Three burial sites were identified as possible locations where Averell might have buried Annette. When reviewed, one was determined to be too close to the highway and probably not the one, another was three days after her kidnapping and ruled out, but the third was the same day as her abduction and on the next day the ground would still be in need of compacting, sodding and watering. This would most likely be the one.

A court order would not be needed if they just dug the ground down to the vault. If they had to go lower, then they would need to get the order. The next day was dedicated to confirming names and cemeteries. Each one of the cemeteries warranted a search, but now the team felt confident Averell would have used recently excavated gravesites. They would be easier to dig and no sod would be visibly disturbed. It was an ingenious and thoughtful plan. So, armed with that information, Jim established the dates that could identify where each victim had been buried.

The Alton Memorial Park south and east of Cleveland, cited as a possible location for Annette, was visited and the specific grave was identified. The FBI had a ground penetrating radar rig brought in and checked the site. A positive result was noted. It could be a body, but the arrangement of the bones was not right. They excavated and found three separate plastic bags, each with human bones that were photographed, inspected and then sent directly to the coroner's office. The remains contained in the plastic bags had decayed and the remaining fluids and gasses in the bags made an on-site inspection unworkable. The bags were transported to the morgue where a team of medical examiners would conduct a forensic autopsy of the remains. The second site, Spring Hill Cemetery where Candice Brighten was buried yielded another three bags with the same body parts in each bag. These first two sites were in northeast Ohio as were the two Portage County burials where Allison Kinsey and Rebecca Markum had been hidden. The burial of Kathy Callen was in the western part of Ohio and both Barbara Harkin and Emily Molin were buried in one of the Finger Lakes Parks in New York state.

The Portage County site was located and the FBI team was searching the area when a pickup truck drove in. The driver parked and approached the four men as they searched the woods. Three men dressed in street clothes and one local police officer.

"You fellas lookin' fer somthin'?" asked Phil.

"Hey Phil, this is being treated as a possible crime scene, so you should stay right here while these boys do their work," said the officer.

"Sure Joe, whatever you say. What kinda crime?" asked Phil.

"Well, it was some time ago, coupla' years maybe. Some fella says he buried a body out here."

Phil stood up straight and looked stunned, "No kiddin', a body. Who is the fella', maybe a guy named Davis, Al Davis?"

"No."

"Excuse me sir, did you have a name of someone who may have been involved?" asked the FBI agent.

"Phil, this is FBI agent Dan Weller, he's in charge of this expedition. Dan this is Phil Samuels, he owns the next farm down the road. Phil does a little huntin' in these woods, both on and off season," said Joe with a grin.

"So, Phil, who is this fella' that you're talking about?"

"Don't know him very good, he stopped in a few times on his way to Cincinnati to visit family. He didn't have no gun with him though, so he just looked around and left."

"Anything odd about him?" asked Dan.

"Well, yeah, sorta, I mean he was standin' here one day, few years back, when I come over and we found a hole in the ground, big open hole, so we filled 'er up so nobody would fall in. Al said he thought it might a been a boar trap. Ain't no boar aroun' here in years."

Dan went to his car and returned with a file. He fumbled through the file and pulled out a picture. "Was this guy with your friend?"

Phil looked at the picture and smiled, "Nope, that there is Al Davis."

"That man's name is Averell Danker. He is a suspect in the kidnapping and killing of at least eight little girls and two adults over a nine-year period."

"Whoa, I thought he was a little off, but not like that," said Phil.

"Do you recall the location of that hole you two filled in?" asked Dan

"Oh, let me see here," and Phil started to walk toward the tree line, "yep, I reckon it'd be right there." Phil was pointing into the woods.

"Show me," said Dan.

Phil walked them about twenty feet into the woods to a small clearing.

"It's growed over some, but I'm sure it was right here." He was pointing at a slightly depressed spot. "See, it's been dug up at some time," he said pointing out the depression.

"How deep was this hole?" asked Dan.

"Best guess, 'bout four foot, maybe five. Not gonna' catch a boar in that, but you could bust a leg fallin in it," said Phil.

The radar was used to scan the area. No results.

"You sure about this location," asked Dan.

"Yep, damn sure."

"Well, there's nothing there," said Dan.

"Well I didn't see nothin' in the hole when we filled 'er up. So no surprise to me."

"There should be two grave sites here," said Dan.

"Oh, okay," said Phil, "let's look around a bit." With that Phil began to rummage through the woods.

Dan was about to ask Phil to please not disrupt the crime scene when Phil shouted out, "Here's another one." He continued through the brush and before the team got to the site Phil identified, he called out again, "And another one. You say there's just two of these," Phil yelled back at Dan.

"Yeah, two."

"Okay," said Phil and he came out of the woods.

The team marked each location and was trying to figure how to get the radar unit to each site when Dan said to Joe, "How did he do that?"

"Do what?"

"He went right to them."

"I don't know, ask him."

Dan walked over to Phil and said, "How did you know where to look?"

"Easy, I looked at the ground, see the way it drops off where there was a hole."

"Yes, but you went directly to each one."

"Oh, I see, well look at the woods, see anything different about where I looked?"

"No."

"Answer is yes, son, you look for a small clearing, about ten to twenty feet into the woods, makes for easy digging and probably nobody will step on it and see the hole."

Both sites were scanned and each site produced a set of three bags. The bags were tagged, everything was photographed and the bags were taken to the coroner's office for inspection and identification.

Phil was quizzed by the FBI at length and he told them everything he knew. Dan had to go to the Finger Lakes Area next and locate two more graves. He spent a few extra minutes with Phil learning what he could about where Averell would look to dig a hole and bury someone. The remains were identified as Allison Kinsey and Rebecca Markum. Once again DNA testing would be conducted.

Dan and his team drove to New York and went to the thruway exit defined by Averell. They followed the direction he spelled out and came to a clearing in a wooded area a short walk through the woods to a view of one of the Finger Lakes. He stood there admiring the view of the lake and remembered that the first grave was marked with some stones. A brief walk about found a pile of stones that fit the description and the ground penetrating radar found the remains.

Dan poked around, remembering what Phil had told him about spotting where a hole had been dug and filled back in. Sure enough, he identified an ideal location from thirty-feet away and walked straight to it. There was a depression in the ground and the radar found a skeletal pattern. The site was excavated, the remains were removed and taken to the local coroner and through dental records, identified as Barbara Harkin and Emily Molin.

Averell's victims were all accounted for and identified. The final confirmation would be by DNA analysis. That was going to take a few more weeks.

In Cleveland Heights, Clare and Dave Shelton were visited by Dan Weller with the FBI, George Penderson and Jim McClarry from the Heights PD. They were invited in and everyone sat around the dining room table. Dan began by telling the Shelton's that Annette had been found. Her remains, along with the remains of the other seven girls, were being examined as thoroughly as possible and then they would be turned over to the family for a proper burial. They were told also that the lead to finding Annette had been through some mysterious source, involving an attorney in Boston.

"Who is the attorney?" asked Dave.

"His name is James O'Leary," said Dan and he proceeded to relay the story as he heard it. "An official report will be assembled and you will be given a copy, if you would like."

"Thanks," said Dave, "How did they . . . ?"

"Apparently the guy who did this opened up to someone, the conversation was taped and sent to us. It's all very mysterious, but we have a tape of the guy confessing to everything. Looks like the confession was not legally obtained and we may have difficulty prosecuting. But that's another story. First, we have to take custody of the guy and then listen to what he says when not coerced, well, that's not your problem. We will keep you informed as to the progress."

"Thanks again," said Dave as the visitors were leaving. Then he and Clare sat down together quietly and said nothing.

* * *

The next week when Jim was in the station, he was asked to join Alex and Sean on the second floor. He walked into Alex's office and sat down, "What's up, guys?"

As Alex was about to speak, the phone rang. Alex answered, "This is Alex Robertson, yes, they are here, I'll put you on speaker "

"Gentlemen, my name is Aaron, and I had to do this last call before I retire. You lads did some fine work, and you should feel proud of what you've accomplished. We have the proof we needed to definitely identify the predator, and we are dealing with him now. I know what we are doing is not legal, but it is just, and I, for one, will sleep well tonight. Again, you are to be commended for your efforts. That's it." and the phone went silent.

Aaron pulled the battery from the phone, pocketed it and threw the phone away as he walked into the Airport Terminal.

* * *

Thirty-Eight

Please, get me outta' here . . .

Adam's work was almost done. The team watching Averell had changed several times and was waiting for confirmation of the information he had provided. When that came in, Adam returned to the Buffalo building and the team began to take the suite apart. Averell was wakened from a sound sleep, cuffed and a hood placed over his head. As a needle punctured his arm, he passed out and was placed in the rear of a black Suburban with heavily tinted windows. The driver, a large man with broad shoulders and beefy hands, dressed in a dark suit and tie, wearing dark glasses, was a real federal marshal taking a few days off to attend to some "family business." He was carrying papers that implied he was transporting a prisoner for some legal proceeding in Ohio. Another man, looking very much like the first, also wearing a dark suit and dark glasses, rode in the middle seat and kept watch on their unconscious prisoner. The drive down I-90 through Erie, Pennsylvania to an equipment yard outside Mentor, Ohio on I-271 took about three hours and was accomplished without a stop. The man drove at the speed limit and never drew the attention of any other drivers or the highway patrol officers.

The trip was pleasant, their guest was quiet and the weather was perfect, a bit of a chill in the air, but the next week was predicted to be warmer than usual. It would be perfect for outdoor activities with temperatures in the high sixties or low seventies during the day and dropping into the fifties at night.

Ben Creighton met the vehicle in the equipment yard and directed it to a remote spot in the parking area. "Package is inside, still out cold," said the driver. "Where do you want to transfer him to your vehicle?"

Ben made sure the yard was all but empty and said, "Wait here while I bring my truck over." He backed his yellow pick-up with state logos on the doors and yellow lights on the roof next to the Suburban. "Let's dump 'em in the back."

"Then what?" asked the driver.

"Then gentlemen, I will gas your ride and you can head back to Buffalo. We will take it from here, and thanks for your help."

"No problem, it was a pleasure being able to assist on this one."

"Okay, when you get back, tell Adam that Mr. 'D' is secured and I will call him in the morning. And be sure to say it that way, he will understand." Ben then pointed them toward the fuel station and said, "Use the blue nozzle and top 'er off, then go inside and help yourself to fresh coffee and bagels before you get on the road." Ben waved to another man standing next to a shed across the parking lot and he approached the truck.

"Is this our guest?" asked the new man as he zipped up his jacket, covering his CHPD uniform.

"That he is, cousin. Now if you would keep an eye on him while I get these fellas back on the road, he should stay out 'til we give the wake-up injection."

"Okay, I got him, do I have to be nice?" asked Sean with a slight grin.

"Not if he wakes up," said Ben as he headed back into the building.

The two men from Buffalo made their pit stop, accepted the refreshments and pointed their Suburban north. They left as they came, completely unnoticed. Ben went back to the pick-up, looked at Sean and nudged their guest with a shovel. Averell made a slight grunt but remained quiet and relatively motionless. They pulled a tarp over him, placed a few blocks on the edges to keep it in place, got in the truck and slowly drove out onto the highway. Ben drove a few miles south with his yellow lights flashing, then pulled onto the median strip where it widened around a large, wooded area. He turned right midway between the north and south bound lanes and drove another three hundred feet, into the woods paralleling the highway, to a small clearing at the base of a hill.

The median was several-hundred-feet wide at this point, with dense tree and brush covering everything, including the hill that rose about sixty-feet above the road surface and extended almost a half-mile down the highway. A driving path, just wide enough for his pickup, allowed Ben to back up close to the top of the hill. He stopped the truck, still surrounded by trees and bushes, set the brake and the two men got out and walked to the back of the truck. Sean looked around, noting they were not visible from the roadway below and nodded his approval. Ben dropped the tailgate and the two men dragged their guest from the truck bed. Averell was now semi-conscious, but not yet able to walk unassisted. They set him on the ground and walked another thirty feet into the bushes to an opening in the ground. There was a ladder protruding from the opening and Ben said, "It's ready, I cleaned it out last week, got rid of the sticks and leaves that were collecting at the bottom."

"What about rain, will it hold water in a storm?" asked Sean.

"This was a construction test pit when they built the road. Something about the flyover supports and drainage. Anyway, they put a sump with a four-inch drain at the bottom and another sidewall drain about a foot higher as an overflow. They run about fifty feet to an outfall on either side of the hill. If you didn't know they were there, you would never see them. It is kinda' dark down there. We had a good rain last week and when I looked, it wasn't dry, but there wasn't any water puddled either. Stays damp down there most of the time, but water drains away quick enough, it won't be a problem."

"So, the drains are clear, not clogged with leaves?"

"Oh yeah, forgot to mention, the little critters probably keep the drains clear, they run in and out all the time."

"So, our guest will be having visitors from time to time."

Ben laughed, "Reckon he will, mice, squirrels, rats, whatever can crawl through a four-inch pipe, just his kind of vermin."

"Okay, ready when you are." The two men dragged Averell over to the edge of the pit. Sean kept Averell on the ground and Ben went back to the truck. He took a rope from the back of the truck over to the edge of the pit and they tied it around Averell's chest below his arms. Averell coughed and spit inside his hood trying to say something. Ben checked the knot and tied the other end of the rope to the back of the truck. The two men then lowered Averell into the pit and climbed down the ladder. The pit was at least twenty-five-feet deep and about ten feet in diameter at the bottom. They untied the rope and started to remove Averell's clothes, cutting his bindings as they went and put everything in a plastic bag. Sean drew a hypodermic needle from his coat pocket and readied it to inject Averell with the wake-up serum.

"He's ready," said Ben.

Sean injected Averell in his upper arm and tossed the used hypodermic needle in a bag with the rest of Averell's clothing. They waited a few seconds and Averell started barking again in unintelligible sounds, trying to speak. Ben started up the ladder with the bag and Sean reached for the hood over Averell's head. He pulled it off as Averell was spitting, coughing and gagging. Sean climbed the ladder with the hood in hand leaving Averell lying on the floor of the pit, naked and completely vulnerable. They pulled the ladder up as Averell finally finished sputtering and regained some ability to speak.

"Where am I?" he gasped as he sat up.

"You're down there, and we're up here. And down there you will stay 'til we let you out," said Ben as he leaned over the edge.

Averell had no idea who these people were, he was confused, disoriented and terrified. He had no idea what was going on, why he was in a dark, damp, muddy place. Why he was naked and cold? He looked up at the opening almost thirty feet above. He could see the sky through the small opening and he felt the clammy cold of the earth around him and he shivered.

"Where am I, what's going on, get me outta' here!" He staggered across the pit reaching for the walls, looking for a way out, there was nothing, no stairs, no door—no way to get to the opening above. He felt sick and began to cough until he vomited, what little was in his stomach was now on the floor of the pit. He stumbled around, scratching at the walls, trying to find something to grasp—anything. The walls of the pit were hard clay and as he scratched at the walls his fingernails cracked and broke and his fingers tore and bled.

Averell fell to the floor and hung his head, trying to understand what was happening. *Was this a nightmare, was this real?* He knew it was real. But who put him here? And why? The police would have put him in jail, he would have rights, he would get a phone call and he would have an attorney. Averell knew this was not the work of the police. Who was Adam? Was he a cop? He remembered the sessions with Adam. Did Adam put him here? He remembered telling Adam about the people he had killed, and where they could be found. *Was that a dream? No, that was also real.* But, the question remained, why was he here?

"Where am I?"

There was no reply.

"Let me out now!"

No reply.

The floor of the pit was hard, moist and slippery. As he moved from side to side of the pit, stepping—slipping—stumbling, Averell could hear the insects and worms squishing and crackling under his feet. They were everywhere, and unavoidable. He called up for the men above, "Get me outta' here! You can't do this to me!" Again, no reply. The insects started to crawl on his feet and up his legs. He brushed them away as much as he could, but they kept coming, crawling, climbing. Averell was screaming for help, begging to be taken out of the pit.

"Please, get me outta' here!" He started to cry as the vomit once again rose in his throat.

Sean and Ben peered down into the pit, "We're going to leave now, but not to worry, someone will check on you in a week, or a month, whatever, but we won't leave you there forever." With that Ben looked at Sean and they both smiled, stood and walked over to the truck, got in and headed down to the hill. At the bottom of the hill, they got out of the truck and dragged some cut brush across the path leading to the pit. They stood silently listening for Averell's cries and hearing nothing, they got back into the truck and drove back to the equipment yard.

Ben decided he would stay late that day and be sure several things were addressed, including the work schedules for the upcoming month. The highway crew that mowed the median and cared for that section of highway was under his direction. He had programmed everybody's activity for the next month in other areas and with the winter snows coming soon, the crews would be very busy plowing and salting the roadway. There would be no opportunity for any activity on Averell's hill until spring at the earliest.

Ben had put in thirty-seven years and was ready to retire soon. He would stay on long enough to be sure that Averell's hill remained undisturbed for a long time and pass the baton on to another cousin who happened to be in line for his job when he did retire.

When Ben and Sean left him, Averell was alive and well. How long he would stay that way was not up to them, he was now in the good Lord's hands.

The Clann had addressed a situation. They did so by stepping out of line several times and if ever accused, they could be prosecuted. They understood and accepted the risk. They also understood if the entire Clann cooperated, the secrets they kept would keep them safe from prosecution. So, the matter of Averell Danker was not discussed and those who knew something, said nothing, and those who knew nothing, didn't ask.

The objective was to find justice, not to replace the authorities, not to become the police, judge and jury. No, the sole purpose was to provide the justice the authorities could not, or would not, deliver.

Sean and Ben sat in Ben's office, shared a cup of coffee and talked about the common cousins between them that neither had seen in too many years. Those who stood up and helped in the search for Annette years earlier, and those that would not be mentioned again who helped in other ways.

"Jim McClarry did a lot of detective work on this long before he was promoted, and thanks to him, we had a lot of information about this character. I wish there was a way to let him know we have taken care of business," said Sean.

Ben thought for a minute and said, "Give it eight years, one for each year Annette was left alone in a cold unmarked grave, and our guest will be given back to the system. I'll be long retired and gone by then and the other key players will back into the woodwork, but our Mr. McClarry will have the satisfaction of knowing justice was served and he played a part in it."

Sean finished his coffee and headed back to Cleveland Heights. Ben checked a few more schedules, made some notes in a logbook and locked up the office. He got into his truck and drove out to the hill with his windows open and listened. He heard nothing. He drove up the road about a mile and turned into a gravel area labeled 'Authorized Vehicles Only' and stopped next to a state trooper watching his radar.

"Hey, Jesse, how's it going?"

"Boring night, Ben, but I think I'll stay right here for a while anyway."

"Try not to fall asleep, if you do, I'll wake you in the mornin'."

They both laughed and Ben pulled back onto the highway and headed home. An hour had passed since he was left in the pit and Averell was cold, hungry, scared and completely and utterly alone. He tried talking to his long-time companion, Stelian, to no avail. He was truly alone for the first time since he lived in the orphanage in Romania.

The sun had moved in the sky and light no longer found its way into the pit. Averell could not see, he could not climb out and all that was visible was the opening above. Total darkness came earlier in the pit than the surrounding area and with darkness came the sounds. The sounds of the little insects scuttling about the floor and walls, crawling on Averell, looking for food. The scratching sounds of animals clawing in the dirt. The sounds of the rats, digging, scratching, in search of food.

No one knows how long Averell lasted in that pit. How long it took for the first critter to reach him, then the second, third, and the rest, to smell him, to bite him and taste his flesh, then to return and feed on him. How long could he fend them off? How long did it take for his mind to snap? How long before the rest of him died and how long did the critters feast on his remains? It could have been hours or days, no one came to look, to check on him, no one knows, and no one cares.

Adam had finished his cleanup of the Buffalo building and went to the airport. His flight was at 8:45pm and he would be back home in Northern Virginia in a few hours. He used his project cellphone and called his contact to give him a final update. Then he pulled the battery and memory card, wiped it clean and tossed it in the trash.

* * *

Thirty-Nine

Do I call you Aaron . . .?

Time passed, Averell went into the pit on the Ohio freeway in September 2000. As was the case with Carl Mason, Averell was left to nature. The insects and other critters that roam the median between the paved lanes going north and south or east and west, found their way to the feast in the pit. Averell was slowly devoured, but how he came to his end is not known. How many crows or roaches or rats participated in the consumption of all but his bones is anybody's guess. As the years passed and new people came to work for the highway department, nobody had occasion to be near the pit, much less to look inside. Ben Creighton retired and moved to North Carolina where he lives today and Jesse is still with the Ohio State Police. The men who participated in the team activities blended back into the world from which they came and Adam was busy back at that unnamed agency with other work involving terrorists. Jim McClarry moved up in the ranks of the Cleveland Heights Police Department and he and Margo moved into a house and started a family. They now have a son and a daughter and live in the neighborhood where Annette and her family lived. The man called Aaron did catch a flight back to Ireland that night in 2000 and returned to his home near Dublin where he lived for the next three years before finally succumbing to a cancer that had been diagnosed while he was living in America.

In the Spring of 2009, another call was made to Jimmy O'Leary, now an associate with the O'Leary firm in Boston and well on his way to becoming a partner. His secretary leaned in his office door and said, "There's a man on the phone who says he wants to talk to you, his name is Aaron."

"Whoa, tell Tom that Aaron is on the phone. Hurry, I'll wait a second before picking up."

"Okay," said Kate and she pushed a few buttons on her phone and gave Tom the message. Tom dropped a file on his desk and as he walked down to Jimmy's office, he told Kate to get the partners to join them, "This might be interesting."

Tom went into Jimmy's office as he was picking up and putting him on speaker, "This is James O'Leary, how can I help you?"

"Would you like me to wait a minute while you call the others into your office, Jimmy boy?" asked Aaron with an Irish brogue.

"I would appreciate that."

"Not a problem, I'm callin' from a prepaid phone that was given to me for this occasion, so no sense tryin' to trace the call. When we're done, I'll be throwin' it in the trash. You do understand, Jimmy boy."

"I do, do I call you Aaron?"

"Well, we use the name because of the history, I'll not be tellin' you my real name, but you knew that."

"Yes, I knew that." The office filled up and Aaron began.

"Gentlemen and any ladies present, my name is Aaron, and the call today is to let you know the whereabouts of Mr. Averell Danker. At least the last place we knew him to be. Start with Interstate 90 in Ohio, between Madison and Mentor. In the median strip there is a hill, a rise with a thick growth of brush at the top. In the middle of the brush, there is a pit. Look in the pit. That's all I have for you, gentlemen. I'll be takin' my leave now, good day." The line went silent.

Tom said, "Okay 'Jimmy m'boy', this is yours to handle," and he laughed as he walked out of Jimmy's office.

Jimmy called the CHPD and spoke to Jim McClarry. "Jim, I have word from one of our cousins. Fella' named Aaron. You know who I'm talking about?"

"I think I do. What did he have for us this time?"

"Grab a pen and I'll read it off, ready?"

"Go ahead."

Jimmy O'Leary read off the location and Jim McClarry wrote it down. "I'll contact the local FBI office and get them in on this, I think the agent in charge was Matt Carver," said Jim.

"Let me know what happens, and Jim …"

"Yeah."

"You know this is all out of bounds stuff. I mean, the Clann really stepped out on this and I expect some kind of heat. Not sure where it will come from—but heat nonetheless."

"I hear ya' cousin, I'll give you a call when we know what's in the pit, if anything."

They hung up and Jim dug out the number for Matt Carver at the FBI office in Cleveland. Matt Carver was pleased to get another lead to follow on this case and eagerly accepted the information Jim had to offer. He asked Jim if wanted the lead on this part of the investigation, "Sure, I'll take it. I'll set up a site visit for tomorrow around 1:00pm. That should allow enough time for everybody to assemble and have the right forensic guy's there."

The following day at 12:30pm, the group was gathering at the equipment yard near the site. Jim was counting noses and making sure that the forensic team was getting prepped on driving into the median strip. A parade of five vehicles was lined up for the ride to the site and highway workers were going to lead and follow with their yellow lights flashing. Jim met Matt Carver at the yard office and the two of them rode with Vince Galley in the second vehicle. They were followed by the forensic van and that was followed by a state trooper car with a couple of local officials. Next came the medical examiner and his assistant and then the other highway truck.

The forensic van and one highway vehicle with ropes and ladders backed up the hill, stopping about twenty feet from the pit. The remainder of the people walked up the hill and gathered at the highway truck to wait for clearance to approach the pit. The forensic team moved ahead with cameras and plastic bags, photographing everything and picking up whatever appeared to be worthwhile trace evidence. Jim knew, as did the forensic team, any trace found at this point had a very low probability of being of value, but procedure was procedure and there was an audience there watching them. When enough preliminary photographs and trace collection was done, the team came back to the truck to get the ladders, rope, lights and other equipment needed to enter the pit. The crime scene specialists wearing the appropriate protective suits climbed down into the pit, setting lights and photographing everything in sight.

The pit, fully illuminated, was now scanned for human remains. The collection of bones retrieved were photographed in situ and carefully tagged and bagged for analysis by a nearby morgue. Some minor excavation was needed to collect the remains that were buried by several years of weather and critters moving bits about. The remains of several rodents mixed in with Averell's were assumed to be those of meal seekers who followed their noses into the pit in pursuit of food. They were either victims of their intended meal or other critters after the same feast. Whatever the case, Averell Danker, in the pit for nine years, had been found and now had been returned to the system that could not arrest, try or punish him.

* * *

Epilogue

Jim McClarry called Jimmy O'Leary in Boston and told him Averell Danker had indeed been found and now, with a few entries in the file, the case of Annette Shelton's murder would be officially closed. This also closed the missing person cases surrounding the other seven girls Averell had taken. Jim called the other police departments and informed them of the developments. He then called Dave Shelton, "Dave, this is Jim McClarry, can I stop by for a few minutes? I have some news for you and Clare?"

Allen Swall retired and moved to Southern California where he whiled away his retirement fishing off the Santa Monica Pier. Ellie and Steve Danker divorced again. Steve moved on to other jobs and never made any alimony payments to Ellie. Ellie found work as a bartender in a dive-bar and lost herself in booze and drugs, passing away about the same time as Averell's bones were discovered. Sarah married a car salesman and had new cars every year for five years. Her divorce settlement got her nothing as her husband filed bankruptcy and never worked again.

The end.

*   *   *

About The Author

John B. Wren worked as a consulting engineer for over 40 years. He began writing in 2009 as a hobby and upon retiring in 2012, turned most of his efforts to writing. He has written six novels, two novellas and six short stories as of the summer of 2021.

Wren was born in Pittsburgh, Pennsylvania, grew up in western New York State, went to college and lived in Northeast Ohio for 25 years and now resides in Northern Virginia with his wife, Lois.

Also By John B Wren

KILLING HIS FEAR

DARRYL'S REUNION

AN TRODAI: SCOLAI

AN TRODAI: LAOGHAIRE

AN TRODAI: CONALL

IMPORT EXECUTE

THE PERDONE COLLISION

BUSINESS OF REVENGE

SHORT STORIES

THE CHAIR IN THE RIVER

A TASTE OF REVENGE

THE WHARF

ANGELA

ASHGROVE

NO WAR

www.ingramcontent.com/pod-product-compliance
Lightning Source LLC
Chambersburg PA
CBHW050553260626
47157CB00002B/539

* 9 7 8 0 9 8 8 9 3 7 1 0 9 *